Not for Sale

by

Iona Morrison

A Blue Cove Mystery

Not for Sale

Cover Art by *Debbie Taylor*

The Wild Rose Press, Inc.
PO Box 708
Adams Basin, NY 14410-0708
Visit us at www.thewildrosepress.com

Publishing History
First Fantasy Rose Edition, 2015
Print ISBN 978-1-5092-0155-6
Digital ISBN 978-1-5092-0156-3

A Blue Cove Mystery
Published in the United States of America

She cut through the cemetery.

It was dark. She could hear someone following close behind her as she wove through the headstones. "Wait up, Jessie." Dylan's voice startled her. "I'll take it from here."

"You can come if you want. Hurry, I know where he is." She picked up her pace. "If you're coming, you'd better keep up." She ran along the trees at the back of the church, remembering that night where she had run not so long ago. Slowing down, she tried to feel her way. That darn tree root was somewhere around there. Closing in on where she thought the gunman was, she got down on the ground and crawled quietly toward the ledge. Matted wet leaves, soggy grass, and mud muffled the sound of her progress. When she came to the ledge, she carefully peeked over the edge. There he was, the snake, stretched out on the ground ready to strike. A dark figure clothed in black, just sliding another magazine into his semi-automatic. She could barely make him out. He had shot out the light in the church parking lot. She slipped her gun out of her holster and took aim, and felt Dylan grab her foot to let her know he was there. Good she had back up.

"If you pull that trigger one more time, mister, it'll be the last thing you ever do." She kept the gun sighted between his shoulder blades. Startled, he yanked his head around toward her voice, his night goggles making him look like a sci-fi character in the shadows. He started to reach for his gun, and she aimed a hair to the right. The warning shot scuffed the leaves six inches from his arm.

Dedication

Dedicated to the great handlers and dogs
at Bloodhound Man-Trackers
under the Elbert County Sheriff's Office.
A special thanks to Frank Hurst,
whose bloodhounds Red (R.I.P.) and Radar
I personally got to watch do a track.
They are amazing dogs.

Chapter 1

Hunched over with arms folded, the young girl whispered into the darkness. "I want to go home, God, please I want to go home. I promise to be good. Please help me." Her small body shuddered as she sobbed. Her tears mixed with the dirt on her cheeks, making muddy smudges.

She had heard once if you tried hard and thought about something long enough you could send your thoughts to someone else. She closed her eyes. Would anyone even listen? She had to try. It was her only hope.

Cradling her small chin into her folded arms, she tried with all her might to concentrate her thoughts. "I need your help. Can you hear me? Please, I need your help," she whimpered the words repeatedly.

"I can hear you. What's your name?" a voice in the distance called out to her.

Someone heard her! "My name is Abigail. Please find me! If they discover I'm not with the others, they will come back for me." The words tumbled out.

"Where are you? I can barely see or hear you. You're fading. Oh no, Abigail, don't leave yet. I need to know where you are and how to find you."

****

Jessie sat up in a cold sweat; she could recall with detail Abigail's small face and hear her desperate cry for help. Was it a vision, a hallucination, or what? It wasn't a dream; she was awake. Seeing the girl reminded her of when she had first encountered Gina several months ago. Another ghost? No, this girl was alive. She was convinced. Troubled by the surreal feeling she turned on the bedside lamp and glanced around the room. Nothing was out of place, but it felt different. She waited and listened for Abigail's voice to come again. There was only silence. Little by little, her tense body relaxed, her head dropped back against the pillow, and her eyes closed. The vision took her by surprise. Vivid details played like a movie in her mind bringing to life one little girl.

She woke up on a dirty old mattress, with several pairs of eyes staring down at her.

"She looks like a little mouse." One of the kids spoke up.

"That's what we'll call her, mouse," the tallest boy in the group added.

"Hey, little mouse, don't cry. It only makes them mad. The big man will start hitting you. They won't feed you either." The young girl with dirty blonde hair held her hand over Abigail's mouth. "Shush, you don't want him to hear you. He's a mean one."

"Where am I?" She gulped for breath as a shudder racked her small body.

"Hell!" the tall boy said and the others nodded their heads in agreement.

In no time, she had learned why the tall boy had called it hell. Scary, like a big hairy monster, the big man's eyes bulged when he yelled. His face turned red all over. She thought he might explode, but he never did. His big fist hit the closest thing next to him. She tried to stay out of its reach. He often thumped her on the back of her head if she didn't move fast enough. It hurt. She lifted her hand and rubbed the spot.

Every day, and sometimes at night, they were forced into and out of the vans. With no windows and no seats, they were tossed around, hitting each other. Were they close or far away from home? Were they just going in circles? She didn't know. She had to find a way home.

She had stumbled upon her hiding space quite by accident a few nights before. Wide-awake, she rubbed her face. Lily had given her a hard whack when she had rolled over. Peering in the darkness, Abigail could hear the man. He was making all sorts of racket. She searched the dark room until she found him sitting in a chair propped in front of the only way out. Sawing logs is what her grandma called it when Grandpa snored.

Being careful not to awaken him or step on the other kids, she crept along the floor. She moved slowly, making her way into a small alcove off the main room. Feeling along the wall, she felt a barely visible gap in the wallboards. She pulled the boards away from the wall. She felt all around the inside. There was a small space just big enough for her to fit in. She tried it to make sure. She fit! A perfect hiding spot, she thought. They would never look for her there. She crawled back to her place beside Lily and lay down. Abigail smiled. Armed with her special secret, all she had to do was wait for the right moment.

The right moment presented itself. It happened that morning when the kids made their way to the vans with only one man watching them. He was on his phone and distracted. The other two were working on the engine of the first van. Some of the kids started fighting, which made the perfect diversion. She slipped away to her space, praying no one would notice. God must have heard her prayer.

Squeezing into the small space, she tried to get comfortable. Her body touched the rough walls and cramped space. Tears filled her eyes. What was that noise? Someone was coming. She held her breath and tried not to move at all. Heavy footsteps thumped closer until he was there in the alcove on the other side of the wall. He was so close she could see his shoes. The only sound was that of her heart pounding in her ears.

"All clear...Let's move these little brats out of here and get our money." Abigail recognized his voice. It was the man with the big hands. They called him the Enforcer.

When the door finally closed, she let her breath rush out but remained hidden. She refused to let herself think about the icky things living behind those walls. There were cobwebs tangled in her hair. How long had she remained there? She didn't know. She waited and waited until it was dark. Cautiously, Abigail crawled out of her hiding place, unfolding her small body from its cramped space. She strained to hear the slightest sound. Working one stiff muscle and then another, she stood up. They were gone, and she was alone.

Thinking about her secret spot now made her skin crawl. Her stomach gurgled, reminding her it had been a while since she had last eaten. Anything would taste good right now. She made a guessing game out of what would be her first meal when she got home. Maybe Mom would order pizza from Angelo's, or Dad might make his great hamburgers with fries. The thought of *her dad brought tears to her eyes. She wiped them on the sleeve of her dirty shirt, a determined look on her face. She would get home.*

She sighed and whispered, "I did it. I found a way."

Suddenly the vision was over and Jessie heard Abigail's voice again.

"It's so dark and cold. I'm afraid they'll come back for me. I want to go home."

"Abigail, you're very brave," Jessie murmured, her eyes strained to see her. "Where are you?"

"I don't know, but I know you can find me. Please try. Please look for me."

"I'll look for you, but you must help me." Jessie found it hard to believe any of what she had just seen was real. She needed to call Matt. "Hang on, Abigail. I'll do everything I can to find you. I promise. Keep talking to me, and I'll listen for you."

****

Jessie's alarm woke her. Rubbing the sleep out of her eyes, she rolled over and reached for her phone as she sat up in bed. She was surprised to get Matt himself on the phone and not his voice mail. At least she knew someone in the police department who would take this story seriously!

"Matt, this is Jessie. I'm sorry to call you so early. Do you have time to see me at the station for a few minutes before work?"

"Long time, no see—does this mean you're through ignoring me?" His tone suggested he was grinning. "Will eight thirty work for you?"

"Fine, I'll be there." Irritated, she hung up without saying goodbye.

She reminded herself not to let him push her buttons. Her feelings for him, she frowned, were all over the place. She opted for distance rather than face her reaction to him. This was about Abigail, and Matt would know if there were any missing girls in the area. They needed to find her. Jessie sighed. The odds were against it. With no general location or no idea where to start searching, what were her chances? Honestly, she could be anywhere.

Jessie got dressed, ate a bowl of cereal, and proceeded out the door. She honked and waved as she drove past the Inn on the way out to the main highway, her morning ritual since she had moved here. Katie probably wouldn't be at the window to wave back yet. A glance at her watch told her there wasn't enough time to stop at Java Joe's for a cup of coffee. She'd catch it later.

She could feel the change of seasons in the air. The mornings were cooler and the trees, once clothed with green leaves, were beginning to show touches of fall's glorious colors. Blue Cove's last summer concert had taken place a few weeks back on Labor Day. The kids were back in school. They would have to work hard to find Abigail before the weather or hunger made it impossible for her to survive.

A few things had changed since the first case she had worked on with Matt Parker. Had it only been a few months ago? She smiled and shook her head, so many changes. She was in the process of negotiating to buy the Cove Bookstore, which had kept her busy the last few weeks. She had several conversations with the owner of Java Joe's about opening a door between the two businesses, which would be profitable for both of them. Jumping into the negotiating process was just what she had needed after the nightmare she had lived through. Keeping busy was a good way to avoid dealing with her feelings for Matt.

He was correct in his assumption; she had tried her best to ignore him. She would have to work through her own embarrassment and ask for his help with Abigail. Better now rather than later, she thought. Molly, the forever-cheerful manager at Joe's, had told her Matt would be her partner at the wedding; it was time for her to face the music.

She walked into the station and found Gary sitting at the front desk. "Hey, sunshine, what are you doing here?" He grinned at her.

"Where's Mr. C?" She glanced over his shoulder down the hall. "Is Joe's little girl still keeping him up nights?"

Gary nodded and grinned. "He's on tonight, and the new kid isn't here until nine. I guess that leaves little old me. What's up?"

"I have an eight thirty with Matt." She pulled a small notebook out of her purse.

"Have a seat. I'll let him know you're here." He picked up the phone, pushed Matt's line, and then hung up. "His line is busy. I'll be right back."

She sat down, crossed her ankles, and waited the few minutes it took Gary to get back. Jessie used the time to jot down some questions she needed to ask Matt. She also wrote herself a reminder to talk to Reba about the vision. Reba, with her sparkling brown eyes and proper manners, had so much more experience in the bizarre than she had.

The last time she had been with Matt was a few

weeks ago. She had given in to a crazy impulse, which was so unlike her. *One incredible evening*, she exhaled, shaking her head. She started running the minute he had started talking about meeting his parents and family.

"Hey, Jessie, Matt will see you now. It's the big office at the end of the hall."

"Thanks, Gary." Walking toward Matt's new office, she felt the familiar heat building along her neck and face. "Get over it!" She stood tall, lifting her head. "You don't want to give him any advantage." She knocked on his open door.

His gaze was intense. "It's been a few weeks, Jess. How are you?" A flicker of amusement lit his eyes. He watched her walk through the door.

"I'm doing well, but I'm not here about myself. I needed to ask you some questions, if you have the time." She sat on the edge of the chair in front of his desk.

"Ask away. I'm all yours for the next few minutes." He smiled, placing his arms on the desk, and waited for her to begin.

She folded her hands in her lap, holding them tight. She didn't want to give way to the desire to slap the grin off his face. "I'm not sure where to start," her soft voice began. "Last night I had an experience. A young girl was calling out for help, and I heard her. I know it sounds strange, but we talked back and forth. I asked for her name, and she told me it was Abigail. I saw what had happened in her life for a few days, which I'm still trying to process. I guess my question is do you know of a missing child named Abigail? I'd say she was twelve or maybe a little older." She opened her notebook and checked off the first question.

"I do remember an Abigail." Matt stood up and walked out of his office. "I'll be right back," he called over his shoulder. When he returned he was carrying a large book. He opened it and flipped through the pages, then pushed it toward her.

"That's her!" Jessie bolted upright in her chair. "Abigail Davis." She stared at the small girl with dark hair and brown eyes. "She was abducted from Blue Cove?"

Matt nodded. "It's an ongoing investigation. She was playing volleyball with her friends on the beach. They described it as one minute she was running after the ball and then she was gone. It was as if she disappeared into thin air. What are you thinking?" He lifted his brows, a thoughtful expression on his face.

"I don't know how, but I saw that volleyball game. She was chasing the ball toward a group of men. They're the ones who kidnapped her. One of the men she described as being big with large hands." She looked again at the photo of Abigail. "I believe she's alive somewhere, but there's not a lot of time. We have a small window in which to find her. She's cold, hungry, and worried they'll come back to get her." Jessie met Matt's skeptical stare. "She can't tell me where she is, not even a general location."

"How are we going to find her, if we don't know where to begin looking?" One brow lifted in challenge.

"I've asked myself that same question. I'm new to all this." She shook her head. "As with our first case, I didn't look for Gina, she came to me, and now Abigail has come to me for some reason. I'm going to keep listening for her. I believe, in time, she may be able to remember something to help us, but she's too afraid right now." She studied the picture of Abigail and took notes. "Her nickname is Abby just like Joe Collin's baby girl. She's almost thirteen. Her birthday is a few weeks away. With any luck we'll find her, and she'll be home to celebrate it."

"How'd she escape her kidnappers?" His eyebrows were up, but he was listening to her at least.

"She found a gap in the wall, barely visible, and was able to squeeze into it. The day they were loaded into the vans to leave, the kids began fighting which caused a diversion, and she slipped away unseen."

"You saw all that?" He raked his hands through his hair. "Geez, Jess, what are you—psychic?"

"No, I know the whole thing is weird—it is to me, too. I'm simply telling you what I saw, but I don't know how or why. I guess we'll have to wait and see when we find Abigail if any of this really happened to her or not. You can hold your judgment on me being whacky until then." She couldn't tell what he was thinking.

He grinned and stroked his chin. "Fate is throwing us together again. I'll send you what I have on the case file for her." He paused. "Is there anything else?"

She nodded. "Abby described her captivity like being in a plane waiting to land, circling around the city until a space opened up. This leads me to believe she must have felt they were going in circles, seeing some of the same area again. What do you think?" She looked directly at him for emphasis.

"Anything is possible." His keen study of her face was making her nervous and she lowered her eyes first.

She managed to continue, glad that she was not blushing. "I think what I'm about to suggest may make the whole idea of finding her more plausible."

"Suggest away, it can't be any stranger than what you've been telling me."

"My friend Frank Wagner has a bloodhound. His dog has had several successful tracks. Do you care if I call him to see if he could help? I'm not sure what Radar can do since we have no idea how much time has passed, or if Abigail is even in the area. If Frank comes, we'll need to talk with her parents and get an item belonging to Abigail with her scent on it."

"I can arrange for the particulars, if you can get your friend here. Who is Radar?" he asked curiously.

"Radar is the dog." She started to stand, but sat back down. "You might want to check and see if there are any other missing children. I did see some other kids."

"Where are you going with this?" He waited for her reply.

"I'm not sure, but I want to consider all the possibilities." She nodded shortly. "I'll start my own research on the subject, but you have the database and the expertise."

"Okay, Jess, we'll work together to find the girl." He grinned, making eye contact with her. "Of course, that means you have to stop running, ignoring me, and hiding from me."

"Let's get something straight." She propped her elbows on his desk and glared at him. "Our little evening took me by surprise. I wasn't sure exactly how to deal with it. I'm not usually so forward." She almost whispered the last part. "However, this is about Abigail, not you and not me. We need to do all we can to help this girl." She stood up and started to walk out of his office. "I'll get over the awkwardness of it, if you can."

"Sure, I can do that, Jess. It wasn't awkward for me, I was damn glad you did it. I'm only happy you didn't know all that was in my head that night." He chuckled, his grin widening when she stopped walking. "You're blushing. Look, we make a good team. And, I'd like to believe we're at least friends."

She nodded, glanced back at him, and walked straight into Dylan who was standing in the open doorway. "Hey, Jessie, what are you doing here?" He stepped aside to let her by.

"I wanted to run something by my friend and your new police chief." She let a hint of sarcasm color her voice. She turned and called over her shoulder. "Oh, by the way, Matt, congratulations. You deserved the promotion."

****

Matt smiled as she gave Dylan a playful shove on her way out. He had to admit he missed their sparring matches. "Dylan, come in for a minute. I need to run something by you."

"What's up?" Dylan sat down.

"Jessie had some kind of vision last night in which a girl named Abigail was calling out for help. She recognized the Davis girl's picture as the girl she'd seen." He pointed to her photo.

"How does she do it?" Dylan had a puzzled look on his face.

"I couldn't tell you and doubt she could either." Matt sat back in his chair, folding his arms behind his head. "Jessie's convinced Abigail is still alive, and we have a short window of time to find her. I agree about the time, but I'm not sure she's alive, seeing as Jessie's last visitor was a ghost." He made a face. "Anyway, Jessie's friend has a bloodhound, and she is going to see if he'll help us with the search. I want you involved in this case from the beginning."

Dylan nodded with a little chuckle. "Okay. Do you think the two of you can work another case together without killing each other?"

"As Jessie so aptly put it, it's not about us, it's about Abigail." Matt grinned. "We're professionals and as such, we work well together."

"Damn, but I do enjoy watching the two of you fight what's so obvious to everyone else." Dylan grinned broadly.

"And what exactly is that?" Matt frowned at Dylan. "People do like to meddle," he said under his breath. "Only Jessie and I can determine if we're right for each other. I like Jessie well enough, but neither of us is ready for a serious relationship. I'm exploring the possibilities, but I'll do it in my own time." He changed the subject abruptly. "I thought you were going to pursue her."

"I have, I am, and so has almost every other single guy in town." Dylan smiled at Matt's frown. "It seems hopeless for all of us though."

"I'll let you know when her friend will be here with his dog. I know time is of the essence." Matt was all business again. He picked up his ringing phone and motioned for Dylan to wait a minute.

"I'm on my way. Has a request for an ambulance been called in?" Matt stood as he hung up the phone. "We have an injured child a few miles from Ted's place. Let's get the team together."

Chapter 2

"Hi, Blondie." Melinda's gravelly voice greeted Jessie as she walked in the door of the church.

"Hey, Red." Jessie looked at her and smiled. Melinda had pulled her red hair into in a precarious ponytail of riotous curls on the top of her head. Her glasses were perched lopsided among the curls along with a pencil she had stuck there.

"Sometimes I miss Gina being around. The church is almost too quiet. The only thing I have to do these days is my work." Melinda sprayed the window beside the door with glass cleaner.

"I wouldn't tell everyone this. I miss her too." Jessie playfully put her finger to her lips. "It's our little secret." She walked down the hall to her office.

She opened the door to a ringing phone and hurried to answer it. "First Community Church, this is Jessie, may I help you?" She straightened her desk as she began to talk.

"Yes, you may, Jessie dear, this is Reba. I was thinking about you today and knew it was time we got together again."

"Nothing surprises me anymore." Jessie laughed. *How does she know?* Jessie shook her head. "I had you on my list to call today."

"You know what they say, 'great minds think alike.' Shall we do lunch at Java Joe's or Angelo's?"

"I wouldn't mind a salad from Joe's."

"Okay, Jessie, I'll see you there at noon."

She heard them talking before she saw them. Pastor John and Pastor Kevin walked in together. "Good morning, Jessie." Kevin smiled at her.

"Good morning. I put a couple of messages in your box yesterday, Pastor John. Did you see them?"

"I did, and I'll make the calls today." Both men walked to their offices.

Jessie was fond of Kevin. He had turned out to be a natural fit with the congregation. He was innovative and had great ideas of how to update the church's programs. Katie especially liked him. She even showed up to church on the mornings when she knew he'd be preaching. She was active in her pursuit of a husband and Kevin was high on her list, even though he hadn't applied. He hardly knew her, much less her list. Jessie smiled.

Jessie sent off an email to her Grandma Sadie telling her about her unusual experience. Another quick email followed, that one to her friend Frank Wagner. She asked him to bring Radar and help with the search. He responded within minutes saying he would call her at five thirty to get more details.

She tried to work, but her mind kept returning to Abigail. Jessie had heard Abigail calling out to her, but would it work the other way around? Could Abigail hear her if she called to her? *"Abby, I need you to tell me something, anything to let me know what has happened to you."* An image popped into Jessie's mind of a small figure lying quiet and still on the side of a road. She could see him breathing. He's still alive! She shook her head trying to clear away the image. His still form kept intruding into her thoughts along with some other images. She was not getting any work done. She was amazed Abby had the fortitude to hide herself once she saw what had happened to him. Abigail had seen him beaten, but never saw what they did with him. How was it possible that she had? Jessie shook her head.

At noon, she knocked on Pastor John's door. "I'm having lunch with Reba. Would you like me to get you anything?"

"I brought my lunch today. Thanks anyway." He looked up from the book he was reading. "Jessie, take your time. The office is quiet, and I can always call you if you're needed for anything."

"Thanks." Jessie walked down the short hallway to Kevin's office and knocked on his open door.

"I'm going to lunch. Would you like me to bring you back anything?" she asked him.

"No, but I'll walk with you as far as you're going. I'm meeting someone at Angelo's for lunch." He smiled at her as he stood up from his desk. "How's your day going so far?" he asked her as they walked toward the foyer.

"I'm a little distracted, but some days are like that." She stopped to let him open the door for her.

"Anything you need to talk about? Sometimes it can help."

"Not yet, but maybe in the future. I'll see if I can work it out myself first." She gave him a grateful smile.

"Okay, I'm available should the need arise. Have a nice lunch." He stopped walking when she did. He held the door open at Joe's for her.

"You, too." She stepped inside, her eyes adjusting to the inside light.

****

"Hey, Jessie, how are you?" Molly greeted her the minute she saw her.

"I'm fine." Jessie walked up to the counter. The first thing she noticed was Molly's edgy look was softer, and her face was beaming. The garish green eye shadow, which was her trademark, was replaced with a warm beige color. Her gothic dark black hair was now light brown with golden honey highlights; even with all her ink and piercings it was a remarkable transformation. "Your big day is coming fast." Jessie couldn't take her eyes off her.

"I know. I'm so excited. Do you like my new look?" She patted her hair. "Kenny wasn't sure at first, but now he just stares at me and tells me he likes the way I look."

"I think you look stunning."

"Thank you." She smiled at Jessie. "I like it too. What can I get for you? Reba's already ordered."

"I want the Cobb salad and an iced tea." Jessie reached for the glass that Molly placed on the counter and squeezed a lemon wedge into it. "I've had the last fitting on my dress for the wedding. The dress will be ready in plenty of time. I like your choice, by the way. I'd wear it again after the wedding in a heartbeat, which can rarely be done with most bridesmaid dresses."

"I know. It's always such a waste, but I think I chose well." She handed Jessie her change.

"Me, too." She looked again at Molly. It was quite a remarkable transformation.

Reba started talking the minute Jessie sat down. "Hello, my dear girl, I know you must have a few questions for me. Let's get started, shall we?" She leaned forward. "I think you and I have come to an understanding of sorts. We don't need to stand on ceremony." She patted Jessie's hand as she said it.

Jessie paused to gather her thoughts, noticing how composed Reba appeared. She looked extremely attractive, with every hair in place. She wondered how many people knew what was brewing under her proper exterior. "I had an unusual experience last night. I thought you might be able to explain it to me." Jessie told Reba about her strange encounter.

"Well, this is an interesting twist on things. Abigail connected with your thoughts, and you heard her. You're definitely progressing along the path." Reba took a sip of her hot tea. "What were you doing at the time?"

"I was in bed but hadn't fallen asleep yet." Jessie rested her chin on her hands.

Reba's eyes twinkled. She smiled at the puzzled look on Jessie's face. "It must have been extraordinary for you to hear her calling, and then to see all those details in your mind."

"It was cool, I guess, but I'm not trying to progress down any path. Gina was enough to last me a lifetime." Jessie tapped her fingers on the table.

"Obviously not…" Reba smiled gently. "Here you are again, back for more. You may not have tried to hear her, but she was trying hard to get your attention; just like you hadn't looked for Gina, but she found you. You have tender heart, girl, and a desire to help. That's the perfect combination for a person in need."

"What should I do?" She watched Reba as she answered.

"Listen, my dear, simply listen, then try to help any

way you can." Reba's smile left her face. "The child is in dire need; her life depends on you. I know you'll do everything you can to help her." Reba closed her eyes for a moment. "Be careful, Jessie, a friend's life is in jeopardy. I'm afraid there are a few bumps and bruises in it for you, too, but lives will be saved."

"I don't know whether to be pleased or scared out of my wits." Jessie searched Reba's face.

"I suppose a little of both. You don't really want to live an ordinary life, do you? I should think not. It seems to me you moved here wanting to make a difference, and you already have. For those of us who are watching up close or from a distance, we can live vicariously through you." She patted her hair to make sure everything was in place. She leaned forward and grabbed Jessie's hand.

"I'm so happy you're buying the Cove Bookstore." Reba abruptly changed the subject. "Your special touch is just what the store has needed for some time. I hope you'll give it a new and happy name. I'll come in often. I love to read." Reba straightened in her chair. "I'll be there to buy an autographed copy of your first novel. If you haven't started the book yet, you should."

Jessie laughed. "It's not a done deal, dear friend. You know way too much." She crinkled up her nose. "I'm glad you weren't my mom. I mean that in the nicest way. You not only have eyes in the back of your head, you have them everywhere."

Reba chuckled. "Didn't your mother?"

"No, but my mom perfected the use of guilt along with a special look that could peel the paint right off the walls. One of those looks and confessions came swiftly, with very little prodding on her part."

"I imagine there was very little to tell." Reba patted Jessie's hand.

"Au contraire, Katie and I managed to get into our fair share of scrapes." Jessie laughed, her eyes crinkling at the corners.

"If you were with Katie, then I can believe you were involved in mischief. Katie has a mischievous look about her." Reba smiled and sipped the last of her tea. "Keep me updated in regards to Abigail. I'll say some prayers for her."

Reba was unconventional and quirky, but she was kindhearted. Abigail definitely needed her as her champion. The odds were tilting in Abby's favor, Jessie thought, as she walked back to the church.

****

As long as he lived, Matt knew he would never get used to a crime scene, especially when the victim was young. The boy was in his early teens and barely alive.

Kip cordoned off the area upon his arrival. Matt walked around the small site. He measured the distance from the road to where they found the boy. High profile and way too close to the highway to commit the crime in that spot. How long had he lain there? He raked his hand through his hair. It was a busy section of road traveled by many people. Matt frowned. At the speed cars whizzed by, the boy was lucky anyone noticed him.

"What are you thinking, Kip? You've been studying the area for a while?" Matt asked him as he approached.

Kip rose from his squatting position. "I think he was dumped here. No blood or obvious signs of a struggle to indicate this is the crime scene. There are tire tracks at the place where he first fell and then rolled. No footprints, only the tire marks." Kip pointed the tracks out to Matt. "He was probably unconscious when they dumped him here." Kip glanced at the injured boy surrounded by medics. "He sustained several blows to the head, with bruising over a good portion of the visible parts of his body."

Matt studied the boy's battered body. "Somebody worked him over, that's for damn sure." He shook his head, his jaw flexed. "The poor kid. He's probably been lying here for a while."

"Hell, is he going to make it?" Bill shrugged his shoulders, his foot kicked at the dirt. "What kind of scum would beat a kid?" Bill's hands fisted at his side.

Matt looked at Jenson. "Are you going to be okay, Bill? You look like you're about to lose your last meal." He waved to get Dylan's attention. "Talk with Officer Mitchell over there and tell him how you discovered the boy.

"I don't want to keep looking at the poor kid, but it's like a train wreck. My eyes keep tracking there even when I don't want them to."

"Is this your first crime scene?" Matt heard Dylan ask him.

"Yes, sir, it is, and I hope it's my last. I have a son about the same age." He swiped at the tears on his cheeks.

"Look, Bill, this isn't easy for any of us and we've seen a few. Give yourself a break. It's natural for you to feel bad." All the officers there nodded, including Matt.

Matt stood next to Kip and watched the medics at work trying to stabilize the boy. "There's a lot of material under the nails. It looks like maybe we could get lucky with some DNA evidence. This kid put up a hell of fight against his attacker. Look at the bruises on his knuckles." Matt pointed them out. "Be sure the hospital uses the crime kit." Matt walked with them to the ambulance. "We'd like to test his clothing. You know the routine in a case like this."

"We'll do it by the book and call you when the evidence is ready for you to pick up."

"Do you think he'll make it?" Matt frowned.

"He's hung in for who knows how long and seems to be stable. One can hope." They lifted the stretcher into the ambulance.

"I'm going to have one of my men follow behind you. We need to get him identified so we can get his family here." Matt stood at the door with him for a moment.

"Sure enough, I have a son. Anyone who would do this to a kid isn't fit to breathe the same air." The ambulance pulled out with sirens blaring and lights flashing.

****

Later in the day, Matt and Dylan drove back to the station. Matt wanted the perp off the street—now. It would help if they could find the site where the crime had occurred. The more evidence they gathered, the more they could piece together what had happened to the boy. Families usually topped the list of suspects when a child was involved. Although in this case, Matt wasn't so sure. Waiting, he shook his head. How he hated to wait.

"What are you thinking?" Dylan watched Matt's face. "You have that look."

"I'm wondering if it's a coincidence that the boy

ends up in our jurisdiction at the same time Jessie has the connection with Abigail. Is it possible they're connected? Sometimes an operation that goes undetected can slip up." He slowed to make a right turn toward the station.

"It's always possible, but they could be two different cases altogether," Dylan pointed out.

"True, but my gut tells me they're related. I think someone got sloppy, and I'm glad.

Chapter 3

Matt sipped his coffee, tapping a pencil on his desk. He tried to wrap his mind around the facts he was reading. A small number of kids had vanished over the last few weeks in the surrounding area. There seemed to be a trend that had begun more than five years ago, a few children from one area had disappeared about the same time. There were no more disappearances for a year. Then another increase in cases occurred a little further up the coast. Now Abigail and others had gone missing. True, there were always children who went missing, but there seemed to be a pattern here. The speed of his tapping pencil increased until it flew out of his fingers across the room.

Matt picked up the phone to call Jessie. He waited, his foot shifting from side to side. "Jessie, this is Matt. Have you heard from your friend with the dog?" He stilled his foot and took a deep breath.

"He's going to call me after work around five thirty. Would you like to be in on the call?"

"Yes, I have a case that we've just started to investigate. I'm wondering if it's in some way linked to Abigail. I want your friend's dog to work the site where we found the victim as soon as possible."

"Can I ask you something?" Her voice got quiet.

"Sure, go ahead." He turned his chair toward the window.

"Was the victim a young boy? Was he still alive?"

"Geez, Jess, how'd you know that?" He snapped his pencil in two.

"I saw it in that whole encounter thing because, I think…" she stammered, "I think Abigail has that picture in her mind. She saw it happen. I'll stop by the station after work so you can talk to Frank, too."

"I'd appreciate it, Jess." He stared out his window.

"You must think I'm odd, first a ghost and now Abigail." She was overwhelmed. He could hear it in her voice.

"I don't get it, Jess, but I don't need to. I appreciate your input. And I'm fairly certain, had you not heard her, Abigail would be just another statistic." He wasn't sure if she wasn't already. "I'm interested in what your friend has to say." He paused when his phone beeped. "Jess, I need to take this call. I'll catch you later."

He clicked off one line and picked up the other. "Matt, this is Kip."

"What do you have for me?"

"The boy's name is Joshua Harris. His fourteenth birthday was a few weeks ago. His family lives in Rocky Pointe."

"Thanks. I'll call over to Rocky Pointe and see how they want to handle notifying the family." He turned his chair around and opened his file, writing *Joshua Harris* in place of *John Doe*. He picked up his phone and asked Joe to get him Carter at Rocky Pointe. While he waited, he looked in the book of missing kids. He found Joshua's picture. Joshua had been missing a little longer than Abigail. He was a good-looking kid with his whole life ahead of him. Hell, life wasn't very fair. Sometimes it flat-out sucked.

Matt grabbed his ringing phone.

"Hey, Matt, this is Carter. What's up? I was told it was a priority one."

"We found a badly injured teen in our jurisdiction. He's from Rocky Pointe. A male, fourteen years of age, named Joshua Harris. He's in intensive care at the Blue Cove Hospital. We need to get the parents here ASAP. How do you want to handle the family?"

"I'll notify the parents and get them over there."

"Carter, he is in the system for missing and exploited kids."

"I'm familiar with the case."

"Would you ask the parents to bring an item of clothing or anything that he recently handled? We have a bloodhound on his way here to see if we can find the real crime site. This was a dump. The kid was pretty beat up."

"Are the parents suspects?

"They could be. I won't rule anyone out. I'm thinking this might be a part of something bigger though and connected to another missing person. We have some strong evidence the lab will be working on."

"Okay, I'll notify the parents and get them over there."

Matt made a list of all the missing kids over the past few weeks from a hundred mile radius. There were a few. Then he circled out a little farther away, added another two weeks and found several more. Some of the kids were older and one was only eleven.

He continued looking over the database of missing children in the same radius to the north and approximate time. He found more. What the hell was going on? He ran his hands through his hair. It had to be connected, but it did not fit a normal abduction scenario. Was it trafficking? They usually went after the poor, illegals, runaways, or prostitutes in major metro areas. This was different. They actually took a kid off a crowded beach in broad daylight and yanked one of the girls out of her front yard. Why take several? Pedophiles usually abduct one. Was there a market somewhere they didn't know about? His bet was on some kind of trafficking.

He wrote an email to Tom Maxwell at the FBI. Matt filled him in on what was happening and what he had found out so far. He asked if his unit had any knowledge of a group working the area using similar methods, or anywhere else in the country for that matter. The email ended with an invitation to come watch as Radar began his track.

He was putting the final additions on his note when Jessie came in. He looked up into a pair of questioning blue eyes. Damn, she was pretty.

"Do you need me to wait in the reception area while you finish up?" She flipped her hair over her shoulder, out of her face.

"No, I'm almost done." He motioned for her to sit down. "I'll be right with you."

She sat down crossing her ankles, took out her small notebook, and opened to an empty page.

"How'd you meet Frank?" He watched her closely.

"I was sent out on a story about an autistic child who had wandered off. I met Frank and his dog Radar when Lt. O'Malley brought him in to find the boy after a search came up empty-handed." She smiled. "It was amazing. Once he got the scent, he was off. Radar followed until he found the boy miles from where he'd started. He was tenacious. I kept up with Frank after that and wrote several stories about his work." Her face lit up. "Bloodhounds are great trackers. Did you know testimonies based on their finds will stand up in a court of law?"

He nodded with a smile.

"Of course you do, but it's not true with all tracking dogs."

"What's your favorite among all of the stories you wrote?" Matt wanted to prolong her enthusiasm on the subject.

"My favorite was Radar's hit on the van of a suspected murderer. His find put the person in jail before he killed someone else. He was with another girl the day they arrested him, who probably would have been his next victim." Jessie frowned. "I found it strange that he was a normal, even somewhat handsome, looking man. I guess I expected him to look like the monster that he was. Did you ever notice how you can't always tell a criminal by looks?"

He nodded and grinned. "It would make it a whole lot easier if they would just stamp criminal on their foreheads. Is that all of the story, or did you get a little off track?"

"Okay, smarty!" She smiled. "The police had suspected him all along, but his van which had been used to transport the body had been cleaned and refurbished. Even after bleaching and cleaning the van, Radar picked up the murdered girl's scent. One drop of her blood made its way beneath the carpet and landed on a screw. The police believe this particular suspect may have killed up to five women. The dog was able to find the body of the first girl buried in a remote area after a couple of weeks." She sat forward in her chair. "If anyone can find the site where the beating took place and locate Abigail, Radar can."

"I'm glad to hear it, sweetheart, because we're going to need all the help we can get." He rubbed the back of his neck. "Where have you been keeping yourself the last few weeks?"

"I needed a break after the whole Harvest Club case. I finally got my life back, with no one to shadow me. I threw myself into getting to know Blue Cove. I got back to running every day and hanging out with Katie. You know regular life stuff. Did I tell you that I'm in negotiations to buy the Cove Bookstore?"

"Is that right? I didn't know. You've been one busy beaver running away from one night with little old me." He chuckled, his eyes creased at the corner.

"I knew you were going to ruin a perfectly good conversation somehow. You just couldn't leave well enough alone." She glared at him, her chin edging up.

"Are you going to run away?" He grinned, winking at her.

"Will you ever let me live it down?" She was starting to blush.

"Probably in time, but in the meantime, I've got to tease you. You turn such a nice color of red. You never answered my question. Are you going to go hide for a few more weeks, ignore my phone calls, and me in general again?"

"No, but if you keep it up, you may wish I would. Every time I think you have some redeeming quality, you up and ruin it." She stood up, threw her hands up in the air, and headed for the door.

"Where are you going?" He leaned back in his

chair, smiling.

"You don't have to worry, I'm just going to get some water and cool off before I give you a piece of my mind. I need to remind myself you're needed to help find Abigail and all this…" She pointed at him. "It's just something I have to put up with to get the job done."

****

Jessie could hear him laughing all the way down the hall. He could make her lose her cool faster than anyone had been able to do. She found herself pacing back and forth in the women's room trying to let off steam. Why did she let him get to her like that? Other people teased her. She would have to try harder. She couldn't ignore him forever, but maybe she could kill him with kindness. As Katie once told her, "You can catch more flies with honey than vinegar." It wouldn't hurt to try using a little honey.

She took her time walking back to his office. Her phone rang just as she sat down in the chair.

"Hey, Jessie, it's been a while."

"It sure has, Frank. I'm going to put you on speaker so the police chief can hear you. His name is Matt Parker, by the way. He may have some questions to ask you."

"Okay. Hello, Matt, it's nice to meet you. What kind of track are we looking at?"

"I have a victim, a young teen who was severely beaten and dumped. I'd like to find the crime site if possible. I think this case and another case of child abduction may be connected. To tell you the truth, Frank, I'm not sure what all we're looking at. We do need to find the girl; we believe she escaped her abductors. With all the variables surrounding her case, the sooner we find her the better." Matt's forehead creased. "I've asked a friend from the FBI if he'd like to be here during the process."

"I'd be happy to bring my dog and give it a shot."

"You might be needed for a couple of days. We'll take care of all your expenses including the usual tracking fees."

"I'll waive the usual fees if you take care of the rest. This one is for Jessie. What time do you need me there?"

"I'm meeting with the boy's parents in the morning. They're with their son tonight, so let's say around ten thirty."

"I'll be there. I'll need something belonging to each of the kids that has their scent on it." He cleared his throat. "Do you have anything you want to add, Jessie?"

"Not at this time. It will be good to see you again."

"Okay, see you tomorrow."

Jessie stood up to leave when the call was over, but Matt asked her to stay a minute.

"Abigail's parents should be here any minute. I'd like you to meet them. Tell them cautiously about Abigail. Don't offer them too much in the way of hope, but give them a lifeline. Do you catch my drift?"

"Yes, do you remember when I talked to Gina's parents telling them about seeing her? I was able to build trust with them; I'll give it my best shot. I do know how to talk with people, seeing as I've been doing it for a while." She forced herself to smile.

Matt answered his beeping phone, still grinning from her flippant answer. "Okay, send them back." He straightened in his chair. "Are you ready for this?" He looked at her when he asked the question.

Jessie nodded and stood up.

A middle-aged couple came in the office. The woman was clutching a teddy bear in a plastic bag. She was petite like Abigail. He was slightly balding, but had the build of distance runner.

"Jessie, this is Stan and Sarah Davis. They're Abigail's parents." Matt stood and shook Stan and Sarah's hands and so did Jessie. "Please have a seat. I've asked Jessie to be here to tell you a story. Before she starts, may we get you something to drink?"

"No, we're fine." Stan looked at Jessie, sitting forward in his chair.

"I'd like to preface our conversation by saying up until today I hadn't seen a picture of your daughter. I didn't know she was missing. What I'm about to tell you may seem odd to you, but I believe real none the less." Jessie adjusted her chair so she could make eye contact with both Stan and Sarah. "Last night I had an unusual experience. A young girl was pleading with me to find her. She told me her name was Abigail. She promised to keep calling out to me and I promised to try and find her." The room was silent.

"Do you think it's our daughter?" Sarah asked, still clutching the bear in her hands.

"Yes. I called and made an appointment with Chief Parker today. I asked him if there was a missing girl. He showed me the picture of Abby. She was the girl I had seen. She is alive, I believe." Jessie touched Sarah's shoulder. "My friend is bringing his bloodhound tomorrow to join in the search for her."

"Is that what the bear is needed for?" Stan directed

the question to her.

"Yes, I've worked with Mr. Wagner before. If anyone can find your daughter, his dog can." She took Sarah's hand. "We're going to do everything we can to find your girl. I think she was able to escape her kidnappers, but she's afraid that they still may come back. I have no idea how many actual days have lapsed since her escape." She maintained eye contact with them. "Why I can see her, I can't explain. I don't claim to have any special abilities. I just think your daughter called out in her desperation, and for some reason I heard her." She tried to let go of Sarah's hand, but she held tight to Jessie.

"Thank you. I know all of you are doing your best to find her." Sarah looked at Matt. "It gives me comfort to know she may be out there. I'll try to listen for her, too." She handed the bear to Jessie. "Please tell your friend thank you for bringing his dog."

"I will, and we'll take good care of this for you and for Abby."

****

When Stan and Sarah left Matt's office, Jessie walked out with them, parting in the parking lot. Getting in her car, she was happy to be in Blue Cove and not in the New York rush hour. She had the added benefit of going home to watch the changing look of the cove as the sun set. Watching the light and shadows that danced upon the water, changing its look from moment to moment, had become her nightly ritual. Before she pulled her car out of the lot, she picked up her phone to call Pastor John.

"Hi, Jessie, is everything all right?"

"Yes, I was wondering if I could have tomorrow

off. My friend is coming to town with his dog to work on a case with Chief Parker. I'm doing some of the research for him. I've already got things ready for Sunday."

"Of course, you have some personal days you've never used. It sounds like it could be an interesting few days. Have you ever seen the dog work before?"

"I have, and it's fascinating."

"I'll see you on Monday. I'll want to hear how it went."

"Okay." Jessie pulled on to the street and made her way home.

She walked into her house, kicked off her shoes, and got a glass of water. The sunset was already changing the look of the cove. Instead of just watching it, she opted to run in it. She changed into her running clothes. Making her way onto her favorite path to the marina, she started her run at a brisk pace. The sun was setting in the west giving an orange pinkish glow to the clouds over the cove. The air had a slight chill, perfect for running. She picked up her pace, her feet pounding the walkway. She reached the zone quickly, the point where everything around her tuned out and she was in touch with the rhythm of her own movement. She loved it. With little effort, she was at the marina turning around and taking in the spectacular color of the evening sky. This was why she had moved here.

"Abigail, look around you while it's still light. Can you tell me what you see? Can you go to the door and look out? I need to see what you're seeing and hear what you're hearing. Please, Abby, help me to find you. I need some clue about your surroundings. Let me see it through your eyes, sweetie. I saw your mom and dad.

They're still hoping to find you. Keep talking, Abby. They love you." Jessie kept talking to Abigail until she arrived home. She sat quietly on the couch listening for her small voice to answer her back.

Chapter 4

Matt was fascinated with the way Jessie handled people. She was good with Stan and Sarah. She had done what he had asked of her. Jessie was a beautiful woman, but that wasn't what defined her. An extra something special within her made her sparkle. It intensified when she was trying to comfort people. He had noticed her kindness when they had worked the last case together. It kept him coming back to her even when he didn't think he wanted to.

He would never be able to describe it to someone else. He wasn't that clever with words. She kept him guessing every time she was around him. Sometimes it made him feel like a tongue-tied high school boy watching an angel, and other times she could skewer him to the wall with her flashing blue eyes and intellect. He was never sure which Jessie would show up. Hell, he rubbed his chin; his reactions to her were all over the place. There were times he would love to love her and times when he would like to be as far away as possible. Who was he kidding, glued to her side was more like it.

"Hey, Matt, are you ready to call it a night?" Dylan interrupted Matt's thoughts.

"I'll be right with you. I need to send Jessie the Davis file." He sent her an email with the file attached.

"You always call her Jessie to everyone but her. Why is that?" Dylan's eyes gleamed with amusement.

"She hates it when I call her Jess, and I love to tease her. I can't seem to help myself." Matt grinned at his friend.

"At least you're being honest. You want to stop for something to eat?"

"Sure, I can use a break from my thoughts. It's been a hell of a day."

"Is Patterson's okay?" Dylan asked as they walked down the hall together.

"Fine with me," Matt said as they walked into the reception area. "Hey, Joe, how's that little girl of yours?"

Joe looked up from the duty roster he was filling in. "She's almost sleeping through the night, finally. I can safely say we're all doing a whole lot better with a little more sleep. People can actually stand to be around us now. No more short fuses, if you know what I mean. I actually come to work looking human, with my hair combed." He laughed. "I got word that I get to start working the day shift after they train the new kid. I'm down with that."

"You do look a lot prettier, that's for damn sure." Dylan chuckled as he headed out the door.

****

Jessie checked her emails and found one from Matt with the Davis file attached. She read it several times. She started to notice a pattern and decided to send an email to her friend Jeremy. She asked him to look into a few things for her. While she waited, she Googled human trafficking and a whole world of information opened up to her. At the top of her paper, she typed the words *Not for Sale*.

Some of what she read in the Davis file and Matt's

notations matched the normal criteria listed in the articles she was reading. Some of it didn't. By its very definition, trafficking was a criminal activity in which humans were possessions, controlled by others, or exploited for profit. One fact stood out in every article; it wasn't good news for woman and children, who were most often the victims.

Was it possible that Abigail was a victim of human trafficking? Jessie shuddered at the thought. Abigail was lucky to have escaped. She would be even luckier if their plan worked out the way Jessie hoped it would and Radar found her. What was happening to the other children she had seen? How could they find them?

Jessie's phone interrupted her thoughts. "Hi, this is Jessie."

"Hey, I got your email. I'm wondering what you've got yourself into now."

She retold the story of Abigail to Jeremy. "Have you heard of anything that might shed some light on what's happening here?"

"The rumor mill is always buzzing with news of investigations, possible raids, and rescues going on. I haven't heard about anything specific to your area, though."

"Do you have any idea what we're looking at? Is it possible they're going to export these children overseas?"

"It's possible, if someone found a specific market that wants these kids. By these kids, I mean they specifically want American children. I've heard of some cases of kidnap and export under those conditions along with the exports tied to the drug cartel." She could hear his computer keys clicking. "There are also some business owners from other countries importing women and kids into this country."

"That speaks volumes, doesn't it?" Frustration filled Jessie's voice. "How do you know what you're looking at?"

"It's not always so easy to spot. You might see it daily and never know." He paused, and she could imagine him running his hand through his curls. "I heard a story the other day about one of my favorite Indian restaurants here in the city. The owners were bringing children and young teens from their own country. Their living conditions were awful. You know, dirty mattresses on the floor, crowded together in one room, and not one had received any compensation for their work."

"How'd the authorities find out?" she asked.

"An anonymous tip to the hotline," he told her. "The FBI raided the place, and the kids are now on their way back to India. It's taught me to be more observant of my surroundings. I went to that restaurant at least once a week and never thought anything was out of order."

"I'm not sure I'd know it if I saw it either. When do they call it human trafficking?"

His answer was quick. "With children the criteria is simple: abducted, transported as a possession, and exploited or sold."

"So why these kids? Do you have any ideas?"

"Do you want my opinion? I don't have any evidence or facts yet." Jessie heard him take a deep breath.

"Yes, I want it."

"It's possible they're a group of our own citizens

abducting these kids. There has to be money involved and changing hands, or they wouldn't risk it. They might or might not look like thugs with machine guns. My guess is since they've been off the radar they could be model citizens and just blend in. Maybe they're an active member of the community similar to those folks in the Harvest Club. The difference is they collect and sell children for some sordid purpose here at home or wherever they find a specific market. We have a few dirty little secrets in this country, too."

"What are we looking at? I'm trying to wrap my head around it."

"I'm guessing some kind of children's porn ring, sexual predators, or some new open market they've discovered. Hell, Jessie, there are people who actually believe that sex with a virgin will cure AIDS. There are some sick people out there."

She rubbed the back of her neck. "I don't get it. How can someone do this to a child?"

"Let's face it, money is the drawing card. You know that from your last case. It always comes back to money. Human trade is an extremely profitable business. Sadly, the human toll makes it staggering."

"Money is always at the heart of everything I guess." She sat down in the chair. "I wonder, are we talking rich enough for someone to be willing to pay off others not to get noticed?"

"You catch on fast."

She jumped back up and paced. "This is our backyard. What's being done to prevent it?"

"There's a small army of heroes who work against time constraints and lack of funds in this area. They're passionate about finding kids and bringing these traffickers to justice. They'll be the first to admit that at times the process is too slow. There aren't enough laws defining what constitutes human trafficking, much less how to get international law to agree on those definitions. It's changing though, and we're tightening the laws here."

"That's good to know." Her forehead creased.

"One good thing, it's created a niche for non-profit groups who are bringing attention to the growing problem and rescuing people. Every person rescued means one less enslaved, and a few more traffickers in jail."

"Another plus and the good guys win again." Jessie smiled.

"How can I help you?"

"See if you can find anything that might tell us why these kids were taken."

"I will, and you stay safe. Say, I've been thinking about heading your way for a little R & R. Am I still welcome?"

"Do you even need to ask? I have a guest room. Just be forewarned my friend is actively looking for a husband. She may add you to her list."

"So is she pretty?"

"Very. Are you interested?"

"It's possible." She could hear the laughter in his voice. "I'll email you the date when I'll be there. You could email me a picture of her."

"I'll think about it, or maybe you should just be surprised. See you soon, Jeremy." She hung up the phone.

Jessie sent off an email to Neil telling him about her idea for a new story. She hoped that by bringing attention to the subject, it might encourage people to notice their surroundings and anything that didn't look just right. Jessie shut off her computer. She wanted a break, and her stomach told her she needed to eat.

She went into the kitchen, opened the refrigerator, peered in, and quickly closed the door. Nothing looked appealing and she certainly didn't want to cook. She sighed, opened it again, and began shifting things around. It didn't help—still nothing jumped out at her saying *I look good, eat me.*

****

She grabbed her sweater, locked the door, and strolled toward the Inn. The full moon was beginning to make its appearance in the early evening sky along with a few twinkling stars. The air was crisp, cool, and refreshing.

Gone were most of the vivid flowers of summer, but the autumn mums and late seasonal bloomers were still in abundance. The colors of autumn were popping up everywhere, and the smell of damp leaves filled the air. She walked around to the front door of the Inn and stood on the large wrap-around porch taking it all in for a moment.

When Jessie finally opened the door and stepped inside, the same pleasure filled her that she felt each time she saw it. The Inn had been restored with meticulous attention to details, from the crown molding down to the wood floors. Katie's uncle had overseen all the work while he was still alive, and Katie made sure it remained topnotch. From its beautiful chandeliers, its fine mixture of traditional and antique furnishings, and the perfect mix of modern amenities, the Blue Iris Inn was a great place for a weekend getaway. She lived right next door and could visit anytime. How lucky was she!

It smelled wonderful. Jessie's stomach grumbled in response. She took a deep breath. Tonight's creation was certain to be another great success. Katie was a fabulous cook. The taste was sure to be as good as the aroma coming from the kitchen.

She followed the sound of Katie's voice, finding her in the dining room. Her hands were waving enthusiastically as she chatted with one of her guests. Her face was animated, her eyes sparkling.

"Hi, Jessie, I'm so glad you're here." She grabbed her and pulled her forward. "I was just telling Mr. Perry some of our crazy antics growing up." A silly grin lit her face.

"Please call me Mark." He stared at Jessie with a besotted look on his face.

"Okay, Mark, this is my friend Jessie. Jessie, this is Mark. He's visiting from Colorado." Katie was amused. She said under her breath, "Another one falls."

"Hi, Mark, it's nice to meet you. Are you here on business?" Jessie gave him her full attention. He looked very athletic and had a nice smile.

"He's traveling along the coast checking it out." Katie answered for him with the silly grin still plastered on her face. "Jessie, I have something for you in the kitchen. Would you excuse us for a minute, Mark?" Katie headed for the kitchen door when he nodded.

"It was nice to meet you, Mark." She followed Katie.

"Why don't you sit down here and eat dinner so that our nice Mr. Perry can talk again. He can't look at you without becoming unhinged." Katie's delight spilled out into uncontrolled giggles.

"You're just being silly. He was captivated by you."

"Oh, Jessie dear, you are so oblivious. If I looked like you, I'd work it. You rendered him speechless."

"You didn't give him time to answer, and you already work it. I don't know a bigger flirt in all my acquaintances than you. You've managed to date far more guys over the years than I ever did." Jessie glanced over her shoulder and laughed.

"That's because I'm normal and not so particular who I go out with." Katie's green eyes sparkled with mischief. "You are the untouchable beauty men may look at but think they can never have. In the end they settle for me."

"You're a goof. I didn't come to let you insult me but rather, to feed me." Both girls laughed, nudging one another. "Please take pity on me, friend, something smells very good. What's for dinner?" Jessie looked at the evening menu card Katie handed her. She had done a beautiful job as usual. Katie was very talented.

Tonight's Menu Includes:
Chicken Breasts on a Bed of Wild Mushrooms
Rosemary Roasted Potatoes
Tomato and Green Bean Salad
Chocolate Raspberry Mousse

"Do I really have to eat alone in the kitchen?" Jessie raised her brows.

"Of course not, I only wanted to tease you about your effect on poor Mr. Perry." She handed Jessie a filled plate, and they walked back toward the dining room. "For heaven's sake, don't sit next to him, he's likely to become mute."

Jessie sat at the far end of the table, away from Mark, with an older couple from Pennsylvania. She enjoyed their conversation but felt self-conscious about what Katie had said. Then she looked at Mark who seemed completely smitten with Katie.

When Jessie finished, she excused herself, took her plate to the kitchen, and loaded it in the dishwasher. Katie joined her. They talked over tea, sitting at the small table. Jessie began to tell Katie about her strange vision and working with Matt to find Abby. Katie's reaction was swift.

"Are you kidding me? You two are actually going to try to work together again. Can it be done without getting one of you killed?" Katie joked, trying to hide her worry. "The last time you did this I almost lost my best friend." Her voice softened.

"But you didn't. Matt saved my life. I have to try to find this girl. You would do the same thing if you were me, and you know it." Her lifted eyebrows challenged Katie.

Katie sighed. "I guess I would. You're still trying to get over the nightmares of your last adventure."

"I'll be all right. This will be good for me." She sipped her tea. "I have a friend coming in tomorrow with his bloodhound to help in the search. He'll be staying at Matt's place because he has space for the dog."

"Is he single?" Katie gave her a sly wink.

"No, sorry, he's married with grandchildren. Although, I do have another friend coming in a few weeks who I told about you, and he seemed interested. You can maybe add him to your list."

"Okay, if you'll continue to bring a fresh supply of

single candidates for my cause, I'll keep feeding you. I'll try not to complain about you working on another case, even though I'll never to get to see you. Is it a deal?" Katie pressed her lips together trying hard not to laugh.

"Do you really promise not to complain?"

"Girl Scout's honor." Katie couldn't contain the smile that widened.

"You were never a Girl Scout." Jessie gulped back an astonished giggle. "You're such a little liar. I almost fell for it. How dumb can I be? I bought the whole 'I had left Mark speechless' routine of yours. He was totally taken with you."

"He was taken with me, asking questions about you, until I got sick of it and excused myself." Katie laughed at Jessie's expression.

"Oh no, you don't! I'm not going there with you again. I need to get home. Thanks for the dinner."

Jessie smiled the entire walk home. Katie made her laugh; it was as simple as that. She pulled her sweater tightly around her. The night air was brisk. Jessie looked up to the night sky awash in moonlight and whispered, "Please watch over Abby tonight and help us find her soon."

Once home, she got ready for bed, gave her emails a once-over, and settled herself in bed. She propped herself up with pillows, picked up a book, and began reading. Concentration was impossible. She kept thinking about a young girl all alone, cold, and afraid.

"Abby, if you can hear me, we're coming. Tomorrow, we'll start searching. You need to look outside when it's light and tell me what you see."

"I'll try," a soft voice replied in her mind.

Chapter 5

"What do you mean we're missing one? I went back and checked the place myself. There was no one there." Eddie slammed his big hand on the steering wheel and stepped out of the van. "We've gone too far to go back. You'd better hope she dies out there. She might be able to identify us."

"I don't know how she could've gotten away, unless it was the moment those damn kids started fighting." Jed glared at Karl who was watching the kids as they ate their breakfast. His eyes darted back and forth between Eddie and the kids, his upper lip covered with a sweaty sheen.

"You damn idiot, Karl. You were on the stupid phone. Not doing your job again." He cursed, trying to slam his huge fist into the Karl's face. Karl shifted and ducked just in time. Eddie's fist hit the van, putting a dent in it. "There was no one inside the shack when I went back in to check. You let her slip away. I ought to shoot you." He pointed his gun at Karl's head.

"Relax, both of you. She has no idea where she is. Without food or water, she probably won't last long. Besides we're almost done with our part; all that's left is to nab two more kids, get our money, and lie low for a while. Thanks to our friend, we don't exist in the system at all." Jed walked toward the kids.

"The sooner these damn kids are out of my hair,

the happier I'll be. I do my job, I move the meat, and I collect my dough. What they do with them is no skin off my back. That's the way I like it." Eddie chuckled, and yelled at the kids to get back in the van, thumping the tallest boy in the back of his head.

****

The clanging of the alarm awakened Jessie. She reached over to shut it off, struggling to open her eyes. She sat up in her bed surprised it was morning. She had actually slept through the night. She had been so sure she wouldn't sleep a wink listening for Abby. She stretched. Smiling, excited, and wide-awake, she wanted to get started.

She got dressed. Wearing her plaid shirt, khakis, and a good pair of walking shoes, she was ready to go. She put on her blue jacket to cover her badge and holstered gun. Matt had told her she needed to have it every time she worked a case. The only thing left to do was Java Joe's for coffee and maybe a scone.

Abby interrupted her thoughts just as she headed out the door toward her car. *"I can see lots of trees and hear the ocean in the distance. The cabin is old and dumpy. It looks like no one has lived here in years. There is no road. A bumpy path is all I can see. Please hurry. I'm so hungry."* A picture came into Jessie's mind. She wrote the details down, not wanting to forget any.

"Way to go, Abby! I can see it. I'm on my way to join in the search. We're coming, keep talking to me." Jessie got in her car; started down the road with a honk and wave as she passed the Inn. She smiled; her car knew its way to Joe's like a horse returning to the barn.

Opening the door at Joe's, she nearly collided with

Matt, who was juggling two cups of coffee and a white bakery bag. "Sorry, I wasn't paying attention." She caught the bag as it slipped out of his hand.

"Now that you're here, maybe we should sit down and drink this." He put both cups on the table without further incidents.

"Thanks, that was nice of you. I guess there may be one or two redeeming qualities in you. I mean a man who buys a girl coffee in the morning can't be all bad." She tilted her head and smiled at him.

"Has your friend contacted you yet?" He sipped his coffee.

"I'm expecting the call anytime." She tried to gauge his mood. "Are the boy's parents at the hospital?" She saw him nod, but he was quiet. "I can't imagine what they're going through. It has to be the worst nightmare for any parent. Did he make it through the night?"

"Yes, he's in a medically induced coma to relieve the pressure on his brain." He paused, leaned forward, and looked directly at her. "I'll be meeting the parents in about thirty minutes at the station. I'd like you to be with me. It should be a short meeting because they don't want to be away from his side. I'm not so good in the comfort department. You have a way with people." He smiled at her making her stomach flutter.

"Matt Parker, I do believe you've just given me a compliment. I'm not sure what to do next." She was about to say something more, but her phone was vibrating, indicating a text. Jessie read the message from Frank.

"Was that your friend?"

"Yes, he'll be arriving on time and will go directly

to the station."

"Good, we can start on the crime scene as soon as we're done with the parents." He twirled the spoon in his hand.

Jessie stood up and grabbed her coffee. "Maybe we should get to the station so we're there when they arrive."

"I guess we should." He looked at his watch. "My job says the parents are suspects until they're ruled out." He stood up beside her.

"If Abigail's thoughts are correct, they had nothing to do with it at all." Jessie watched him. "I guess until we find her and hear the details from her lips, we'll never know for sure."

He held the door open for her. His brows creased. "The one good thing in all of this is every day he survives, his chances of a full recovery increase. He was barely alive when we found him." He closed the door behind them.

"There you go…" She smiled at him. "He just made it through the night, so his chances went up just a little."

"Jess, you do know that you need to carry your gun and badge all the time you are working a case with me." He glanced at her, seeing neither.

"I have the badge and the gun." She opened her jacket to show him.

"That probably means you had to remove it from the box in your closet where you put it after the last case."

"What, are you psychic?" She grinned at him. "I'll see you in a few minutes," she turned to say, but he was already in his car.

****

Jessie pulled in to the lot and parked just as Matt was walking in the station. Kip opened the door for her.

"Hi, Jessie. Matt told me to tell you to go right to his office as soon as you got here. I'm looking forward to seeing how your friend's dog is going to work the crime scene." He smiled at her.

"I am, too." She breezed by, thanking him for opening the door.

"Good morning, Jessie." Dylan nodded at her. "Are you ready to get started?"

"I am," she called over her shoulder, heading toward Matt's office.

She tapped lightly on the door, and he gestured for her to come in, not looking up from something he was writing. Jessie observed his concentration, not wanting to distract him. He was every bit the professional now. This part of Matt she could relate to and appreciate. She wouldn't want to be on his bad side.

She knew in her heart Joshua Harris couldn't have anyone better on his side. Matt would see that justice was done. She was proud to work beside him on the case.

Jessie pulled out her notebook and wrote Joshua's name at the top of a page. This would be the first article in a series of stories about the kids. Joe knocked on the door, and Matt looked up.

"The kid's parents are here. Do you want me to bring them back?" Joe inquired.

"Yes, and, Joe, ask them if you can get them anything. Is Carter with them?" He nodded and turned to walk back to the reception area.

"I hope I'm ready for this. I don't want to fall

apart." Jessie could feel the tears already starting to gather. She pulled a tissue out of her purse just in case.

"I'm counting on you, Jess." He gave her a warm glance. "You can do it."

The parents stepped through the door, and Matt stood to face two strained, worried faces. The woman was clutching a baseball glove and a picture frame. The man held on to her as if trying to pour what little strength he had into her.

"Martha and Colin, this is Police Chief Matt Parker. He's in charge of the investigation." Carter introduced them.

"I'm sorry to meet you under such hard circumstances." Matt shook their hands. "This is Jessie Reynolds. I've asked her to write a story about your son. We want to bring his story before people, in hopes that if anyone saw something, they'll come forward."

"You never know what might trigger a memory for someone," Jessie added.

"Please be seated." He waited until they were comfortable. "Can you tell me when your son went missing?" Matt's deep voice filled the silence. Martha sniffled, and Jessie reached over, handing her a tissue.

"It was a couple of weeks ago." Colin spoke up, his words halting. "Josh had gone to play basketball at the school with a few of his friends. He rode the bike we had just given him for his birthday. He had just turned fourteen, you see. We bought him the helmet and bike he had always wanted." Colin patted his wife's hand as she sniffled. "I'm sure glad we did that now. The police came to the door with his bike. They found it lying on side of the road, but the helmet wasn't with it. They thought maybe he had been abducted right off his bike."

Jessie went and sat down beside Martha, putting her arm around the woman's shoulder as shudders racked her body. "Who would do such an awful thing to a child?" Her words were barely audible. "His doctor is optimistic but cautious."

"There are people who can help you." Jessie spoke softly to her.

"And we're going to do everything we can to find the person or persons who did this," Matt told them.

"I know of a family support group for victims of violent crimes. There's a chapter in Rocky Pointe. I took the liberty of writing it down for you." She handed Martha the address. "I also gave them your name, so they can contact you and help during Josh's stay in the hospital. They will help as little or as much as you would like. I hope you don't mind." Jessie's soft voice calmed Martha.

"Thank you, it was nice of you to think of us. Our lives stood still the day he went missing. I knew in my heart that he was okay up until a few days ago. Then suddenly, I lost hope I'd ever see my boy again. The phone call telling us Josh was alive but in critical condition gave us a little hope back." She turned a teary gaze on Jessie. "I believe you understand."

"I do." Jessie squeezed her shoulder. "My friend is coming today with his bloodhound to search the area where your son was found. We'll find the crime scene if it's anywhere in the vicinity." Jessie glanced over at Matt and their eyes met. "There is no doubt in my mind that Chief Parker will find the people who did this to your son." She saw the corner of his lips turn up.

Martha handed Jessie the baseball glove. "He carried this with him all the time."

"I'll make sure you get it back so he can use it when he gets well." Jessie placed the glove in the plastic bag on Matt's desk and sealed it.

Martha turned the picture of her son around to show Jessie. "He is such a handsome boy, isn't he?" Martha's voice cracked.

"Oh, Martha, he's a very fine-looking young man." Jessie's eyes filled with tears. "Can you tell me some of your happiest memories of him?" Josh came to life in his mother's words. Jessie carefully wrote the details in her little book. Colin added his own stories of his son. "I want people to know your son. I'll do my best to do justice to his story."

"Thank you. If you're done with us, we would like to get back to our son." Colin helped his wife stand when Matt nodded. "I don't know if talking to him helps him, but it sure does us."

Jessie handed Martha a card with her phone number. "I'll stop by and see you while Josh is in the hospital. I'll sit with him so you can have some time off."

Matt handed them his business card. "I'll make sure you're kept up to date on the status of the case." As Colin and Martha Harris left with Carter, a lingering sadness still filled Matt's office.

"Thanks, Jess, that was an ingenious idea about the support group. They're going to need some assistance in the next several weeks." He frowned. "I get mad that some jerk can randomly hurt a family's life with little or no regard." His eyes flashed with anger. "For what? Money, power? Only God knows what goes through people's minds during such awful unspeakable acts. I have yet to figure out how Chief Anderson did what he did, much less some of the others I've helped put away over the years."

Dylan walked into Matt's office. "How'd it go with the kid's parents?"

"It wasn't easy. There's no way they're suspects in this case. I hope that dog can tell us more."

Jessie cleared her throat. "I believe the one who can tell you the most is Abigail. She saw it, which is another good reason we need to find her. This morning she sent me a picture showing me her surroundings. Are there some abandoned cabins in the area where you can still hear the ocean?" Jessie looked at her notes. "She showed me many trees and a road that was more of an overgrown pathway."

"More than a few, I'm sure." Matt looked skeptical.

"Sent you a picture, how?" Dylan looked at her, puzzled.

"In my mind...I know, weird, huh?" She smiled at his expression. "It must be the drinking water in this town." She looked at her phone when it buzzed, reading a new text. "But don't fry your brains trying to figure it out. I can't, and it's happening to me." Amusement lit up her eyes. "By the way, Frank's in the parking lot if you want to get started."

Chapter 6

Matt walked with Jessie to the parking lot. They found Frank standing beside Radar, a large handsome bloodhound with soulful eyes wearing his sheriff's harness proudly. Frank's kind face, with faded blue eyes, acknowledged their greeting, crinkling the abundance of fine lines at the corner of his eyes and lips. It emphasized the smile that seemed permanently imprinted on his face.

Jessie introduced Frank to everyone as soon as Dylan and Kip joined them. Frank fit into the group, naturally talking with ease to each of the officers. After hearing a little more about the case, he was ready to put his dog to work.

"How do you want to do this?" Matt asked Frank.

"When I get on the scene, the first thing I'll need is a scent article. The less it's handled by others, the better it is for Radar."

"I have the shirt the boy was wearing at the time he was beaten and his baseball glove."

"Radar is a great with finding human remains. Once he has the scent, he can find something as small as a drop of blood or even a tooth." Frank grabbed dog treats, stuffing them into his pockets.

"We're not sure how long ago the boy was dumped at the scene, and the girl has been gone for about two weeks," Matt explained.

"We have successfully run a two-week-old track both in training and on a case. Radar is a scent discriminating K-9. This means, a person he's tracking can't hide even in a crowd. He'll walk right up to them and touch them on the hand with his snout."

"I'm looking forward to seeing him in action. My friend works with a patrol dog. His German shepherd works well on a hot track. He becomes less effective as time passes and the more people cross over the track. His dog's training emphasized bite work, and he's great in apprehending a suspect." Kip stroked Radar as he spoke.

"A good rule of thumb in considering what dog to use is a patrol dog is a general practitioner with emphasis on bite work and apprehension. The bloodhound is a specialist trained to do one thing, hunt for people. His handler devotes one hundred percent of his training on search work. Regular training allows the handler to learn his dog's body language to determine if the dog is on or off scent. They learn to work as a team." Frank paused for a moment adjusting the harness on Radar. "As you can see, this is one of my favorite subjects. I'm still amazed how my dogs work."

"How long did it take you to train him?" Dylan made his way into the conversation.

"I worked with him for about one year before we did search work, but I actually train him on a weekly basis still. I have a five-month-old puppy doing puppy tracks and training alongside Radar."

"He looks ready to get started." Matt bent down holding out his hand with a treat for Radar. "I have a chocolate lab. You can get pretty attached to these guys."

"You're telling me. I have a Belgian Malinois, Kilo, who is my drug dog. I have two bloodhounds, Radar and Red. They're some of my best buds, aren't you, fella?" Radar looked at Frank with tail wagging, and bayed in response. "I'll load him up and follow you out to the site."

"Do you have everything you need for the dog?" Matt petted Radar.

"Yes, sir, I do."

"Kip, you and Dylan ride with Frank out to the site. Jessie and I will be there directly so don't start him until we're there. I need to pick up an order of sandwiches on my way out. I can't have anyone getting hungry while this is in progress. Frank, you're the handler; you tell us what you want to do."

"Okay." Frank shook Matt's hand.

"Let's roll." He pushed Jessie playfully toward the car. She gave him the look, the one her mom had given her often enough.

The order was ready and waiting at Patterson's. Matt paid and was back in the car in less than fifteen minutes. They got to the site just as Frank was unloading the dog.

"Your friend seems nice." Matt pulled his cruiser in behind Frank's Durango.

"He is the best. I've known him a few years and have gotten to know his family. He works a case extra hard when he knows there are kids involved. He has two grandsons." She opened the car door to step out.

She went over to Radar and stroked his head. "How are you doing, big boy?" She fussed over him. "Are you going to work hard today, Radar?" She handed him the treat that Frank had placed in her hand.

His tail wagged in response.

Matt took out the plastic bag containing the shirt that the boy had worn and the baseball glove. He handed it to Frank. "There may be more than one site involved," he cautioned.

"It doesn't matter. If the boy was anywhere in the vicinity, he'll find the track." Frank directed Radar to the site where they had found Josh. He took off the dog's harness, handing it to Kip. He had him sit down. He knelt down beside Radar placing the shirt on the ground near him, and let the dog sniff it and the ground around it. "Find it, Radar. Let's get to work."

Frank attached the line to Radar's collar. Immediately his head bent—nose to the ground—suddenly he'd raised it up in the air where he picked up the scent and started for the road. "What do you want us to do?" Matt asked.

"Someone needs to follow in my SUV; it has the dog's food and water in it. One or two of you can walk the track with me."

****

Jessie and Kip walked behind Frank as the dog pulled him along. Dylan drove Frank's vehicle and Matt drove his car with their lunch in it. Radar kept his nose to the ground and followed the road for close to two miles when he suddenly veered left off onto a barely visible path. He was tugging hard on the line and pulling Frank along at a quicker pace.

"You have to be in some kind of shape to do this for long periods of time. Your friend's getting a real work out." Kip grinned.

"I can't imagine what his arm feels like at the end of the day." She called out to Frank. "Do you always keep him on the line?"

"Most of the time, especially near the highway. I always do in an area I'm not sure about. If we're working a large open area, I'll sometimes let him offline on rare occasions." Radar tugged on the line, sniffing up in the air, moving faster. "I think he's on to something." Frank adjusted his pace to keep up with the dog.

She called Matt. "Frank thinks he's on to something; he's pulling hard."

Frank halted the dog for a minute. He got the water out of his SUV when the vehicles pulled up behind them. He made the dog drink. "How far have we gone?"

"Close to three and half miles…" Matt checked his odometer.

"He won't stop unless I force him to, but he needs to stay hydrated. Jessie, you're a runner. Do you want to run with him?"

"Sure, but won't he get too far ahead of me?"

"He's trained to keep you in sight, and he'll pace himself to you. We'll follow in the car." Frank put him on his long line. "Here's a radio. Stay in touch."

"Jess, remember to use caution. I doubt they're in the area, but you never know." Matt made eye contact.

Jessie took a swig of water and put the bottle in Matt's car. "Let's go find him, fella." Jessie took the end of the line in her hand. Frank let go of Radar's collar and gave him the command. They took off running together.

They kept a steady pace for a while, but then Radar's pace picked up; just like Frank had said. He slowed, coming back to check on her and kept her in his sight. They came to an open area. Radar was looking up in the trees, then sniffing head down around the area, until he finally sat down.

"Frank…" She keyed the radio. "He just sat down. I don't know where we are in relation to all of you. He's found something."

Matt jumped out of his car a few minutes later followed by Frank, Kip, and Dylan hot on his heels. Matt carefully searched the area where the dog was and found a couple of pooled areas of dried blood. "This could be the place all right." Up went the crime scene tape so that they would not compromise the evidence still intact. Matt placed the call to Marcy and the crime team, giving them their location.

"Good boy." Frank patted Radar's head, taking him over to the shade where he lay down. Frank filled his water bowl and set it in front of him.

****

"What are you thinking, Matt?" Dylan asked.

"Finding the blood evidence on this site points to the fact that they had to be somewhere in the area. The boy couldn't have run too far before they caught up with him here."

"If the site is in the area, Radar will find it. Radar can retrace all the places this boy has been to recently," Frank called out, overhearing their conversation.

Matt walked a few yards away, squatted down next to a recent set of the tire tracks where two vehicles had stopped. "It looks like the vehicles stopped here and one adult took off running." Dylan and Kip both came to look. "Here are two sets of footprints." He pointed them out. "It looks like maybe three adult males."

"One of them must have stayed by the kids, these

prints don't lead anywhere." Dylan pointed out the stationary prints.

"Look at all the smaller prints. They must have made the kids stand outside and watch what they did to Josh; that's one hell of a way to control them, keep them afraid. There are quite a few prints, but too overlapped to tell how many kids we're talking about." Kip walked the length of the tracks from the front tires to the rear tires. "A long wheel base might indicate a truck or van; transporting kids, you wouldn't want to be noticed, most likely a van with no windows."

They walked back to the car and Matt reached for the water and soda, pulling the cooler out of his car. "We may as well eat while we're waiting for the team to get here to process."

All of them sat down on whatever they could find. Lunch consisted of a turkey, avocado, and tomato sandwich, a piece of fruit, and something to drink.

"Watching your dog work fascinates me," Kip addressed Frank.

"A bloodhound tracks by smell. They can distinguish human scent days after they have been in the area even across water." Frank spoke proudly.

"He was quiet the entire track. I thought they barked all the way during a track—at least they do in the movies." Jessie smiled at him taking note of his grin.

"Actually, at one time they did, but too many dogs were lost that way. It gave the bad guys the advantage; they could hide and pick off the dogs and their handlers when they came into view. We train the dogs to be silent during the track. The only reason he bays is to let you know he's found what's been asked of him."

"You get a helluva workout holding on to that dog." Kip chuckled. "I got tired just following you."

"You've got that right, and with each passing year it gets a little harder. I'll keep doing it as long as I can." He rubbed his knee. "I have arthritis in this knee. Sometimes it slows me down. My dogs take it all in stride." He paused. "How'd you like running with him, Jessie?"

"It was cool. He would get out ahead, pull hard on the line, and then come back to me, taking off again." She ate a bite of her sandwich. "I hope we can find where they had all the kids before they were here, it might help us in finding Abigail. I know she holds the key to the other kids' identities. She might be able to give us a description of her abductors."

"Like I said, if it's anywhere in the vicinity, Radar will find it. He's been routinely utilized at cold crime scenes. He's one of the best with decomp. If it's out there, he'll find it."

"I, for one, am impressed." Dylan stood up to stretch.

"Me too…" Kip stretched out his long legs. "I'm anxious to see what he does in the next part of the track."

Once the rest of team was in place doing their job, Frank could proceed with the next phase of the track.

"Okay, Frank, let's see if he has one more find left in him today."

Frank led them to the tire tracks. He knelt beside the dog, back on the line, and let him smell the shirt and glove again. "Find the boy, Radar."

The dog's routine began again. He sniffed the ground where the vans had been and started down the path where they had come from. He sniffed the air, then his nose was down smelling at ground level until he caught a scent, then he pulled on the line moving more quickly. Frank kept pace with him, working in tandem. After about fifteen minutes, they rounded a corner into an area where an old barn was standing. Frank let go of the line. Radar ran to the barn and started baying, trying to get in.

Matt and Kip, with guns drawn, cleared the site before they let anyone else go in. They had been there. The remnants of their stay had remained. Matt called Dylan.

"Dylan, when you wrap it up there, we have another site to process straight down the path from where the tire tracks are. It took us about fifteen minutes to walk here, so it's not far. Look for the old barn. Whoever is done there, send them over. It looks like this is one of the places where they stayed."

"What's on your mind, boss? You have that sound about you."

"It has to be someone who knows the area well. Someone passing through wouldn't know these old paths, much less where they lead." Matt looked around.

"I wonder if they have taken kids from the area before." Dylan sounded thoughtful.

"I think we may be dealing with some locals. None of this fits the normal profile, but maybe we're in new territory. We'll be writing a new playbook as we go along."

"Tom Maxwell just got here. He's following us down to look over the site."

It didn't take long for the small group to get there. Matt strode over to talk to Tom when he got out of the car, and filled him in on the morning's progress. Tom was almost as tall as Matt was, with brown eyes and broad shoulders.

"I'm sorry for not getting here earlier. I had a few things I had to take care of before I could leave the office. A lot of paperwork, I'm sure you know how that is." He shook Matt's hand.

"I do now." Matt laughed. "I want you to meet the man who is working the track for us." They walked together to where Frank stood with Radar. "Frank, I'd like you to meet a friend of mine with the FBI. This is Tom Maxwell." They shook hands. "Tom, this is the other hero of the day, Radar."

"It's nice to meet you, Frank. You have a good-looking dog here." He put his hand out for the dog to sniff it. "He's a damn fine animal. You must be pretty proud of him."

"I am, especially on days like today when things go well and he gets down to business without any shenanigans." Frank smiled.

"Did you train him yourself?" Tom asked.

"I did. I have two dogs, which I have trained in search and rescue. I also have a dog trained to find drugs."

The two men walked toward the barn to have a look around. Marcy was busy taking pictures. Dylan was helping one of the newer officers with measurements and drawings.

"How did you hear of Frank? There are so few really good dog handlers to go around," Tom asked.

"He's a friend of Jessie's, the woman that helped me in the last case with the Harvest Club. I told you about her. She is a writer with a great instinct for digging up facts. I don't think you ever got to meet her."

"I don't remember if I did or not." Tom stopped to shake Dylan's hand. "Is she here now?"

"Believe me, if you met her, you'd remember." Dylan chuckled.

"Why's that?"

"She has a face you can't forget, and a..." He stopped when he saw the look on Matt's face.

"Several of my officers are taken with her." Matt changed the subject. "She's going to have to tell you how she got involved in this case. I don't think you'll believe it."

"Sounds good, Matt; if you don't mind I'm going to go check into the motel. Call me and let me know where you want to meet for dinner. I want to hear all you've got on this case so far. We're beginning to hear more in the rumor mill about this kind of activity. If you ever want to switch over to the FBI, just let me know." Tom laughed at the scowls he got from the rest of the team.

Matt walked Tom over to his car. "Let's meet at six thirty at Anthony's on the waterfront. I'll call for reservations now."

"I'll meet you there." Tom got in his car.

Matt called Anthony's.

Matt informed Dylan and Kip of plans to take Tom and Frank out and invited them to come along. "Have either of you seen Jessie?"

"I saw her walk down the path a while ago." Frank pointed in the direction.

Matt started down the path. He wanted to ask Jessie to come to dinner tonight, and tell her to invite

Katie so she wasn't the only woman. It was short notice, but it wasn't a date after all. He rounded the bend in the path and saw her sitting on a fallen tree. She looked deep in thought and very vulnerable.

Chapter 7

Jessie had followed the pathway down around the bend, away from all the activity at the barn. She needed to be alone. Once again, she found herself overwhelmed with the strange occurrences happening in her life. If this case went like the last one, she would hardly have time to process one event before the next came along. She leaned her shoulders against the smooth trunk of a young alder. Why did she have a girl talking in her head? She sat down on a rock close by and closed her eyes. She had never been interested in the paranormal. She was a journalist, for heaven's sake, who dealt only in facts. Why me, she wondered.

As she stared off into space, her thoughts turned to the words Katie had said in fun the other night. Was she aloof, did she scare men off? She hadn't had time for a real relationship, between building a career and wanting to date someone who was a least as intelligent as she was. She frowned. Maybe she was just being too fussy. Anyway, what man in his right mind would want to hang out with a woman who talked with ghosts and had a girl running a movie reel in her head? She did an internal eye roll.

"What are you doing here all by yourself?" Matt's voice startled her.

"Gathering wool, as my grandma would say."

"Have you worked it all out?" He grinned, his hand

pulling a leaf from the tree. He twirled it for a moment, checking it out. He let it fall and watched as the golden leaf floated to the ground. "You looked like you were about to take someone out. I was hoping it wasn't me."

"I can assure you, I wasn't thinking about you." She smiled, glancing at him.

"That's nice to know. I'd hate to think I could cause such a scowl."

"I wonder where this path goes from here." She changed the subject rapidly. "It looks a little like the road that was more of an overgrown pathway that Abigail described."

"I take it the subject is now closed." He leaned against the tree watching her. "Yes, I can see that it is."

"Really, there's nothing to talk about. I'm just trying to figure out why this crazy stuff has started happening to me." She rubbed the back of her neck feeling a pinch of pain starting in her head.

"It could be just like Reba told you."

"Meaning…" Her eyebrow arched up.

"You are a caring person, Jess. Maybe you are simply hearing cries for help that the rest of us miss. Don't make it something it's not. It is what it is. Did you go looking for Gina's ghost or Abigail for that matter?" He pushed away from the tree and walked toward her.

"Of course not!" She shook her head. "It just happened."

"I proved my point. You are being sought out because you care." He sat down on the rock beside her. "I'm taking Frank to dinner, along with Tom. I'd like Tom to meet you. Why don't you join us, and see if Katie wants to come along."

"That would be nice." She smiled at him. "That way I could spend some time with Frank." She looked down at Matt's hand next to hers. "I'll see if Katie's free. What details should I give her?"

"We'll meet at six thirty at Anthony's. I'm picking up the tab." His hand brushed her hand. "Stop worrying. I think you're pretty normal; most of the time anyway." He grinned when she jumped.

"Ha, ha, aren't we funny." She stood up quickly.

"In the meantime, we should probably make our way back." He stood beside her and motioned. "After you, sweetheart." He chuckled as she glared at him. "I see you're back to normal."

They strolled toward the crime scene. Matt veered off toward the barn, and she walked to the car. She saw Kip lean his hip against the Durango as he talked to Frank. She had never noticed how tall he was before.

"Hey, Jessie," Kip called out to her. "Where have you been? Matt was looking for you."

"He found me." She stopped to talk to him. "I walked down the path a little ways." Kip had a nice face, she thought, one with a lot of character. His grayish-blue eyes always focused on whomever he was talking to with interest. She had noticed that earlier when he was talking to Frank. Kip was his nickname. His given name was Keith Peterson; but Kip suited him. She was tall, but she still had to look up to see his eyes.

"So, will you be at dinner tonight? Anthony's is a pretty swanky place on the waterfront."

"I'll be there. That reminds me. I need to call Katie." She pushed Katie's number on speed dial.

"Hi, Jessie, what's up?" Katie's cheery voice came over the line.

"Matt told me to ask you if you want to come to dinner tonight. He's taking Frank, Tom, his friend from the FBI, and a few others for a meal at Anthony's."

"Dinner is already started, and my assistant can take over for me tonight; sure I'll be there. Anthony's is a really great place, lots of atmosphere, and a wonderful crème brûlée that is out of this world."

"What should I wear? I mean, should I dress up, or what?" Now she had done it. She couldn't keep the words from flying out of her mouth.

"Of course—umm—I know, you have to wear that little red dress I made you buy the last time we went shopping in New York, and those killer heels."

"I'll think about it, but I think it's a little too fitted for an evening out with all the guys. I should have never let you talk me into buying it." Jessie sighed. "What are you wearing?"

"Don't give me that, Jessie, you look terrific in it, wear it! It accentuates your curves without being indecent, as Sadie would say. I'm wearing the great little number I bought. You don't see me afraid to wear it, do you? I swear, Jessie, you better wear that red dress or I'll make a scene, and you'll wish you had."

"Do you want to ride with me?" Jessie changed the subject. That was the only way to stop Katie once she got started.

"No, I'll drive in case I need to leave early. What time are we supposed to be there?"

"Six thirty. See you there." Jessie hung up and headed for Matt's car to wait.

****

They left the crime scene, and Jessie got back to her car with about two hours to make it home and get ready. She needed to shower and to decide what to do about the red dress. Katie would never let her hear the end of it if she didn't wear it. It was a great dress, but it seemed a little on the short side, or maybe she was just too tall. The color was great on her though.

Jessie was ready with a little time to spare. She had her hair pulled up in a cascade of curls to show off her small diamond earrings from her dad. She had to admit the dress was a knockout. She glanced one last time in the mirror trying to tug it down another inch. She put on her lipstick, grabbed her evening bag and a shawl to keep off the evening chill, then made her way to the waterfront and the restaurant.

****

Katie paused in the entry to the restaurant scanning the room for Matt and the others. They were over by the big window. No Jessie? Good! She smiled as she made her way across the crowded dining room. Matt introduced Katie to Frank and Tom. She knew everyone else including most of the other people in the restaurant.

"Save me the seat next to you, Dylan. I'll be over in a minute." She sat down next to Matt.

"Where's Jessie? I thought you two would come together?" He reached for a roll from the overflowing basket.

"I wanted to get here before her." She leaned close to Matt and lowered her voice. "I wanted to see everyone's reaction."

"Reaction to what?" Matt grinned, searching her face. "What are you up to?"

"Remember I told you that I have a theory I'm working on." She tilted her head back and glanced at him. "You are probably the only guy who I know who

72

seems to be immune. Jessie has no clue what she does to men, but I watch it happen all the time. I came early to see what happens tonight. Every time she gives a guy her full attention, he is rendered speechless, or gets all twitter-pated as I like to say."

"Why would you say that?" Matt gave her a quizzical look.

"I have the joy and honor of fielding the questions that they ask about her. None of them ever asks her out. They think she's out of their league. And then I get asked out by the very same guys." She smiled at him. "I'll think you'll even find it a little hard tonight, when you see her. But then again, I've been wrong about you before. I bet your good-looking friend Tom will be interested though." She looked up at him through her lashes.

"I thought you were her friend." He grinned, chucking her on the chin. "You little minx…"

"I am. I absolutely think she's the best. Her father did a real number on her. She's shy when it comes to relationships. Not you, of course. You're one of the guys and when she's with you, she is too." She laughed at Matt's puzzled expression. "Guys always wanted to date her, but she never gave them any encouragement. She's not pushy like me."

"Is that so?" His brow lifted in challenge.

"You're about to see my theory tested out. Jessie has just arrived." Katie gave Matt a sly wink and scooted to the chair beside Dylan.

Katie smiled at how insightful her little experiment actually was. No male at the table could take their eyes off Jessie. Matt was the worst. He acted nonchalant, but Katie noticed his eyes kept drifting to Jessie. She knew her hunch had been right.

She almost laughed out loud when Matt introduced Jessie to Tom. His expression was comical. Katie had seen it often enough.

"Tom, this is Jessie, the lady I was telling you about earlier."

"Uh, nice to meet you…" Tom tipped his head to her.

Katie looked at Matt and mouthed the words. "See what I mean."

"Behave." He frowned at her.

Jessie walked over and said something to Frank, laughed at something Kip said, and smiled at Dylan on her way back to the chair next to Matt.

"You're late." He growled at her.

"Don't start on me. It's just now six thirty. I didn't get home until late. I had to get ready you know."

"It must have worked," he said taking a breath. "You look like a girl."

"If that was a compliment, I think you could use some help." She giggled, patting him on the arm.

He turned away from her and changed the subject. "Frank, as I watched you earlier with your dog, I wondered about a couple of things."

"What do you want to know?"

"I noticed you took off his harness and changed to a collar when you started the track. Why did you do that?"

"Bloodhounds tend to get depressed if they don't find the person they're looking for alive. When I'm doing decomp work and looking for blood evidence or a body, the change in collar alerts Radar to the fact he's looking for decomposition and not a living person."

"Wow, he understands all that by changing from a harness to collar." Kip looked impressed. "Does every trainer do that?"

"The group I work with all train their dogs the same way. It changes how the dog works the track. Tomorrow if we look for the little girl, Radar will wear the harness, and he will know he's looking for a living person."

They asked Frank more questions about Radar. Katie reached across the table to grab Jessie's hand. "You look sensational. Red looks so much better on you than me, and I love red."

"You look pretty great yourself, Miss Donovan. That color brings out the red in your hair."

"Did you notice not one of these guys said anything? I guess we'll have to give each other compliments if we want any."

"Matt told me I looked like a girl," Jessie whispered.

"Are you kidding me?" Katie giggled until they all turned to look. She faked a cough. "What are you thinking of having for dinner?" Katie picked up the menu.

"What's good here?" Jessie glanced over at her and smiled.

"What's not is a better question."

Katie wondered what was going on in Matt's head as he watched them. She knew he was the perfect man for her friend. But Jessie was oblivious, and Matt wasn't much better. He was very interested. Katie could see it. Even with all of her helpful nudges, they weren't getting it. She was going to have to step it up a notch.

When Matt asked Jessie to tell Tom about how she

got involved with the Harvest Club case and this new one, Katie started plotting how to get them together.

Jessie told them about her encounter with Gina's ghost, her near-death experience at the hand of the former police chief, and about Abigail, the little girl now speaking inside her head.

"Are you a psychic?" Tom's voice sounded disappointed as he asked it.

She chuckled. "Absolutely not! I'm a church secretary who is still trying to figure out if I'm weird, though." All three men laughed.

"Whatever it is, she made a world of difference in our first case, and with Frank's help we're moving forward in this one." Matt leaned back in his chair.

"What are we looking at for tomorrow, Matt?" Frank asked.

"I'm hoping we can take a shot at trying to find the girl. I'm not sure what can be done, but we have to give it a try." Matt placed his arm over the back of Jessie's chair without thinking about it. "Do you have any ideas how we should go about it?"

"We need to go back to where we were today. She was probably there with the other children. That might be a good starting point." Frank paused. "Do you have something that belongs to the little girl?"

"Yes, her parents brought something." Matt realized where he had placed his arm and quickly removed it, knocking Jessie in the head. "Sorry..." He dropped his arm to his side. "Tom, do you want to ride along?"

"You bet." He turned and watched Jessie and Katie stand up.

"We'll be right back!" Katie smiled in a flirtatious

way. "Don't talk about us while were gone." She winked.

****

Several sets of eyes followed their retreat. "Frank, how long have you known Jessie?" Tom asked.

"Several years. I met her when my dog did a track to find an autistic child."

"Was she always so unconventional in her approach to cases?"

"No. I know she is struggling with the experiences she's having now." Frank looked after her with fatherly concern. "She told me as much. However, she has always been intuitive, caring, and good at what she does. I simply think it flows from who she is." Frank fidgeted with his napkin.

"You're right about that. She's nice to pretty much everyone." Kip nodded.

Dylan laughed, "Everyone except for Matt, that is. The two of them argue all the time. Of course it doesn't help that he calls her Jess and teases her all the time."

The girls' return, along with their dinner, saved Matt from any further embarrassment. Steak and lobster all around, except for Jessie. She had a grilled chicken breast on a bed of greens; followed by the crème brûlée that she shared with Katie.

"What time are we going out tomorrow?" Jessie turned to look at Matt.

He tried to focus on the question, but her steady gaze was making it hard. "Frank, what time would you like to get started?" He turned away from her.

"The earlier Radar starts the better—how about seven thirty?"

"Seven thirty it is." Matt looked around the table

and everyone nodded.

After dinner, Jessie went to the other end of the table and pulled up a chair to talk to Frank, which gave Matt a chance to observe her and listen. He noticed Dylan, Kip, and Tom were also interested in that end of the table. Katie just smiled and kept winking at him.

"See what I mean?" She giggled.

"What's so funny?" Dylan turned to look at Katie.

"I was just thinking of a conversation I had earlier, nothing important."

A little while later Jessie stood and gave Frank a hug. "I'm so glad I had some time to catch up with you. Please give your family my love. I'll see you tomorrow." She walked around to Katie. "I need to get going. I want to finish my story about Joshua. The article needs editing, and then I have to send it on to Neil. Thank you, Matt; I appreciate being included tonight and dinner. It was nice to meet you, Tom. I'll see you all tomorrow." Katie stood up and left with her, stopping Jessie's progress along the way to talk to everyone she knew.

****

With the bill paid, the men walked out together. Tom headed back to his motel room, Dylan dropped Kip off at his car, and Matt drove with Frank back to his place. Matt's house stood in a slightly wooded area on a hillside with an unobstructed view of the cove. His parents had given him the house when they moved to Boston, but after his remodel, the place did not even resemble the house of his boyhood years.

"I didn't get a chance to tell you earlier. Your house is amazing. Dylan told me you did all the work yourself." Frank sounded impressed.

"I did, it was my therapy time. I love restoring and remodeling things. Working with my hands is a great stress reliever for me." He ran a hand along the glossy wood trim around the window. "I had a contractor work on the exterior and the windows facing the cove, but the inside work was done by me."

"You did a great job, especially with all the woodwork and built-in bookshelves. It's fine craftsmanship."

"Thanks, I'm proud of it all." Matt smiled, his gaze sweeping around the room.

"I love the way you restored your truck, too. It's a beaut." Frank had noticed the quality of the leather on the seats.

"That was a fun project. I've always liked older cars and trucks. There's a lot of my heart and soul in that venture." He looked over at Frank. "I think Jessie's Mustang is sweet. Someone did a great job with it."

"Speaking of Jessie..." Frank paused. "Jessie's a pretty woman, but more than that, she's sweet."

"She sure is." Matt nodded.

"She tends to protect herself. She is very careful about men. I saw the way some of them were looking at her tonight."

"They would have to be blind not to notice. She's damn pretty." Matt drummed his fingers on the windowsill.

"Mind you, she's not weak; she can take care of herself. In fact I've seen her go toe to toe with any man who challenges her."

"Boy, don't I know it." Matt chuckled. "I got on her wrong side early on. She got eyeball to eyeball with me and put me in my place for sure. We still fight each other some, but I believe we're friends. We work well together." Matt dimmed the lights in the living room.

"Watch over her for me, will you?"

"I'll watch over her."

"Thanks, Matt. I love Jessie. She's like my own daughter." Frank's expression was pensive. "Jessie greatly admires her Grandma Sadie, whose life was pretty interesting. Has she ever told you about some of the things she has done in her life?"

"No. Although, I have talked to Sadie and I can well imagine."

"Jessie admires her values and qualities. She is the one person Jessie wants to emulate." Frank sat down in the leather recliner. Radar plopped down at his feet.

"I doubt she realizes it, but she already does." Matt smiled and turned on the news.

Chapter 8

Jessie enjoyed her evening but was happy to be home and wearing something comfortable. She was more of a jeans girl than a dress-up girl. She checked her messages and found one from her Grandma Sadie. A brief glance at the clock told her it was early enough to call her.

"Hi, Grams, are you watching your favorite show?"

"It's not on tonight, some awful special took its place. By the way, I got your email and see you're back in the thick of it again."

"It's weird." She paced as she talked. "I don't know why it suddenly has started happening to me again. I did the same work in New York and nothing like this ever happened to me."

"There are so many investigators in New York, great people working on so many cases. Maybe a smaller town with fewer resources needs an extra edge in solving its crimes. You are just what Blue Cove needs right now. Gina needed you, and now this sweet little girl does, too. I must admit it's a slightly unconventional method, but if it works, who cares. What matters is the crime is solved."

"I hope we can kind find Abigail in time. It's getting colder at night. She's been without food for several days."

"You'll find her, Jessie. Things like this happen for

a reason. If you heard her call, you were the one meant to hear it, as strange as that may seem."

"You always help to put things in perspective. How are Mom and Dad?"

"Fine, but as usual they're trying to tell me what's good for me and what's not. I'm seventy-five for heaven's sake. If I want to eat a long john with chocolate frosting once in a while, I think I should be able to do so without a lecture about how it's full of fat and sugar." She snorted. "I've earned that much in my life. At least while you were here, they were too busy telling you how to live your life. Now they have way too much time on their hands."

"Stand your ground, Grams. As long as you don't eat like that very often, who cares?"

"That's what I say, besides, I walk every day and that's more than I can say for those two. I complain, but you know I love them. I wish they would find another project besides me."

Jessie giggled. "Think of one quick so they don't drive you crazy."

"Maybe I should send them out to check on you."

"Now, that's just mean." She groaned. "There must be something in town or at church you can get them involved in. Is there a disaster somewhere in the country?"

Sadie laughed. "You do my heart good, Jessie girl. I hope someday you'll be calling to tell me you're getting married. I want to dance at your wedding."

"Don't hold your breath, but maybe Katie will give you a chance to dance. She's actively, and I do mean actively, pursuing the matter."

"Well, I guess that's better than nothing." Sadie

sounded disappointed.

"I did go on a date of sorts tonight with Katie and five guys." Jessie smiled imagining the look on Sadie's face.

Sadie laughed. "A sort of date with five guys at once. Are you interested in one of them maybe?"

"I'm interested in all of them as friends, and we'll see if anything else develops."

"Was that nice Matt Parker one of them?"

"Oh no, you don't, you'll get no more information from me." She smiled and slapped her thigh. "You'll have to get by on what I gave you."

"All right then, I'll have to get my information from another source." She chuckled. "You stay in touch, and call me when you find the girl."

"I will. Grams, I hope you're coming for Thanksgiving. Katie is planning a big feast for everyone."

"We plan on it. Goodnight, sweet girl."

Jessie smiled as she hung up. She emailed her article on Joshua for edits. Then she would send the article to Neil and Max at the Blue Cove paper. She was just starting the framework and the first paragraph of Abigail's story when she heard a light tapping on her door. Jessie glanced at her watch; it was almost ten, a little late for a visitor.

"Jessie, are you still awake?" She heard Katie's voice.

Jessie opened the door. "What are you doing here?"

"Everyone is settled down for the night, and I saw your light on. I wanted to talk." Katie sat down in one of the floral chairs.

"What's up?" Jessie sat across from her on the couch.

"Did you enjoy the evening?"

"I did." Jessie smiled. Katie was up to something. "They're a great group of guys."

"I absolutely love that place, and the company would be hard to beat." Katie laughed, fanning herself. "You hang out with some good-looking guys."

"Yes, and they're good friends too."

"Uh…" Katie paused. "I wanted to tell you I was sorry for teasing you the other night. You're my best friend and about one of the nicest people I know. I think I got on a kick after your grandma called me the other day."

"Sadie called you?" Jessie blinked.

"Yes, she does every now and then to make sure you're all right. Anyway, she wanted to know if you were dating. She kept saying she wanted to see you get married. Even though you don't see how guys like you…" Katie smiled, shaking her head. "No, you don't. You're the best, and you'll fall in love when the time is right."

"I could say the same thing to you. You don't have to sell yourself; anyone can see you're one of a kind. Besides being pretty, you keep life interesting; you're one of the funniest people I know."

"Listen to the two of us." Katie laughed aloud. "We're a part of the mutual admiration society. Are we square?"

"Of course, Katie, I thought long and hard about what you said. It all comes back to I'm not ready yet. I like working, writing, and the cases I get a chance to work on. I want to own the bookstore, and I enjoy being around all the guys who are my friends. I'm not in a hurry."

"Would you consider dating once in a while so I can tell her you've been dating?"

"Sure, every time I go to dinner with someone, you can say I went on a date."

"Boy, I'm glad I got that off my chest. Although, I might have made another teeny mistake..." Katie put on an innocent expression.

"Just what kind of mistake are we talking about?" Jessie had a look of utter frustration on her face.

"I might have mentioned my theory to Matt and told him you were a little naïve when it came to men."

"You didn't..." Jessie sucked in a quick breath. "You know how he teases me, and you've handed him more ammunition to use against me. Katie, how could you?"

"I'm sorry, friend. Open mouth, insert foot. I don't stop to think before I act."

"Look, Katie, I'm not as naïve as you think. I have seen the way men sometimes look at me. I don't like it. I don't want someone to like me just because of my looks." She threw herself back onto the sofa cushions, arms crossed. "I have a mind, and I am intelligent. I want to be more than just a body with a face. All that fades. My grandma Sadie is one of the most interesting people I know and people still love her for that, even though she's not young and beautiful." Jessie leaned forward.

"Sadie's great!"

"I do understand people are attracted to each other by looks, but there has to be something more. The man who wins my heart will have to love my mind as well as the rest of me. He will at least have to hold an intelligent conversation with me for longer than a few seconds." Jessie lifted her chin.

"Okay, I'll quit bugging you. If I start to say something to you in the future about this subject, just give a quick kick under the table." Katie giggled. "Maybe I'm the one who has been naïve, I actually just understood and agree with what you said."

"You know me and my soapbox." Jessie smiled. "Women have a lot to offer and I can see how all the emphasis on having the perfect body has been bad. I've done stories on the down side of it when young girls starve themselves to maintain a certain size. Now, there's an epidemic of woman over fifty with eating disorders."

"Again I agree with you, but I have to admit I'm vain. I like it when someone tells me I look great."

"I do, too, but I want them to like more. Do you know what I heard a man say on the news the other day?" Jessie frowned.

"I'm afraid to ask, but I'll take the bait. What did you hear?"

"He actually said 'One of the worse things that happened in history is when men gave women the right to vote.' Can you imagine a bigger jerk? If I had been interviewing him he would have heard a few choice things."

"On that note, we both can totally agree." Katie stood up. "I guess I'd better get back to the Inn, and you have to be up early and ready to go. I'll see you tomorrow." She started out the door but turned back suddenly. "Hey, we're doing the last barbecue of the season tomorrow at the Inn. My famous ribs are on the menu. I'll give Matt a call in the morning to let him know so everyone can eat here tomorrow night. Even if he doesn't want to, you should come." She waved as she walked out the door.

"I'll be there." Jessie shut and locked the door. She wondered how long it would last this time before Katie was back to matchmaking. With the click of the dead bolt, an amazing idea popped into her head—the perfect addition to her story about Abigail. She jotted down her idea and thought about it until her head hit the pillow. She slept peacefully for about an hour and then it was downhill from there.

Jessie tossed and turned through the night. Abigail's cries for help filled her dreams. She awakened with a renewed sense of urgency. She crawled out of bed and headed for the shower hoping it would revive her. It was bound to be a long day.

"Hang on, Abby, please, sweetheart, hang on."

By seven, she was dressed and ready to go. This had to be the day they found her. Abigail wouldn't last much longer. She called Frank's number.

"Good morning," he answered.

"Are you ready for another day of tracking?" Jessie smiled at his cheery voice.

"Both Radar and I are chomping at the bit to get started. We're here, Jessie. Are you on your way?"

"I'm on my way. I had a rough night. I could hear Abigail's cries all night in my dreams. She's fading. We have to find her quickly." She choked back a sob. "I don't know how much longer she can hold on."

"It'll be okay, Jessie. We'll give it our best shot. That's all we can do. Pay attention to your driving and I'll see you in a few minutes."

****

Matt looked at Frank. "What's that all about?"

"Jessie had a rough night. She said she could hear Abigail's cries all night. She's afraid she won't survive much longer."

"We'll just have to find her then, won't we?" Matt looked around the group. "Dylan, you pick the sandwiches up at Joe's. Kip, you ride with Frank out to the site. I'll wait for Jessie and Tom and bring them with me. Oh, and before I forget, Katie wants us all to have dinner at the Inn tonight. It's their last barbecue of the season, so count yourself invited if you don't already have plans. Let me know so I can give her the number."

Matt watched them all depart, wondering where Tom was. Jessie was just pulling into a parking space. He called Tom and got his voice mail. *"Hey, Tom, this is Matt. Did you want to ride with us or drive out to where we were yesterday? Let me know. I'll wait a few minutes to hear from you."*

"Good morning, Mr. Parker." Jessie smiled at him.

"I heard you had a rough night?"

"You could say that." A furrow creased her brow. "Abigail's cries got weaker as the night progressed. If we get close to finding her, we might need a doctor or an ambulance on call. I think she's going to need it."

"I'll put a call into dispatch, if we do."

"We're going to need it today. We have to. We have very little time left." She shivered.

"Tom's here. We can get started now." He opened the door for her to get in.

She shook her head no. "I'll get in the back. Tom's legs are longer than mine; he'll need the front seat."

Matt opened the back door for her and closed it as she got in.

Tom approached Matt's car. "Sorry I'm late, I flat out overslept. Did you have to wait very long?"

"Not long, the others left about ten minutes ago. Let's roll." Matt started the car.

"Hi, Jessie, how are you?" Tom turned to look at her.

"Fine…" She smiled, glancing at him. "And you?"

"No complaints." He turned back around and clicked his seatbelt.

"Matt, Katie sent a text wanting to know how many are coming for dinner tonight. She already knows I'm coming."

"She texted me too and knows I'm coming," he told her. "Tom, are you in?" Matt glanced over at him.

"Sure, I'm always up for food."

"Tell her probably everyone who was there last night." Matt watched Jessie in the rearview mirror and smiled at her concentration.

Matt started Tom in on college football and in the midst of their argument glanced in the rearview mirror to see how Jessie was handling this all-male conversation. She was sound asleep, her head propped against the window.

Chapter 9

She was startled awake by the sound of her phone alerting her to an incoming message. Rubbing her eyes to focus them, she tried to grasp what she was reading. Abruptly Jessie interrupted their heated debate. "Matt, two children were snatched off the streets in New York City a few hours ago. The authorities have activated an AMBER Alert. It says two dark-colored vans were seen in the vicinity by witnesses."

"How'd you hear that?" he called back to her.

"A news update on my phone." She could see his facial expressions in the mirror. "What's the probability that it could be the same guys?"

"Anything's possible." He looked thoughtful. "Does it say whether the victims were boys or girls?"

"One of each…" Her eyes narrowed.

"What are you thinking?" He glanced at her.

"They had to replace Joshua and Abigail. There must be some kind of quota they have to make." She paused. "I wonder if there is an entry or exit area from New York used by traffickers."

"We've been aware of traffickers leaving from the Long Island area." Tom turned to look at her. "But we have nothing firm as of yet. We also have heard rumors about an underground distribution center. A little like a warehouse that moves the kids through to their new location. We haven't found it yet."

"I wonder if that's where they're taking the children." She bent her head over her phone as she continued to read.

"The places are constantly changing. It's a fluid situation. Here this week and gone the next as the heat turns up." Tom turned to look at her. "It used to be somewhat predictable, but the market has grown so large, with some crimes overlapping. It's constantly changing with new areas for law enforcement to tackle."

"We found that in our last case, too."

"They won't want to be too visible right now," Matt added. "It would be risky driving the vans in the city with the present AMBER Alert." Matt made the turn and headed to the barn they had found during the track yesterday. "What, if any, details were given?" Their eyes connected in the mirror.

"Witnesses said the kids were literally grabbed right off the street in broad daylight." She read on, taking note of the key facts.

"Sounds familiar, doesn't it?" Matt asked her.

She nodded. "We need Abigail! Any description she can give to us would be helpful at this point." Jessie continued to scroll through the information on her phone.

****

As they approached the barn area, Jessie could see Frank standing by Kip with Radar already in his harness. Dylan was just getting out of his car. She opened the door, jumped out as soon as the car stopped, and walked over to Frank.

"Is he ready to get to work?" She patted Radar's head.

"Yep, are you?" Frank looked at her sleepy eyes. "Do you want to walk the track with me?" He hooked the line to Radar's harness.

"I sure do!" She walked away from the others a little ways and spoke to Abigail. "Come on, Abby, we're going to need your help. We're on our way. You need to start talking and keep talking to me. Can you hear me, Abby?"

"I'll try, but I'm so tired..." The words came into Jessie's mind.

"Sweetheart, you have to stay awake. Tell me what the men looked like or anything that comes to mind. Can you do that for me? Abby, please, you have to stay awake!"

"I'll try."

"The dog is going to start looking for you. What's the first thing you want to eat when we find you? Think about that, Abby. But just keep the thoughts coming," Jessie whispered.

"I want...a milkshake." Her voice brightened just a bit. *"Chocolate..."*

Jessie followed Frank and Radar into the barn. Frank bent down to give Radar his command. He held the bear in his hand and let Radar smell Abigail's scent. "Find her, find the girl."

They stood back and watched as the dog went through his routine. He sniffed all around the barn and started out the door. Jessie and Matt walked with Frank. The others followed in Frank's Durango.

The dog headed down the path that Jessie had walked the day before. After going close to two miles, Radar veered off onto another path. Making a turn to the right he circled back toward the main road.

"Are you sure, boy?" Radar lifted his head in response, but then he went back to work, and continued his track on the new path. "He's still working it."

Matt kept pace with Frank and they talked, while Jessie lagged behind. She was getting nothing from Abigail and that had her worried. Several *what if* scenarios played through her mind like a bad movie. She became more determined with each step she walked. They had to find Abigail not only for her, but for the lives of the other children, as well.

Frank paused, stopping Radar to wait for Jessie to catch up. "Are you all right?"

"Yes, I was trying to contact Abigail, but I'm not getting anything anymore."

"Keep your head in this, Jess." Matt frowned at her.

"That's what I'm doing!" She frowned back at him.

"Is he still on the trail do you think?" Matt asked Frank.

"I have no reason to believe he's not. If he comes to the end of the trail, he will sit down. If I give him the command again and he doesn't move, that will be the end of it. Are you ready?" Frank was looking at Jessie.

"Sure, let's kick it into gear. Don't worry. I'll keep up." Her chin edged up as she walked past Matt. He smiled at her back. Her sass was in place.

"Find her, fella, let's get to work." The dog was off again. Radar worked slowly along the highway for a few miles and then he started pulling harder. "I think he's on to something," Frank called over his shoulder as the dog veered back to the left on to another small roadway. He took them further into a wooded area until he came to an open area where there had been a campfire recently. He circled the clearing several times and sat down.

"They were obviously here at some point." Frank pointed to the area.

"It looks that way." Matt walked over to where the fire had been and looked around. The others branched out, combing the area for any evidence. "Frank, do you want to take a break or eat as you walk?"

"I think we should keep going while the dog wants to work. He's still into it, and I don't want him to lose interest. I'll give him some water, and then we'll start up again." Frank set the dog's water bowl in front of him.

Jessie listened to them talk, but she wanted to hear Abigail. She concentrated her thoughts. *"Abby, we're at a place where there was a campfire. Do you remember the place? Are we getting any closer?"*

"Yes, I can remember it," her soft voice answered. *"We kept going in circles so I don't know if you are close or far away."*

"Frank," Jessie called to him. "Abigail mentioned it felt like they were going in circles. I'm not sure what that will mean to the dog, but I thought I should tell you that."

"He should still come out okay. He's an off-scent dog; he takes the scent from the air not just the ground. He can move out as much as thirty feet from where they've walked or have been. He won't circle as often as they might have." Frank looked at Matt. "I think we should get started again."

"I'm ready." Jessie stood up and grabbed a bottle of water.

"I'd like to walk with you this time." Tom stepped

forward. "I'd like to see this dog working up close. It's really pretty fascinating."

Frank knelt beside the dog and held out the bear. "Can you find the girl, fella? You've done great, Radar." He gave his dog a treat. "Let's bring the girl home."

For the next hour, it seemed they weren't making any headway. Jessie found herself losing hope. Abigail had been silent since lunchtime. Radar suddenly lifted up his head and started pulling down another odd little path, which went farther into a wooded area.

Jessie heard what sounded like water in the distance. She could see a dilapidated old homestead a little farther up the bumpy overgrown road. Radar was pulling hard.

"Frank, let him off the line and I'll run with him. I think that's it up ahead. It looks like the place she told me about." Jessie felt a rush of adrenaline and took off running.

Frank didn't need to give a command; the dog was already running. When he reached the cabin he circled it baying, keeping Jessie in his sights. She practically tore the door off its hinges in her haste to get inside. Breathing hard—she forgot to draw her gun—her eyes adjusted to the dark interior, but Radar found her first. The dog whined and whiffled at a small heap in a dim corner.

Curled up on the floor, the small skinny girl lay still and motionless. "Abby, precious girl, hang in there." Jessie held her breath until she felt a pulse. Matt burst through the door followed closely by Tom. She looked up at him, Abigail's head cradled in her lap, tears rolling down her cheeks. Radar leaned into her other side, his nose on her lap.

"Well, I'll be damned; I would never have believed it possible if I hadn't seen it with my own eyes." Tom shook his head at the scene in front of him.

Matt knelt beside Jessie. "Is she still alive?"

"Yes." She blinked away the tears.

Matt put in a call to Joe and told him to send the ambulance. He gave him the mile marker where they had veered away from the main highway. "Tell them it's more of a path than a road, but the vans made it back here. They should be okay." He hung up after giving a few more orders.

Jessie looked into Matt's eyes. "Thank you for believing in me. Most people would have thought I was crazy, but not you." She smiled at him.

He nodded, reached out, and gently pushed a curl back that had fallen into her eye. "Your hands are full right now." He cleared his throat. His voice sounded gruff. "To my credit, I did have a little experience with this strange side of you once before." He gave her a sly wink.

"Ha, ha..." She rolled her eyes at him.

Frank finally reached the house, panting. "Way to go, Radar!"

Dylan followed Frank. "Is she okay?" Jessie put her fingers to her lips.

His voice startled Abby, and her eyelids fluttered open, filled with terror. "It's me." Jessie stroked the hair back from her face. "We found you; you're safe now." Abigail's body went limp, but Jessie could feel a nice steady pulse.

Matt gently lifted Abby out of Jessie's arms so that she could stand and sit down in an old chair in the room. Jessie got comfortable, and he handed Abigail right back to her.

"Abby, I'm so glad we found you. I promised I would try. As soon as you're better, you will have to have your picture taken with the dog who found you. He's your hero," she whispered. "You'll have to meet all the people who worked to find you. I hope when you are awake and feeling better you can tell us about the other kids so we can find them too."

Jessie rambled on talking to her until the paramedics arrived on the scene and took over. Jessie rode to the hospital with her. With an IV dripping fluids into her body, her vitals were already getting stronger on the ride back to town.

****

Matt could hardly believe what he had just witnessed. Stan and Sarah Davis were going to see their little girl again. At least he could deliver some good news. Matt watched the ambulance until it was out of sight. He took a breath and made the phone call to the Davis household.

Sarah answered the phone. "Mrs. Davis, this is Chief Parker."

"Is everything all right?" Her voice cracked.

"Yes, I wanted to let you know that your daughter was found alive today. She is en route to Blue Cove Community Hospital right now." Matt heard the phone hit something and then the distant sound of Sarah screaming for her husband.

"Hello, hello!" Stan shouted into the phone. Matt repeated the information to him. "How is she? Is she okay? You found my little girl. Thank you, oh God, thank you."

"We'll know more after she's been checked out."

"How can we ever thank you?" Stan's voice broke.

"It's my job, and I'm happy we found her."

"We'll get right over there. Thank you, thank you." Matt could hear Sarah still crying in the background.

When he went back inside the old shack, Kip and Tom had already made drawings of the site. They found the place where Abigail must have hidden herself. The tiny space concealed her perfectly with very little room to move or stretch. How had she done it? They bagged up what they could see, but there was very little visible evidence.

Matt gave directions when he called Marcy and Gary on how to get there. "Kip, you'll need to wait here. Marcy and Gary are on their way."

"Do you think she'll be okay?" Frank patted Radar's head.

"Thanks to Radar, yes, I think she will be."

"Honestly, I thought the chances of finding the girl were about zero. I'm so glad I was wrong, and I was here to witness what I just did. I'll be talking about what I saw for a long time to come." Tom leaned down to pat Radar's head.

"Since Jessie is riding in the ambulance with Abigail, I'll need to pick her up at the hospital. Frank can you drop us off at my car?"

"Sure thing." He nodded.

"Did you see how small the space was where she hid?" Dylan squatted down to get a closer view. "She must have been petrified. What a brave thing to do, especially after seeing Josh get the crap beat out of him!" Dylan shook his head.

Matt nodded and walked over to Frank. "Your dog

did a hell of a job." He leaned down to pet Radar. "You did great, big fella." As he stood, Radar got up and leaned his head into Matt's hand. "I thought for sure we were just going around in circles." He patted him on his head. "I can see now that the circle was ever tightening. Abigail had told Jessie that it felt like a plane waiting for its chance to land, flying in a holding pattern over the city."

Everyone but Kip got into the SUV. They drove back to the barn to pick up the two patrol cars. "Frank, I'll see you back at my house. Make yourself and the dog comfortable." Matt climbed out of the car. "Do you remember how to get there?"

Frank nodded. "I'll be fine once I get back to the main road. I'll follow you out from here."

"This has been some day." Tom heaved a sigh as he shut the car door.

"It sure has been. I'll drop you off at your car and then catch up with you at the Inn for dinner. Katie said to be there by five thirty, dinner's at six." He gave Tom directions on how to get to the Inn. "I need to swing by the hospital to see how the girl is and to pick up Jessie."

"Jessie is something."

"Yes, she is." Matt smiled, knowing what Tom was about to say.

"If you're not interested in her, let me know, because I sure as hell am." Tom hopped out of the car and closed the door before Matt could reply.

It would seem that everybody was. Of course he was and had already told her as much. He was waiting on her to be ready, and losing patience as more men flocked around her. She didn't see it.

She constantly surprised him, and he enjoyed her

company. The only thing that held him back, even a little, was keeping her safe. He had messed that up the last time. That's as far as he would let his thoughts travel. He walked into the hospital room and saw Jessie talking to Stan and Sarah Davis.

"Where's Abigail?"

"They're cleaning her up." Jessie smiled at Matt. "Thanks again for all your help." His pulse quickened.

It was moments like this when she made him feel like that tongue-tied high school boy. "Jessie, you're the reason we're here right now. You're the one who heard her, asked Frank to come, and was persistent enough to drive a sane person whacky." His grin softened the gruffness in his voice.

A few minutes later, the nurse wheeled a freshly scrubbed young girl into the room and helped her into her bed. Her parents were overwhelmed the minute they saw her and so was Abby. Matt and Jessie stepped out into the hall to allow the family a private reunion.

The shift nurse popped her head out of the door a few minutes later. "Could you both come back in for a minute?" Matt nodded.

"Thank you, Jessie, for hearing me and, Officer Parker, for looking for me." Abigail's voice was thin and weak, but her eyes glowed. "Reaching a person through my thoughts seems crazy now. I heard it was possible somewhere. I've never done anything like that before."

"It was a first for me, too." Jessie took her hands. "I'm so happy you called and I heard you. We won't try to figure out how."

"I'm just glad we found you." Matt smiled at Abigail, glancing down at her.

"I thought I was going to die and never see my parents again." She glanced at her mom and dad and smiled. "I was so scared those men would come back." Abigail shuddered. "I'm happy you found me, too!"

"Are they treating you good?" Matt patted her head.

"Uh-huh." She nodded. "Later on, the nurses promised to bring me a chocolate milkshake."

"A good milkshake goes a long way to making things better." He smiled at her. "How would you like to meet the real hero who found you? I've got permission to bring him up here tomorrow if you'd like."

"That would be way cool!" Her eyes suddenly filled with tears. "Did you find Josh?"

"Yes, we did. Did you see the men who beat him?'

She nodded, her voice barely audible. "I was scared." Abby wrapped her arms around Jessie and cried. "That awful man wouldn't stop hitting and kicking him." She sobbed. "Josh was nice to me. He was my friend."

"Did you see them push him out of the van?" Matt asked her.

"No, they kept him with us. We could see him all time. Karl held a rag soaked with water to his lips. He kept telling the man named Jed they needed to get him help, or he would die. At night, we could hear him groan until one day he got quiet. They left the morning I hid, with him in the van. I never saw him again. He isn't dead, is he?" Abigail cried out.

Jessie hugged Abigail, but Matt answered her. "He's alive. He's right here in this hospital. He's a little too ill for visitors just yet."

"Does the hospital have someone who can talk to her? God only knows what she has witnessed." Matt spoke quietly to the nurse. "Was there any molestation?"

"No." The nurse shook her head. "Thank God, she has enough to deal with. Doctor Henderson mentioned earlier that he would send the hospital psychologist to talk with her before he releases her. I would imagine she'll need some counseling for a while."

"So it would seem." He walked over to Abby, bending down to look her in the eyes. "We're going to leave you with your parents so you can eat and rest. We'll be back with Radar to see you tomorrow. I want you to think about anything that might help us to find the men who did this to you, and the other kids who still need to be rescued."

"I will." She yawned, and smiled up at him.

"You don't need to worry about them coming back. I'll have a police officer outside your door all night so you can sleep. Okay?"

"Okay." She yawned again.

****

"You're pretty good with kids. If you keep being so charming, she may develop a little crush on you." Jessie leaned close to speak softly.

"How about you, Miss Reynolds, do you think if I'm real nice, you might develop a little crush on me?" He grinned at her.

"It's possible, Mr. Parker, anything is. I wouldn't hold my breath if I were you, though." She chuckled, tilting her head to look up at him.

"That's what I figured, so there's no incentive for me to be nice to you." His grin widened. "You wouldn't want to up the ante, would you? Make the work a little interesting." He raised his brows.

"That sounds a little like a challenge. I have to admit, I've always loved a good challenge." She grinned at him. "I'll have to give some thought to it."

"You do that, sweetheart, but while I wait, I'll follow your wise words and not hold my breath." He stepped through the open elevator doors after her.

Chapter 10

Jessie ran through the door, checking her watch as she did. She had just barely enough time to take a hot shower, dry her hair, and dress before she was due at Katie's for dinner. It had been a remarkable day. She had gone from feeling hopeless to complete elation in a few moments' time. Holding Abigail in her arms was pure joy, unlike any emotion she had ever experienced before. It was as if she had found a part of herself. Abby had been the girl in her head for several days. She wondered if this would be the only time she'd hear a call for help, or would someone else call out to her?

She had no clue. At this point Jessie wasn't sure how or what had made this possible. It was better not to think about it too hard. She checked her image in the mirror. Everything seemed to be in place. Barbecue was a word that evoked casual: jeans, t-shirt, and a light sweater. She passed inspection.

Jessie heard a tapping sound on her back door and opened it to find Dylan and Kip standing there with silly grins on their faces.

"We've come to escort you to dinner. You have the dubious distinction of being one of the guests of honor." Kip bowed. "After you…"

"What on earth for?" She laughed as they replaced their grins with an attempt at a serious look.

"It's that head thing of yours that helped to save a

young girl." Dylan's lip thinned as he fought a smile.

"Knock it off, you two." She bit her lip trying not to laugh.

"Really! Katie told us to get over here and escort her best friend quickly. There are people dying to meet you." Kip was grinning ear to ear. "Now get a move on; we don't want to experience the wrath of Katie."

"Let me get my key." She grabbed her sweater, locked the door, and stuck the key in her pocket, pulling the door closed behind her.

"Aren't you just a little in awe of how this day went?" Dylan watched her face light up.

"I'd be lying if I said I wasn't. Of course, I am. Watching Radar work is amazing every time."

"We at the precinct think he's pretty great, but we also think you're pretty great." Kip tucked her hand through his arm. "That little tidbit about the plane circling to land brought hope into a day which was becoming dismal at best."

"We're glad you're on our side and not with the bad guys. Besides, you make the station a whole lot prettier," Dylan whispered in her ear. "Try to enjoy your moment. Tomorrow, we have to get busy trying to find the other kids." Dylan pulled her other hand through his arm. She walked to the back of the Inn, sandwiched between the two men that she had come to know as friends.

Katie was watching the path and as soon as she saw them headed their way, she let out a cheer. People at the Inn clapped. Jessie paused, blushing.

Frank stepped up beside her and spoke in her ear. "They did the same thing to me."

"You deserve it for your work with the dog. You're

a team after all."

"You deserve it for hearing the cries of a girl, for believing it was real, and getting others to believe it as well. It would seem we're in a stalemate. We both need to just enjoy the evening."

"Hey, Jess, nice shade of red." Matt approached her. He put his hand over her mouth and smothered her indignant protest. "Don't say it; you'll just regret it if you do. See how I'm helping you grow?" Jessie rolled her eyes, her pulse quickening as she walked away from him. His hearty laugh followed her.

Looking around, Jessie saw that Katie had once again created magic, not just a meal. Twinkling lights adorned the garden area, some hidden in colorful paper lanterns. The empty tables, dressed in bright colored cloths waited for people to settle around them and enjoy the beautiful fall evening. The atmosphere was humming with the talk and the laughter of the Inn's guests. A pleasant night in the making. She sighed—the perfect end to a textbook day.

Jessie made her way toward the buffet table. She filled her plate with several of the wonderful salads, arranged with care alongside a variety of amazing looking desserts. She saved room on her plate for Katie's special melt-in-your-mouth barbecued ribs. Her plate filled, she strolled to the table that Katie had pointed out to her earlier and found the place card with her name on it. Tom, Matt, and Frank brought their plates to the table, soon to be followed by Dylan and Kip. Conversation was minimal until they had consumed their first plate full. What talk there was centered on the food they were eating.

"Katie sure knows how to throw a great feast."

Dylan headed back for yet another plate filled with ribs.

All the beautiful little details were lost on them, Jessie smiled to herself, but not the taste of some great food. Her smile broadened as she watched them go back several times for more.

"What are you smiling about?" Kip stood up with his plate, but waited for her answer.

"I was thinking about the amount of food you guys can consume. I can only imagine how much it would cost to feed you if you all lived in the same house." She laughed.

"My mother knows. She raised four of us boys. She used to call us the bottomless pits." Kip headed for the buffet.

Tom looked at the text on his phone. "Jessie, I thought you'd like to know the FBI is watching the Long Island area. They're keeping certain areas under surveillance. There is an active ongoing search for the two vans. With any luck, maybe we'll be able to rescue all of those kids." He smiled at her. "By the way, that article you wrote about the Harris boy was great. Your old news station featured the story on air today. It has people in New York looking for them. Tips are pouring in on the hotline."

"That's great news." She turned to look at Matt.

"Right about now, I bet they're feeling the heat breathing down their necks."

"I certainly hope so. I wish them at least as much discomfort as they inflicted on Joshua and Abigail." She frowned. "Although, there are still other kids' lives at risk so I guess I had better hope they don't get too stressed and take it out on one of them."

"Matt, the bureau's trafficking taskforce would like

to work alongside your team in this process." Tom read another text. "The optimum word is work with and not run roughshod over you guys. Even I know we haven't always had the best reputation working with the local authorities." Tom's brows furrowed. "We want to help find the kids before they're relocated. I know you have your hands full, Matt, and we have some excellent resources." His hand tapped on the table. "The main thing is that we find those kids." Jessie nodded in agreement.

Katie stopped at their table and whispered in Jessie's ear. "I have a lot of guests who would like to talk with you and Frank. Do you think you can make the rounds?"

"Come on, Frank, we have some schmoozing to do." She grabbed his arm and took him around from table to table to answer their questions.

****

Matt listened to the conversation around the table but started losing interest. His eyes kept drifting in the direction of Jessie. She laughed at something a guest said to her, and he couldn't stop his lips from smiling right along with her. He knew what he wanted to do. Hell, he should have thought of it days ago.

"What's got you smiling, Mr. Parker?" Katie sat down beside him.

"Just lost in thoughts, I guess." He turned his attention to her. "It turned out to be a great day. With any luck maybe we'll have a few more in the works."

"Oh, call me naïve and embarrassed! I thought you were smiling because you were taken with the sound of Jessie's laughter." Her mischievous green eyes sparkled.

"Are you trying to stir up trouble again?" He chuckled.

"Not really. I think you'd be perfect for my friend, but she'd never buy it. I can't get you to see it. So what good am I?" She stood up laughing. "I can see my work is done here." Katie walked away smiling.

Matt grinned. He was glad Katie wasn't looking in his direction now. She had busted him, and she knew it. Guarding his growing feeling for Jessie was getting harder to do. Maybe it was time to let it show.

Tom stood up to leave. "I need to get back for an early morning meeting. I'll coordinate with you as soon as I have my team in place. I want you to be in on getting these perps even if they're out of your jurisdiction. Give some thought to your theories. We'll talk." His eyes drifted toward Jessie. "Tell her I said goodbye."

"Will do…" Matt walked Tom to his car. "I'll let you know any information I get when I question the Davis girl." They shook hands. "I want to find the one who beat Joshua Harris."

"I have to tell you, Matt, I came down here thinking to maybe give it all up. I feel renewed after seeing Abigail's rescue today. I want to find those kids in a bad way. When I get back to the office on Monday, I'll be pushing to get this started. I'll be in touch." Tom got in his car.

"Okay." Matt walked back toward the group. "Hey, Frank, I'll be right back, and then we'll head back to my place, okay?"

"I'll be here. I'm too tired to move." He rubbed his tender knee.

Matt walked over and stood beside Jessie as she

finished her conversation with Katie. He grabbed her elbow. "Tom said to tell you goodbye. So I'm telling you." He smiled at her. "I've come to walk you home and then take Frank back to my place. He's tired."

"You don't need to walk me back—I can walk there myself." She tried to shake his hand free from her arm.

"Yes, I do. I have something I need to tell you. Say goodnight, Jess." She walked away from him toward home. Matt kept pace with her, glancing over at her from time to time. "Do you think you'll hear any more thoughts like Abigail's?" His hand grabbed her hand.

"I have no idea. I don't know how any of this works." She moved over a little on the path trying to pull her hand free.

"How come your hands are so soft?" He rubbed his thumb over hers.

"I'm a girl."

"Believe me, I've noticed." He gave her a crooked grin. "I guess we'll just have to wait and see if anyone talks in your head again." He grinned as he pulled her against his side, resting his arm over her shoulder.

When they got to her back door, he took the key out of her hand and unlocked the door, then held it open for her to walk in. "Goodnight," she said and started to shut the door.

"Not so fast. I told you we were going to have a nice little talk." He put his foot in the door. He pushed it open, walked in, and stood directly in front of her. He leaned down so he could look directly into her eyes. "I want to have a serious chat with you." He moved closer still until his lips were within mere inches of hers. "If I remember correctly, I told you we were meant to be

110

together. I'm getting a little impatient with you dragging your feet. I've made an important decision. Do you want to hear what it is?" He watched her begin to shake her head no. "Oh yes you do, sweetheart, because it definitely concerns you."

"All right! I'll bite. What's this great decision?" She looked flustered.

"I think you're purposely dragging your feet and ignoring me, thinking I'll give up like all the other guys have over the years." She shook her head no. "Yes," he said. "But my mind is made up! I'm not waiting much longer, nor am I going to let you drag this out for months." He grinned. "I'm going to turn on the charm and make it hard for you to say no. In the end you're going to love it." He leaned in closer and gave her a quick kiss. He chuckled at her expression, turned around, and walked away.

Matt felt her eyes boring into his back. He was still smiling when he got back to Frank. "You look awful pleased with yourself, Mr. Parker." Katie eyed him.

"I've won another round with my sweet little adversary." He grinned when Katie gave him a puzzled look. "Thanks for a great meal." He tipped his head to her. "We'll be seeing you around." They walked to the car.

****

Jessie was dumbfounded as she watched him leave. She shut and locked the door. What was he up to now? She leaned against the wall. One thing for sure, she didn't want the added stress of trying to figure him out now. If she was honest, she found it more than a little exciting. She fanned her over-heated face with a piece of paper. "Charm me...if you only knew just how you affect me already." She took a deep breath to calm her racing heart.

Matt wasn't teasing her. He was serious, and the look on his face convinced her of that fact. Something there might be nice to explore. Jessie went to her computer and wrote for a while trying to put the evening behind her.

A light tap at her back door got Jessie out of her chair to check.

"I see you're still up." Katie studied her as she opened the door.

"Yes, what's up?"

"I could ask you the same thing? Matt came back to the Inn looking rather pleased. He had a grin a mile wide. What happened between you two? Fess up."

"Nothing! He was in some strange mood, rambling on about who knows what." Jessie gave her an innocent look.

"That's odd. Matt said he had won another round. I wish you two would stop fighting. You have to work together on this case, and he needs to watch out for you. I don't want anything to happen to you. So promise me not to fight. Okay?" Katie planted her fists on her hips.

"He's won nothing!" Jessie frowned but changed what she was going to say when she saw the look on Katie's face. "Please don't worry, we're friends now." She bit her lip.

When Katie left, Jessie went to bed. Faces from Abigail's dreams filled her dreams with faces and pictures of children. Nightmares really. What was happening to the other kids? She awakened knowing she still had a job to do. On standby was where Matt and his weird proposal would have to go for now.

Chapter 11

The look on Jessie's face last night had been priceless. Matt smiled to himself. She had been surprised all right, but he felt like a million bucks. From the first day he had laid eyes on her, he had struggled with his instant attraction to her. He paused to pull his shirt over his head. Yeah, he had grumbled, lectured, and tried to push her away. He had put up a valiant fight.

I surrender! He threw up his hands and headed for the kitchen. He had stated his intention clearly. She would get used to the idea in time. He grinned. This might be fun after all, and it was worth the battle. He had almost lost her once, during their first case. Life was too short to wait for her to get around to it.

Matt walked into the kitchen to the smell of freshly brewed coffee. He poured himself a cup. "Thanks, man…" He saluted Frank and pointed to his cup.

"I always get up early at home and start the coffee. It's the least I could do to say thanks for your hospitality. This beats a motel any day for me and Radar." Frank took a sip of the dark hot brew.

"The hospital gave us the okay to visit this morning. I want Jessie to have pictures to go with the story she's writing." Matt leaned his hip against the counter. "The sooner we get the information out there, the better. People tend to make mistakes when the pressure's on." He took a swig of his coffee and popped a bagel into the toaster. "Will that work for you?"

"Sure, Radar loves attention." Frank smiled. "He plays the role of hero well, believe me." Frank topped off his cup.

Matt's phone vibrated in his pocket. He looked at the caller ID and took the call. "Good morning, Jess, how'd you sleep?" He laughed at her grumble. "That bad? I had a great night. I got a lot off my chest, and I slept better than I have in years." He grabbed the toasted bagel, placed it on a plate, and handed it to Frank.

"Zip it, Matt. Are you trying to irritate me?" Her voice sounded sharp on the phone.

"That would be affirmative." He grinned. "Hey, we have the hospital's approval to take Radar up to meet Abigail. I want you to come along so you can write the story. Marcy will take pictures." Matt pushed the jam and cream cheese toward Frank.

"Sure, okay..." She sounded distracted. "I wanted to talk to you—" He cut her off.

"Just a minute, Jess." He handed Frank a knife and then walked out of the kitchen. "I wanted to talk to you too, sweetheart." Matt grinned as he imagined her expression.

"Would you please be serious?"

"I am very serious."

"Let me try this again." She exhaled a long breath. "Abigail was in my head again, and I saw lots of the kid's faces. So I need to take a look at the book to pick out their photos."

"Sure, I'll bring it along with me. Why don't you ride with us? I'd like to see if Abigail's picks are the same as yours." He sat down on the edge of the leather couch.

"When will you pick me up?"

"That's what I'm trying to do." He couldn't resist and then laughed when she moaned. "I'll be there at ten thirty. Talk to you later." Matt hung up and made a couple of calls.

****

He couldn't take his eyes off her when she walked out the door. She looked like spring in the midst of an otherwise gray autumn day. Her hair bounced softly with the sway of her hips, her blue eyes sparkled almost as much as her smile. He felt a catch in his throat. Focus, he told himself, but it wasn't helping. He frowned. When it came to Jessie, all sense of discipline eluded him.

"Good morning." She smiled at them as she slid into the backseat and closed the door. She looked over her shoulder to the crate in the back. "Hi, Radar, are you ready to be lavished with lots of praise today?" The hound's head popped up, and he gazed at her with his soulful eyes.

"He's always ready for attention." Frank looked in his mirror at her.

Matt chuckled. "What male isn't?"

"You'll have to help me out with directions." Frank approached the stop sign.

"You've got it, Frank. You'll need to take a left when you get to the sign and head back toward town." Matt looked over his shoulder at Jessie. "The book is on the seat. You can write the page number and child's name on the notepad with it." Matt turned back around.

Jessie marked the pages with the pictures of several

115

of the kids including Lily, a boy named Austin, and the youngest child taken, Olivia. By the time she was through, they were pulling into the parking lot of the hospital.

Matt opened the door for her while Frank got the dog out. She handed him the book and pad. "It looks like you found quite a few." He closed the door behind her.

"Which means Abigail will be able to identify several of the children and hopefully her abductors, as well." She walked past him toward Frank and Radar at the back of the SUV. "Hey, fella…" She stroked the hound's head. "Are you ready for this?" His tail wagged, slapping against her legs. With Radar's harness in place, they all walked toward the hospital.

Marcy was waiting with her camera, clicking pictures the minute they entered the doors. Radar took it in stride—all the hands reaching out to stroke him, kids running up to him, and an elevator ride up to the fourth floor to the children's waiting area. After a brief stop at the nurse's desk and a promise to take Radar to see the other children, Sally, one of the young volunteers escorted them to Abigail's room.

"Oh, Abby, you look so much better today." Jessie walked over to where she was sitting. "Did you sleep well?" Abby shook her head no.

"I had a bad dream." She frowned.

"I'm sorry, maybe you can take a little nap later." Jessie touched her shoulder.

"The doctor told my mom I get to go home tomorrow." She smiled up at Jessie.

"That's good news, honey." Jessie smiled back, sitting down in the chair next to hers.

"Is that the dog that found me?" She looked around Jessie and pointed to Radar.

"Yes, would you like to meet him?" Matt motioned Frank over with Radar.

At first, she was timid, but Radar pushed his head into her lap, and she hugged him. "Thank you, oh, thank you for finding me." She giggled when he licked her face. Her small hands stroked his shiny red coat. She whispered what a fine dog he was. Matt noticed the moisture in Jessie's eyes and handed her a tissue.

Marcy got several great shots and went back to the station to arrange them. Frank and a nurse took Radar around to some of the other children's rooms. Abigail looked through the book. She picked out the same faces as Jessie had plus a few more. Jessie took a deep breath after hearing Abigail's version of what happened to her.

"At least now I know I'm not completely weird." She smiled at Matt.

"That has yet to be determined." He grinned but didn't let her see it. "I still don't know how you managed to get all of those details in your mind."

"If you figure it out, let me know. I'd love to know how it happens." Jessie bent down and whispered in Abigail's ear as Jared, a local artist, walked in the room. "I'll be back in a little while. I'm going to go find Radar. Jared needs your help now."

"How can I help?" Abby looked at her, puzzled.

"You can tell him about the men who took you, and he will draw a picture of them." She patted Abby's shoulder. "I know you can do it."

"Jessie's good with her." Jared plopped down in a chair and opened his sketchpad. Matt nodded and watched Jessie until she left the room.

****

By the time Jessie and Frank got back to Abigail's room, she was sound asleep. Her parents had gone home, and Matt was the only one left in the room.

"Hey, are you guys ready to leave?" Matt kept his voice low as they walked in the door.

Jessie nodded.

"How'd she do?" Frank inquired.

"She was a real trouper! She filled in many of the missing pieces. As you can see, we wore her out." Matt stood and gathered up his files. "We have three composites we'll be able to put out to local agencies and news outlets." He held up one for them to see. "She gave us some detailed information that will help us compile the charges against them."

"You look concerned. What are you thinking?" Jessie studied him.

"They'll come after her. She knows too much." He frowned. "They're probably on their way back now. I have no clue what we're up against."

"Are you going to keep her in protective custody?" Jessie turned to look at the sleeping girl.

"We'll keep her safe." Matt motioned toward the door.

"I believe you will." She smiled at him.

"Frank, would you mind being on call if you're needed to come back again?"

"Sure thing. You call, tell me when and where, and I'll be there."

"Great…" He gave Jessie a playful push to get her moving toward the door. "By the way, Marcy said you can take a look at the pictures. They're ready. We'll stop at the station on our way back."

"Keep her safe." Jessie smiled at the police officer sitting outside the door.

He nodded. "We will."

****

Jessie loved the photos and picked several to accompany her story. She chose one of Abby hugging Radar, a great single shot of her, and one with Frank, Radar, and Abby together.

"If it's okay with you, Matt, I'd like to stop by your place first." Frank spoke up as they left. "Radar has been confined for a while and needs to be fed."

"It's fine by me. Will that work for you, Jess?" Matt closed the door behind her.

"I don't mind." Jessie's interest was piqued.

She had heard it said that a person's place could tell you something about them, and Matt's house spoke volumes. She was impressed and speechless, which didn't happen to her often. It didn't square with her perception of him. Each of the rooms he showed them he had meticulously planned. She could tell by listening to his descriptions that he was proud of his work. The quality was outstanding, and the window placement took advantage of a view that was breathtaking. The gourmet kitchen was a chef's dream with its large professional gas range and deep sink. Who wouldn't want to cook in a kitchen like this? Katie would go nuts.

Next, Matt showed her the gardens. Jessie could only imagine how beautiful it would be in the summer. "I'm sorry, Jess." He reached for his phone. "I need to take this call. Continue to explore, you'll enjoy it."

Jessie found Frank sitting on a bench on the edge of the property. She sat down beside him, content to watch the sun reflecting its glorious colors over the cove.

"Hey, you two, I didn't realize it was so late. Is anyone hungry besides me?" Matt's voice startled her.

"I'm never one to turn down food." Frank chuckled.

"How about you, Jess, are you up for it?" Matt touched her shoulder.

"Sure…" She stood and walked toward the car with them. "You must be very proud of all the work you've done on your house. It's impressive."

"Thanks, I am. It was my after-hours therapy sessions over the years. Since our last case I've started working on the master bedroom and bath."

****

After dinner, Matt dropped Jessie off and she got back to work on Abigail's story. It was late when she finished the final draft. She sent the final copy on to Max and Neil, with a note telling them they were free to print it. She had seen the composites and the AMBER Alert issued earlier with pictures of all the children. With any luck, the tips would start coming in.

Chapter 12

Jed walked away from the others to answer the call. He wiped the sweat dripping down his face on his sleeve, a scowl marring his otherwise handsome face. He clenched his left hand so tightly that it made marks where his fingernails dug into his skin.

"To say I'm not happy with you guys is a hell of an understatement." He coughed. "Which one of you goons beat that kid?" He swore under his breath. "You're a damn bunch of morons."

Jed exhaled a long breath. "He was dead when we left him."

"Wrong."

"Oh geez, that's bad, man." Jed kicked the tree he was standing by. "You know how Eddie gets when he's mad. He was out of control. Karl and I couldn't stop him."

"Did you try?"

Jed evaded the answer. "The kid tried to run, and by now you know the rest of the story."

"It's all over the news. Half the city is looking for those two vans and the three of you."

"I don't know what else we could have done."

"Whose freaking idea was it to take the two kids off the street—in New York—in broad daylight? You guys screwed up."

"What do want me to say? It's all I've been

thinking about, and I can't change a damn thing." Jed ran his hands through his hair.

"Our drop sites are hot and getting hotter. The kids can't come here now. An AMBER Alert is showing the kid's photos nonstop. You idiots are going to be stuck with those kids for a while."

"Where are we supposed to take them?" Jed leaned against the tree.

"You'll have to come up with a plan." His voice was icy. "It's your lives on the line. Did you know they found the girl? She's alive."

"Oh hell, she knows what we look like." Fear filled Jed's voice.

"You should have thought about that before you let her get away."

"Damn, what else could go wrong?"

"Your ugly mugs are showing up on the news for everyone to see. A woman reporter broke the story on the boy. She had some kind of dream, and they brought a bloodhound in."

"Hell, what am I supposed to do about all this?"

"You're going to drive those vans north out of the city taking the back roads. I'll meet you at our usual spot, with a couple of different vehicles. I want Lutz gone. Do you hear me? Destroy the vans or abandon them, I don't care, but remove the plates first."

"What do you mean about wanting Eddie gone?" Jed held his breath.

"Waste him—I'll put him in the system so when they find him it'll take the heat off us for a while."

"How am I supposed to get rid of Eddie? You heard what he did to that kid."

"You figure it out. Just get it done," he hissed. "Get

those kids, and get out of here! Jed, you'd better not let me down." The phone went dead.

Jed walked back toward the others. Karl and Eddie were watching over the kids playing some crazy game. "We have to get out of the city. They're looking for the vans and watching our drop-off sites." Jed watched Eddie's face. "We have to take the kids with us until our next orders come through." Jed filled them in on the details, all except one.

"The hell you say." Eddie's fist doubled up. Jed wasn't fast enough. The blow knocked him to the ground.

"What was that for?" He picked himself up off the ground slowly, his eye already swelling up. "You're the one that messed everything up by beating that kid." His face hurt, and his eyes watered. Jed turned and walked away. Eddie had just made it easy to kill him, and Jed couldn't wait.

Chapter 13

"It must have been something when you opened the door to the old shack and found her." Pastor John spoke to her the minute she walked through the office door. He held the local paper in his hand, opened to her story.

"It was one of the most amazing experiences of my life." She placed her purse down on her desk and went to sit beside him. "I wish Josh had been found earlier, though. He's still fighting for his life."

"What an awful thing for his family." His brows furrowed. "I can't help but think of my own son. If Rick had made better choices, everything would be different now. One wrong turn can change someone's life forever." He shifted in the chair, glancing away from her.

"It still has to hurt." Jessie touched his shoulder gently. "Rick's story would have been completely different if he hadn't come into contact with the Harvest Club."

He cleared his throat. "I heard a rumor that you are negotiating to buy the book store. Will we be losing you?"

"I am. I was going to talk to you about it as soon as I knew for sure. I'd like to continue working here for a while if you want me. I enjoy the people and would certainly miss not being here at least a few days a week." She smiled at him.

"Let's see, you're writing for the paper here in town and your old company in New York. You're working with Matt Parker on some of his cases, you work here at the church, and you want to add running the bookstore to the equation." He chuckled. "I've always heard it said that if you want to get the job done, ask a busy man. I would have to amend that to a woman. I'm sure if you want to stay, we'll find a way to make it happen." He looked at her and smiled. "You could consider working part-time. The board would be happy, too. They were just saying we needed to trim our budget, but talks of trimming the budget are in every meeting." He chuckled again.

They discussed some of the details from the weekend and she retold it again to Pastor Kevin when he came in. Everyone who stopped by wanted to talk about nothing else. Jessie was ready for work to be over by the time five o'clock rolled around. She leaned back in her chair, stretched her arms up over her head, and folded them behind her head.

Her cell phone rang. Unfolding her arms, she reached her hand into her purse to grab it.

"Hello, this is Jessie."

"Hi, Jess." Matt's voice came over the phone. "Could you stop by here if you're not home already? Tom sent me his plan, and I'd like your input."

"Sure, I'm just getting ready to close up now. I'll be by in ten or fifteen minutes."

"See you, Jess." She couldn't help but smile. Jessie cleared her desk off, unplugged the coffee, grabbed her purse, and walked out of the office, locking the door as she went.

Melinda was standing in the hall. Her glasses had slipped halfway down her nose and she was looking over the top of them, as usual. "Hey, Blondie, the front door is all locked up so just go out the side door."

"Okay. Are you done for the day?"

"I will be soon." She smiled, bending over to pick up a piece of paper off the floor.

Jessie had almost made it to her car when she noticed the dark SUV idling near the front of the church. In a blink of an eye, she saw the gun come out the window. She dove to the ground as two shots popped. It had happened so fast that by the time she looked up, it was in time to see the vehicle speed from view. She could see the scrapes on her knees and elbows. Her purse was on the ground, and the contents had scattered everywhere.

She grabbed her phone, sat up taking slow measured breaths. Before she panicked, she calmly called Matt. "Someone just shot at me and tore off in a dark-colored SUV with tinted windows."

"Are you kidding me?" He cursed under his breath.

"Do I sound like I'm kidding?" She took another deep breath.

"Where are you? Are you all right?"

"I'm in the church parking lot. I'm fine except for all the parts of me that hit the pavement." Her voice was shaky. "I didn't know I could fall that fast."

"Get out of sight in case they come back around. I'll be right there."

Jessie gathered the contents of her purse and got into the car to wait. A few minutes later, two police cars raced into the parking lot. Matt and Gary got out of the cars.

"Now what did I do? People are always shooting at me." She gave him a lopsided smile as he yanked the door open. "Is this what my life is going to be like from now on when I hang out with you?"

"They weren't shooting at *me*. It's more likely I'll be shot, hanging out with you." He grinned, clenching his fist. "Your articles must have stirred up the hornet's nest, and they came to pay you a call."

She looked at her knees. "Wouldn't you know it, I would have to do pavement diving on a day when I didn't wear pants or a long sleeve shirt."

"It's a darn shame to mess up such pretty legs." He glanced down at her bruised knees.

"Leave my legs out of it. Don't you have some bad guys to catch or something to do?" She felt the heat building along her neck, and the space between them was closing in on her.

"I'm doing it right now." He cleared his throat. "I'm questioning a victim and gathering facts. Although, I'm not sure we'll see them again. I imagine you were being warned, and they hightailed it out of here."

"Okay, then, you should be on your way."

"Not so fast, Jess, let's see if we can find the bullets and any other evidence. Show me where you were standing." She stepped out of the car and walked over to where a pen still lay on the ground.

"It was close to here because things fell out of my purse when I went down. This is my pen." She bent to pick it up. Gary was already looking around the parking lot.

"Did the bullet go off to the left or right of you?"

"It felt like one just missed me."

"Well now, that changes everything." He followed what might be the trajectory of the bullet and found the patch of raw wood where it had embedded itself in the trunk of tree not too far from where she had been standing. "I think we can safely say they weren't just warning you. They were trying to kill you. May I offer you a word of advice?" His expression was grim. "Start carrying your gun so you can shoot back. Be aware of your surroundings." Gary found a second bullet a little farther back on the asphalt, a 9 mm round.

"I saw the car, and I saw the gun come out the window or believe me, I wouldn't be standing here." She rubbed her arms. "Don't go getting any bright ideas that I need anyone watching me every minute of the day. I know how to use a gun now. I don't relish using it, but I will." She put her hands on her hips and looked him in the eye. "It might feel little awkward at first, but if push comes to shove I could do it to stay alive."

"I won't put anyone on you for protection unless they try something else, but I'm glad I left one on Abigail and her family for a few days." He looked puzzled. "I knew they would be coming back into the area again. I didn't think they would try to hit you. Are you going to be okay?"

"It's a little disconcerting to be shot at twice in less than five months, when it had never happened once in the twenty-six years before this." She walked back toward her car. "I guess this is my new normal."

He opened the door for her. "I don't want any harm coming to you. I've just gotten used to thinking of you as my girl." He laughed when she groaned.

"You're not going to let up, are you?"

"I believe that's my plan, and if you remember, I

told you right up front how it was going to be." He started to close her door but stopped midway. "I think you need to be at the practice range nightly for a while. I want you comfortable with your weapon." He paused again. "Move over. I think we should go by Abigail's and make sure they're okay. I'll bring you back here to pick up my car and follow you home just in case they're still in the area."

Matt could shift from playful to serious in a matter of seconds. She knew he was every inch the cop right now. She had to admit she liked it when he took charge, just a little.

Jessie was relieved that Abigail was fine. When she finally got home, she was happy to be there. Dressed in a pair of comfortable sweats and slippers, she sat down at her computer. Somehow, she wanted to find a way to do justice to all the people taken and sold into slavery in the world's human trafficking market, people who unlike Abby would never see their homes again and were lost to their families forever.

She stared at the blank page for a long while. Words weren't formulating right, and she found herself writing a sentence and then deleting it. Someone had tried to kill her, again. That was the most pressing thought in her brain. They were back in the area. Were the kids here, also? Tom said the FBI was watching some places in New York. Maybe it had gotten too hot in the city.

She needed to think. If Matt thought she was in danger, he would camp outside her house. She smiled. She couldn't catch her breath when he was around. He made her nervous and off balance. Okay, new plan. She would practice at the gun range daily and get used to her weapon. She was in over her head, and this was no game. She had to think like a cop, not just a journalist or a secretary. It had to be a part of her nature if she wanted to live.

Chapter 14

"I can't believe you missed her." Jed looked in his rear view mirror for the umpteenth time.

"I did the best I could with the car moving." Karl wiped the sweat from his brow. "I've never shot at anyone before."

"Yeah, yeah, whatever..." Jed slowed down to make the turn on to the dirt road. "I hope it scared her, at least. Maybe she'll keep her damn nose out of where it doesn't belong."

"I'm glad I missed her, Jed. I'm no killer." Karl stared out the window.

"You're an idiot. What do you think happens to these kids? Maybe we don't murder them, but we sell them. What kind of people do you think would buy kids? Do you think that they all grow up nice and happy like our kids?" Jed glanced in the mirror again. "I try not to think about it, ever!" Karl didn't turn.

"You're dumber than a door post." Jed laughed. "There's no way I can stop thinking about it. Every time I see my kids I'm reminded." Jed slowed down. His back ached from the constant vibration and bumps. "Hell, we'll need another car. We won't be able to drive this one anywhere near town. She might have gotten a good look at it."

"I wonder when they'll find our friend." Karl fidgeted with his seatbelt.

"Soon, and I hope it takes some of the pressure off of us." Jed looked at Karl. "Could you sit still? You're worse than a damn kid."

"I don't know why I'm so nervous." Karl glared at Jed. "Anyway, I'm glad they took the kids for a little while. At least it's quiet enough to think for a minute."

"There's no way we could have killed Eddie with all those brats running around." Jed rubbed his temples.

"My wife acted strange last night when I talked to her. She kept asking me if I was still out of the country." Karl frowned.

"She probably saw the mug shots on the news and thought it looked like you." Jed chuckled. "My wife doesn't answer the phone at all. I guess that part of my life is gone for good."

"What are we going to do, Jed? We're not murderers, not really. I mean if you don't count Eddie."

"I can't believe you're so naïve, Karl. We've destroyed so many lives; hell, we took their kids. Where have you been living, man? You've been taking the money." Jed pulled over to wait for their contact. "They should be here with the brats soon."

"I don't want to face it. I feel bad about everything I've done." He stretched his arms over his head. "It's damn depressing to me. I want to believe that I'm a decent person." Karl took off his seatbelt and opened the door to stretch his legs. The minute he opened the car door, the glass exploded inward and a bullet struck him. He fell forward out of the car, arms and legs splaying, then sprawled face down in the dirt.

That low-life had set them up! Jed felt a crushing tightness in his chest. No wonder he'd offered to take the kids off their hands. Killing Eddie was just a ploy, a set-up to kill them all. Jed gunned the engine, wrenching the car around as more bullets hit the SUV. The passenger door slammed closed, but didn't latch. His mind was screaming at him. Too many bullets for just one shooter. A side window shattered, then the rear window. Somehow, he managed to get out to the highway alive. He could feel the bile rise in his throat as he gunned the engine, and he forced himself to breathe deeply. Think, think—he had to come up with a plan. He ground his teeth. All right, he was going to outsmart them and take them down with him. First thing he needed was a different car and a place to lie low. He knew the area well. He had been all over the area often enough as a kid looking for the next place to party where the cops couldn't find them. He smiled grimly. He knew just the place.

He braked hard, pulled off the road on the other side of the highway, and drove behind a bunch of tall bushes, branches clawing at the side of his car, then hid his vehicle. He pulled his Glock from its concealed holster under the seat and checked the magazine. Full. He nodded, his face grim. Crossing the road, he concealed himself among the scruffy bushes so he could watch. He rubbed his arms to keep off the chill. Why hadn't he grabbed his jacket off the seat? Karl was dead. His stomach churned.

Hell, he had just made fun of him a few minutes ago. Karl never really had the stomach for this line of work. Jed had kept him around only because they were friends. Damn, he blinked hard. Swallowed. Jed kept his eyes peeled. There. Dust. He remained out of sight, watching two vehicles get closer. He held his breath as the two vehicles stopped a few feet away from him.

"Which way did he go?" One of the drivers jumped out of the car.

"I don't know. He cleared out too fast." The second man stepped out of his car.

"I was so sure we would get them both."

The first man walked toward the other. "No one told me when they hired me that we would kill people."

"Not you, man, you're just along for the ride. The boss won't be happy that Jed's not dead along with the other two." He turned and spat. "I'll be damned if I'm going to tell him. Let's split up and keep looking."

"What are you going to tell him?" His eyes darted around the area.

"There's nothing to tell," the taller man said. "I won't fail. I always get my man. He's dead." He glared at the other man. "I'll head back toward town. You go in the opposite direction, and we can meet back up here in about an hour. He'll be looking for a different car so you'll have to keep your eyes open. Don't touch him. You call me. He is mine. Do you hear me?"

When the first man turned to get back in his car, Jed clamped his lips tight to keep from making a sound. He was angry—hell, he knew the little two-bit low-life. He lifted his Glock, aimed two-handed. *Your turn, suckers.* He got the first one square in the head. The second man spun around taking a bullet in the shoulder. Jed fired twice more as he fell, hitting him in the torso. He stood and moved cautiously into the road, looking down on the moaning man who lay curled in a puddle of blood on the gravel roadway. "You double-crossing bastard, my face is the last one you'll ever see." He sighted on the man's wide eye and pulled the trigger.

****

"Hey, this is Matt." Matt picked up his cell phone on the second ring.

"Matt, we have what appears to be a homicide just outside of town by highway marker 165. Kip called it in. There are two vehicles on fire with a body inside. Dylan is on his way there with Marcy now."

Matt turned on his lights, heading down Main Street. "Tell them I'll be right there. Oh, and, Joe, call the coroner and have him meet us there."

"Will do—" Matt had already hung up.

****

When Matt arrived on the scene, the fire truck had already extinguished the flames. "What are we looking at?"

"It looks to me like a murder with the fire set to cover it up." Kip pointed to a hole in the window. "The bullet went through the side window and struck him in the head while he was sitting in the van. The rest will have to be done through forensics." He bent down to pick up an empty matchbox on the ground. He bagged it. "Do you think he's one of the guys who took Abby? Why would they be back here and not long gone?"

"Maxwell said the FBI was watching several locations in New York. They had to get out of the city. I knew someone was back in the area because Jessie was shot at in a drive-by."

"Is she okay?" Dylan stood up quickly.

"Yes, other than a few scrapes and scratches from pavement diving, as she called it." Matt smiled thinking about how she had looked when she had said it. "I'm glad I sent protection for Abigail when she left the hospital. They probably were hoping to get both of them."

Dave Lewis arrived with his assistant. They carefully removed the remains from the van. He promised to give Matt a call once they'd identified the body and the cause of death.

"When you get the vans to the impound lot, tell them to check for any prints and the VIN. Sometimes the perps take the plates and forget all about the VIN." Matt headed to his car. "Dylan, call me when you wrap this up."

****

Sitting in his office, files spread out on his desk, Matt was waiting on the new name soon to be added to the file in this case. If he were a betting man, he'd bet a few dollars on the victim having something to do with the kids. His working theory was that this guy had screwed up. Someone had wasted him, changed vehicles, and burned the vans to cover their tracks. If that were true, he could hardly feel sorry for the sick bastard.

Matt picked up his phone. "Joe, get me Maxwell at the FBI."

"Sure thing, Chief, this may take a while. It usually does."

Matt turned his chair to face the window. It was all back in his jurisdiction again. Where were the kids? Here, or out of the area?

His phone beeped. "Dylan's on line one, and I'm still on hold for Tom."

"Thanks, Joe."

He hit the button on the phone for line one. "Are you done, Dylan?"

"We've done about all we can here. The tow trucks are here to pick up the vans. We're getting ready to start back, but we want to go over the area one last time."

"Any surprises?"

"Not yet, but we still have to go over the vans."

"Okay, we'll see you when you get back. Just a minute. Joe is at my door. He's trying to reach you. I'll put him on speaker."

"Dylan, there's a report of gunshots fired out on Homestead Road." Joe glanced briefly at his notes. "The call just came in from the Homestead Estates area. You aren't too far from there. Can you go check it out?" Joe asked.

"I'll check it out and get back to you." Dylan hung up.

"Tom is on line two." Joe walked back toward the reception area.

Matt switched lines. "Hi, Tom."

"Have you had time to look over the proposal with Jessie?"

"Not yet. I have a developing situation here. Someone shot at Jessie, but she is doing fine. I have a murder victim who I believe is one of the trafficking suspects and two burnt out vans. I think they've come back into the area to get the girl."

"I'll be there with a team as soon as I can make the arrangements. Are there any signs of the kids?"

"There was only one body in the vans. I'm thinking they must have realized they were hot and dumped them."

"You may be right about that."

"My unit was finishing at the crime scene when a call came in about shots fired in another area. Dylan should be there soon. I'm waiting to hear from him." Matt doodled on the edge of his notepad.

"Sounds like you could use some extra hands."

"You've got that right. Hey, Tom, do you want to hold on a minute? A call is coming in." Matt put Tom on hold. "Dylan, what's up?"

"You're not going to believe this." Dylan paused. "The gunshots were for real. We have three victims, there are two near the highway. One of them is dead and the other looks critical. Another victim is down the road a ways near the estates."

"Is the third victim dead?

"Affirmative. It looks to be a hit from a high powered assault rifle. The same kind of rifles we found in the cars of the two males near the highway. Both rifles had large capacity magazines. There's a lot of firepower here. The guy still breathing was found near the main road. When the rest of the team finishes up at the other site, they can join us here. For now, it's only us. I have a call in to Lewis and an ambulance is on its way. We may need some lights."

"I'm on the phone with Maxwell. I'll be right there." Matt's jaw flexed.

"Okay, see you in a few."

"Tom." He switched back over. "I have another crime scene with two dead vics and a critical. I need to get out to the site." Tension filled him as he stood up. "I think whoever this group is, they're turning on each other."

"Sure thing, we'll be there to help as soon as I can get the team together."

Matt grabbed his jacket and headed for his cruiser. He waved at Joe as he ran out the door, hopped into his car, and had the lights on before he'd left the parking lot. What was going on!

Chapter 15

Jessie had just shut down her computer for the night when she heard a light tapping on her door. She opened it to find Reba Thompson standing there in her robe and slippers with a wild look on her face. Jessie was concerned. She started to ask a question when Reba lunged toward her.

"Oh, thank God, you're all right." She grabbed Jessie in a big hug. "I had Lawrence bring me over because I couldn't take it anymore. I've been worried about you all day."

"Why?" Jessie pulled out of her hug to look at her.

"I had this feeling you were in grave danger. It started this morning and wouldn't go away all day. A few hours ago, it was so strong, I was almost positive you were lying injured somewhere."

"Would someone shooting at me be a good enough reason for the feeling?"

"Oh, goodness." Reba clutched her chest. "When did this happen?"

"It was around five, when I was leaving the church after work."

Reba's forehead creased. "There is a very troubling aura over Blue Cove today. I don't know what's going on, but it's not good, my dear." She took hold of Jessie's hands. "I need to go. Lawrence is waiting. But I had to make sure and to see for myself you were okay."

"Shaken and angry, but I'm okay." Jessie smiled, taking a hard look at Reba for the first time.

"Be careful, it's far from over." She hugged Jessie again before she left.

That was simply strange. Reba knew so much sometimes it scared Jessie. She didn't want to have that kind of knowledge. She smiled wryly. There was a lot of truth to the old saying that "ignorance is bliss." The little bit of "extra knowledge" she had experienced was enough to last a lifetime. Although, when it helped change an outcome for the good, well, that was different.

Jessie walked into the kitchen to put the teakettle on. She went through the familiar motions of getting her cup and a tea bag as she waited for the water to boil. Her mind on the other hand, was a lost cause, filled with thoughts of shots fired, troubling auras, and what it all might mean. The sputtering whirr of the whistle and a loud knock at the door startled her.

She turned off the kettle and went to open the door. "Matt! What are you doing here?"

"I needed to make sure you were all right." He stepped through the door. "It's been a hell of a day since you were shot at, and I needed to see you." He rubbed his temples. "Do you have time to talk?"

"Of course, come in." She motioned to him. "You're the second one to come by tonight to make sure I was okay."

"Oh, yeah, who was the other one?"

"Reba Thompson." She sat on the couch across from him. "It was the strangest thing. I opened the door to find the neat, fastidious Reba dressed in a robe and slippers. She looked so strange to me. When she saw me, she hugged me. She mentioned there was a strange aura over Blue Cove. What do you suppose she meant by that?"

"Oh, I don't know—maybe a drive-by shooting and a few murders in one day could make for a strange aura."

She jumped up. "What? Is Abigail all right?"

"Relax. Abigail is fine." He reached over to pull her back into her seat. "We have two burned out vans, no kids, and three murder victims so far. There are very few answers at the moment." He ran his hand through his hair. "There's one man who might have some answers if he lives long enough to tell us." He leaned forward in the chair and watched her. "Seeing you, sweetheart, makes it all seem better."

Jessie turned her eyes away from him and fidgeted with the pillow. "Would you like some hot tea or something to drink? I was just making myself a cup when you knocked."

"Water would be great. Make you a little nervous, do I?" He grinned, watching her play with the fringe on the throw.

"What do you think?" She gave him a stern eye. "I admit I'm not comfortable with this side of you." She marched into the kitchen. He was close on her heels.

He watched her make the tea and got his own glass from the cupboard. "Look, Jess, I mean it, I find a certain peace with you except for when we're fighting, of course." He chuckled. "That's why I'm here now, no other reason. You're a kind person. Sometimes the world just stinks. I need something stable and steady to remind me there is still some good somewhere. My plan aside for the moment, I need your thoughts and observations on these murders."

She relaxed. "Okay, I can do that."

Matt told her what he knew so far and watched her face. "So what do you think?"

"Is it possible that the kidnappers are being picked off for messing up?" She sipped her tea. "Let's see, they lost Abigail and they beat Josh, leaving him for dead. Several witnesses saw the kids abducted off the streets of New York. How dumb can they be? I would call that drawing attention to an operation that had been under the radar."

"I believe it's very possible, but who are the ones doing the killing? The two with the rifles killed the man on Homestead Road. But who shot them? Who shot the man in the burnt out van? Where are the kids? And where is and who is the fourth man who shot the shooters?" He drank his water down. "Was he shot at first and then became the shooter?"

"Those are all good questions. Let's start with the last one and let me know what you think." She picked up her notebook and pen from the table. She answered his quizzical look. "I think best on paper."

"Well, Jess, if the one who shot the two near the highway was first an intended victim, then he's somewhere in the area, which makes it still dangerous for you and Abby. It's hard to figure out the next move of a fearful and cornered animal acting on instinct, much less a man." He stood up and paced. She looked at him with questioning eyes and he grinned. "I do my best thinking when I'm moving."

"Has the dark SUV been found? He was probably one of the men in the vehicle. I think he was the driver. If so, he'll need to get another car quick. He also has to have a place to lie low for a while—which means he would obviously know the area. It would help to know the names of the other two men so you could question their families." She saw his grin widen. "What? Don't you like the way I'm thinking?"

"I like everything about you, including your brain. That's why I'm here." He laughed. "If you must know, I was thinking criminals would go dizzy with your line of reasoning, but somehow you always get there in the end."

"Moving on, where are the kids?" She watched him pace.

"If I had to make a guess, I'd say someone up the chain has them. They're still somewhere in the area. They may have transferred the kids when they changed the vans. I think they're still here because their departure site is being watched." He stopped in his tracks. "But who knows? These guys aren't doing anything the way I think they should. We don't even know what they have in mind for the kids."

"Hmmm." Jessie was speedwriting. "That leaves your final question. There has to be someone who hired the three suspects in the first place. They obviously didn't like the job the kidnappers did this time. Especially the fact they left someone alive who could identify them."

"They were in the area to clean up the mess. Here's how I see it. We have two possible kidnappers and one of the hired guns dead and the other is barely clinging to life." Matt ran his hands through his hair. "We'll have to wait to see if any of this pans out. But at least it's one way to look at it." Matt smiled at her. "My gut tells me the first three guys were being set up.

Information will probably trickle out about them in the days ahead, with evidence that leads us *away* from the more important people, the ones who are actually selling the kids." He clenched his fist. "I want *them*."

"Was any DNA found under Joshua's nails or on his clothing?"

"Yes, but nothing in the system was a match."

"Is that unusual?" Her eyes fixed on his face.

"Not if he doesn't have a record, which is a little hard to believe considering the kind of men these guys seem to be." He sat back down in the chair.

"Could someone wipe out their record if they had the know-how and enough money?"

"Anything is possible, but it would be darn hard."

"Not for the right person. After Chief Anderson, I won't doubt the ability of good men to turn bad—when there's money involved." She took another sip of her tea.

"I hear you. We'll have to listen and work our way through the fabricated evidence to get to the real. Are you thinking about getting Jeremy involved?"

"He already is doing something for me, and when you figure out the victim's identity he can do a search." She pursed her lips. "He knows his way around almost anything."

"We have to get the main guys, or we won't save the kids in the long run."

"Without them, it will be like putting a little bandage on a gaping wound. You might stop the flow for a short time, but they'll grab others later. It sounds to me like this group might be turning on each other." She closed her notebook and placed it on the table.

He took his glass into the kitchen. "Thanks, Jess,

for listening to me. Be sure to lock up when I leave." She followed him to the door. In one smooth move, he turned and kissed her. Before she had time to protest or react, he closed the door behind himself leaving her breathless in his wake.

Jessie locked the door, leaning against it. She couldn't figure him or her tangled emotions out. She liked Matt, but she didn't like the feeling of being out of control. He always made her feel off balance. She needed a plan, a little distance, and a new project to work on. She frowned and pushed away from the door. What she really needed was the old Matt who lectured her—him she could deal with. This new person, who was nice and kissed her when she least expected it was not so easy to figure out. He made her nervous!

****

Matt wasn't sure he liked the feeling of needing to see her. He couldn't seem to help himself. In the midst of all the death, he needed to know life was still present, and Jessie represented what was good about life to him. He hadn't planned to go there when he left the station; it just happened. Now he didn't want to go home. Eating alone didn't sound appealing. Determined, he walked back to Jessie's door and knocked.

"I thought you were gone for the night." A surprised look lit up her face as she opened the door.

"I thought I was too! Look, I need to go eat and I'd rather not eat alone. It's been a bad day. Would you go with me?" He raked his fingers through his hair.

"I could make you something here." He shook his head no.

"I'm in a strange mood. I don't trust myself to be

alone with you." He managed a grin. "Come with me."

"Okay, I'll be right with you." Jessie changed into her jeans and a sweater.

She hurried back to where he waited. "Ready to go?" He opened the door holding the screen open for her.

She flashed him a smile. "Where are we headed?"

"How about I surprise you with someplace new?" He glanced at her and she nodded.

They ended up at a small café down on the wharf. "You can get the best chowder in town here." Matt handed her the paper menu.

"I just finished eating not long ago, so maybe I'll just have hot tea."

He shook his head no at her. "If you don't like seafood chowder, then try a bowl of the chicken tortilla soup. It's good too!" Matt gave the server their order. "I received a text while I was waiting for you. They found a dark SUV abandoned a few miles outside of Rocky Pointe riddled with bullet holes and shattered windows. I want you to have a look at it. I'm having it towed here to have it dusted for prints."

"Okay, but it all happened so fast. I'm not sure if I'd recognize it."

"You are pretty observant. I think you'll be able to help." The server placed a basket of bread on their table followed by the steaming bowls of chowder.

"I imagine he dumped it after he shot the guys who shot his partner." Jessie reached for the crackers.

"He had to know the police in the area are searching for it." Matt grinned, grabbing her hand. His thumb rubbed across her palm. "I mean they were stupid enough to shoot at my girl." Jessie rolled her eyes. "I can't help myself, Jess, you make it so easy." He watched the familiar red flush creep up her face.

Jessie retaliated by a quick kick to his shin. "I couldn't help myself either." She smiled and then frowned at him.

"You know, eventually, I'm going to win this."

"I'm not willing to concede anything yet." She laughed. "Just ask my dad. I can hold out for a long time. You may be sorry you ever started this."

"I don't think so, sweetheart. I'm nothing if not persistent. You've heard it said that for the man it's all about the thrill of the chase. Your resistance only makes it more intriguing to me. The gauntlet has been thrown down, and I love a good challenge." He waggled his eyebrows at her. "We'll see who the last one standing is. If I have my way, we'll both be winners and it'll be settled to our mutual satisfaction."

Chapter 16

Settled to our mutual satisfaction. She knew what Matt was suggesting. She fanned her face. She was in way over her head where he was concerned. How could she go toe to toe with him? The more she resisted, the more interested he became. He was able to gauge her reactions and anticipate her moves even before she came up with them. No comfort zone here; it had been obliterated. Intrigued, fascinated, and feeling slightly impulsive, she waited eagerly for his next move. She found the flirtation exciting. Matt stirred up strong emotions in her. She didn't know whether to kiss him or slap him. He made her feel safe but troubled at the same time. She liked it! She smiled. What would he do next?

If Matt was the worst challenge she faced, then life was good. Following Matt's directions, she turned on to the street where the impound lot was. Her handsome adversary was leaning against the fence. He pushed away and started walking toward her, grinning. All a part of his next move, she thought. As soon as she pulled her car into a parking space, he opened the car door.

"Good morning, sunshine. The vehicle I wanted you to look at is out back." He grabbed her hand and pulled her along.

She studied the SUV, walking around it. "That's

the one, all right. Who could forget those fancy spokes on the wheels? I thought it was a little strange when I saw them. Why would you want fancy spokes if you didn't want someone to notice you?"

"Beats me." He shrugged. "None of what they've done makes much sense."

"Wow, would you look at all the bullet holes. How'd he make it out alive?"

"I asked the same thing." He grabbed her hand and forced her to stop walking. "How come you didn't mention that little detail about the wheels to me the other day at the church?" He tilted her chin up so he could see her eyes.

"I don't know, umm…maybe it was because you were in your crazy game plan. I had been shot at and wasn't thinking too clearly." She frowned, her forehead creasing.

"So what you're saying is I made you lose your train of thought?" He chuckled, giving her a playful nudge. "Looks like I'm making headway."

Her brows rose. "Are we done here?" she snapped. "I should get to work." She turned on her heels making a beeline for her car. He was doing it again.

He got there first and opened the door. "Look, Jess, I'm trying to keep things light. I know there's a lot going on right now. Why don't we go out to dinner on Friday night? The two of us, like a real date. I can be real charming, and we might even have a good time." He gave her an engaging grin.

"You, charming…" She giggled, her face lighting up. "That might be something to see. Friday it is."

"I'll pick you up at six thirty." He smiled as he closed the door.

****

He watched her drive away. He then turned to Bob, the officer standing by the gate. "Let me know if you find any prints." Bob nodded. Whistling a tune, Matt walked back to his car. He spent the rest of the morning on the phone with Coroner Dave Lewis and Tom Maxwell.

Three bodies were in Dave's capable hands. One victim was in surgery. It was still too early to count Joshua out of the woods yet. His doctor was a tad more optimistic today than yesterday. Josh was making progress, but it was slow. A small piece of good news mixed among the bad. Matt smiled, tapping his pencil on the notepad.

Matt went over the details in his head. Tom had promised to get his team to Blue Cove to help. The lab at the bureau had agreed to put a rush on some of their lab results. He could use all the outside departmental help he could get. Forensics would supply part of the story. The results would help him build the case. The why would come only after a thorough investigation of the suspects' lives. He enjoyed this part of his job; sorting through the evidence until a true picture of the crime emerged. Gary interrupted his thoughts.

"Joe wanted me to tell you Dave is on line one," Gary said as he stuck his head in the doorway on his way to Dylan's office.

He reached for the phone. "Dave, what do you have for me?"

"I have a name for one of the murder victims. Victim number one is from the burned-out van. Unbelievably, he showed up in the system when we ran the DNA match again this morning. Not there yesterday, but he's there today. Seems a little odd, don't you think?"

"Strange, but I can't say I'm surprised." He tapped his fingers on the chair. "I'm sure he's supposed to lead us off track and take the heat off the others.

"His name is Eddie Lutz. He has quite an extensive record if we're to believe the information in the system." Dave sounded doubtful.

Matt turned his chair to look at the window. "I'm sure some of it is real. Some has probably been manufactured for our benefit, but we'll get to the truth."

"I'll get back to you on the other two as soon as I have something. I heard they were able to pull a lot of prints off the van."

"Good news, thanks, Dave. We'll talk later."

It didn't take them long to gather information on Eddie Lutz. Eddie was a man feared by family and friends. A big, violent man, just as Abigail had described him. Matt imagined the brute kicking and pummeling Josh in an angry fit. It made him physically sick to think of it. The vein in his neck pulsated; his hand fisted. Those who stood by and did nothing were just as guilty as Eddie was. Matt relished the idea of making them pay, if they hadn't already.

Picking up his phone, he dialed the church. "First Community Church, may I help you?"

His hand unclenched at the sound of her voice; he felt the tension ease. "Hey, Jess, would you look something up for me? You can get Jeremy involved, if you want. We found out the identity of one of the victims. I want anything you can find on the guy."

"Sure, I'll send Jeremy an email, and we'll get started on it."

"There will be a couple more before too long. Eddie Lutz is the man we're looking at right now. I'll send you the address we have listed for him so you can pass it on to Jeremy." He opened up his email and began to type. "Look, sweetheart, I really appreciate it. It's going to be crazy the next few days. I hope you don't mind a few late night visits for perspective's sake."

"I'm okay with it." She sounded wary. "Say, if you're too busy for our date on Friday, we can postpone until another time."

"Oh no, you don't! Friday is on, come hell or high water. I'll really need it by then."

"I was just thinking about you."

"I just bet you were." He grinned. No way would he let her out of it. "I'll see you, Jess, and keep your eyes open. Our missing shooter has to be somewhere in the area."

He emailed her the information. Her instinct for a story was great. As a combination, Jessie and Jeremy together would find things others would overlook.

****

Jessie had a lunch meeting with the Realtors, Bert Feldman and Sally Wallace. She was pleased with how things were going. Feldman represented the owner of Joe's. He let her know the owner was receptive to the open door concept of joining the bookstore with the coffee shop. He thought it would be a boon for his business, as well as hers. Feldman told her the owner was out of the country, but he would have some estimates of the shared costs the next time they met. Sally handed Jessie the figures to look over for the bookstore. They agreed on another day to meet.

Jessie walked back toward the church after lunch, going over the details in her mind. She was one step closer to having roots in Blue Cove. She loved this town; she wanted to be a part of it in every way. Jessie was so busy in her thoughts, with all the changes she wanted to make to the store, she wasn't paying attention. The white car parked in front of Patterson's, with an occupant watching her wasn't even on her radar as she walked up the steps into the church.

Her phone rang. She shuffled the contents of her purse, grabbing it after several rings. "Hey, this is Jessie."

"Hi, I got your email. I've already started tracing the information. I thought that maybe I should come there for the next couple of weeks and help. Are you still open to my coming?"

"Of course!" She smiled. "You don't even need to ask, Jeremy. I have a guest room. You're more than welcome to stay there. I'd love to have you."

"I'll be there Saturday afternoon as soon as I can summon the energy to get up." He chuckled. "You know me. I'm a night person with no active brain waves until the afternoon."

"I'll see you when you get here. I'm sure my friend Katie will be very happy to hear that you're coming." She sat down at her desk and got to work.

Maybe she should let Matt know Jeremy was coming. She picked up the phone.

"Hi, Jess, what's up?" he asked.

"Jeremy called. He is coming here on Saturday so he can help. He'll be staying in my spare room. I thought you would want to know he'll be available."

"Sounds good, I could use his help right now. I'm

not sure about him staying with you, though. How good looking is he?" She could hear the laughter in his voice.

"You can stop teasing me." She frowned at the phone. "Jeremy's just a friend. I guess some would call him handsome. I don't think of him like that. He's a friend, a really good friend."

"How good a friend are we talking about?"

"Goodbye, Matt." She hung up on him, smiling.

Jessie watched as Melinda stopped the vacuum that she was pushing down the hall, a bucket in her free hand. "Hey, Blondie, what's got you smiling?" Melinda walked into the office lugging her cleaning supplies. She set the bucket on the floor and plopped down into the chair in front of Jessie's desk.

"Just lost in thought I guess." She smiled as Melinda pushed her glasses up on her nose. "What's up?"

"I'm going to clean the offices just as soon as you all leave." She took the pencil out from behind her ear and grabbed a scrap piece of paper from Jessie's desk. "Next time you order office supplies I need a few things." Melinda scribbled on it and handed her the list.

Jessie looked the list over and slipped it into the drawer. "I'll take care of it. I should place an order in the next couple of days. I don't mind if you want to get started cleaning. It won't bother me. The pastors are both gone for the day."

"Actually I wanted to sit for a while." Jessie noticed that Melinda seemed preoccupied.

"Is something bothering you?"

"You know how I said things have been pretty quiet around her since Gina left?" Jessie nodded. "Last night I wasn't so sure. I thought maybe she had come back, or we had another visitor. There were some strange things going on. I heard several doors open and close. I thought it was my imagination, but then lights popped on and off." She scratched her head. "I don't know what it was, maybe some kids goofing around."

"Did you tell Pastor John about it?" Melinda shook her head no. "I think you should, just in case someone is getting into the building at night."

"I didn't want to bother him." She frowned trying to arrange her ponytail back to the top of her head.

"You should tell him first thing in the morning. It could be kids, but we should make sure."

"All right, I'll either come in and talk to him tomorrow or call him at home." She heaved herself out of the chair. "I'll get started cleaning and say my goodbyes now. See you tomorrow, Blondie. Oh, and I'll close up and turn everything off."

"I guess I'll leave then. See you." Jessie shut off her computer, grabbed her purse, and walked out of the church to her car.

Chapter 17

Jessie was going to let the information from Melinda slide, but she remembered what Matt had said about keeping her eyes open. Once in the car, she grabbed her phone out of her purse, put it on the holder, and said, "Call, Matt." She loved this new gadget from her dad. It was a hands-free way to talk. It was great, especially with all the new laws cropping up about driving and cell phone use.

"This is Matt." The sound of his deep voice made her smile.

Jessie repeated what Melinda had told her. "So what do you think, should we be concerned?"

"Maybe, maybe not, let's err on the side of caution." He sounded distracted. "A lot of people come and go in the building. It could just be kids, but it could also be something more. Just a minute, Jess." She could hear someone talking to him in the background. "Sorry for the interruption. I'll send Kip to check for any places it would be easy to break in."

"Okay, Mr. Parker, I did my civic duty." She chuckled. "I'll leave it in your capable hands. I'm on my way home to run before it gets too dark. Talk to you later."

****

Matt had a second name to check out. Dave Lewis called with the second victim's identity and preliminary info. Gary had already contacted the authorities in Evansville. Matt wrote the name Karl Hampton on the top of his file. Dylan had found Karl's body alone three miles in on Homestead Road, with a single gunshot to the head. Shards of glass imbedded themselves in the side of his face and neck. A large piece of glass had nicked a major artery. Matt's brows furrowed. If Karl was anything like Eddie Lutz, people were standing in line wanting to murder him. Too many suspects made it hard to narrow down the field.

He turned his chair to look out the window and laced his fingers behind his head. Why Blue Cove? He didn't get it. How many years had this been going on? This ideal small town was fast joining the ranks of the larger cities in terms of crime. Maybe it was easier for criminals to work from the shadows of small towns like his where people weren't as observant because they felt safe. Blue Cove was just off the main highway, not too far from several major cities, a great location, close to the action. Matt grabbed his phone as soon as the thought hit him. She answered it on the second ring. "Jess, are you home yet?"

"I'm just about to my turnoff, why?"

"Head back toward the station and keep your eyes peeled for a car that might be following you."

"You're freaking me out, Matt." She was silent for a moment. "A car behind me just pulled onto the shoulder. I'll turn around." Her sigh came over the connection. "I'll be there in a few minutes."

"I'll wait in the parking lot for you." He stood up and headed out the office door. "Keep your eyes open, Jess! My gut tells me he's in the area. You, Josh, and Abigail are a threat to him. The kids are under protection, you aren't. You could be his target, for now."

"He'll just have to move on. I'm not going to be anyone's target again." He smiled briefly at the irritation in her voice. "My life is just getting back to normal, and it's going to remain that way."

"Now, Jess, you know it doesn't work that way." He pushed through the station door.

"Well, it should!" Another few moments of silence passed. "Darn." Her exhale sounded loud in his ear. "That car that pulled over is following me."

"That's why I wanted you to come here. Keep talking to me, Jess." He paced back and forth, eyes fixed on the turnoff from Blue Cove Drive.

"He's hanging back so I can't get a good view of the plates or the model."

"Just keep talking to me." He could hear the tension in her voice and felt his anger rise with it. "Where are you?"

"I'm on Main Street, about to make the turn onto Blue Cove Drive."

"Can you still see the car?"

"Yes."

"How far back from you?"

"A couple of cars back. Hang on." She paused. "I turned and he's following me."

"Stay cool. Just keep coming to me."

"Don't worry. I'll bring him your way. I don't want him."

Matt smiled. Her humor was still intact. He stood, feet apart, watching up the street. "I see your car. Is he still following you?"

"He's hanging back a little ways and hasn't made

the turn yet."

"Does it look like he's going to turn?"

"No such luck, he went straight." He could hear the relief in her voice.

Matt disconnected as she turned in to the parking lot. He motioned for her to roll her window down as he walked up to her car. "Did you get the make or model of the car?"

"You're asking me?" She was clearly tense. "I think it was white, yes, it was white. It could have been a Honda or Toyota. They all sort of look the same to me." She sighed. "It was midsize and nondescript." She noticed his frown. "In my defense, I could remember that black SUV only because of those fancy spokes on the wheels, but this car was like millions of others on the road. He never got close enough for me to see a license plate or anything."

"You can do better than that. You drive a sweet Mustang. Think again, Jess, give me something to go on." He gazed at her and winked.

"Like I said before…" She frowned. "It was white, midsize, hmmm, a Toyota Camry." She looked up under her lashes at him.

"Are you sure?" He watched her closely.

"Yes, it was a Camry." She nodded, and he knew she had guessed.

"Ideally, it would be great to keep him in the area. He may lead us to the others. But not at your expense."

"How kind of you." Her voice sounded sarcastic even to her.

He leaned on the open window, eye to eye with her. "At least for now, he doesn't know where you live. Wait here, I'll follow you home to make sure we keep it that way." He stood up and started to push away from the car.

She grabbed his hand before he left. "You do know, if he has my name it's pretty easy to find out where I live? A click of a mouse is all it takes."

"I know." He gave her a wry grin. Darn, she was smart. "I was hoping you would forget that little bit of information so you wouldn't worry."

She made a funny face at him. "Like that's ever going to happen. I've looked up so much information on the Internet about people. I'm fully aware that people can do the same about me." She grinned, tilting her head back. "I wasn't born yesterday, you know."

"Believe me, I'm fully aware that you're all grown up." He couldn't resist and tried not to grin. "And may I add, quite nicely in all the right places." He stepped back from the car. "Stay right here for a minute, I'll follow you home." He enjoyed the rosy blush spilling across her face.

****

Jessie watched him walk back in the station, out of sight for a few minutes. Her phone alerted an incoming text. Katie wanted her to come to the Inn for dinner. She texted back that she was waiting on Matt. Katie told her to bring him. Matt walked out of the station carrying several folders. She motioned him over to the car. "Katie wants you to come to dinner."

"If you're going, I'll go too. Tell her that I'll be there." He took his keys from his pocket. "I'd like to go over some things with you afterwards if you have time." He waited as she texted Katie. "Let's get going. I'll be right behind you. Keep your eyes open."

"You, too…" She put the phone down and shifted

the car into gear. She pressed her lips together. She had missed her run. At least she didn't have to make dinner, or be alone for the evening.

She pulled into her parking space and Matt pulled right next to her. They walked through the gardens up to the Inn. "We got a make on the car," Matt said as he opened the door for her.

"What? You saw him again?" He nodded his head yes. "Where? I didn't see anything." Matt put a finger to her lips. He excused himself when they walked through the kitchen door.

Katie pulled Jessie aside. "After tonight, you're going to have to thank me big time. This couldn't have worked out better if I had planned it."

"I don't even want to know." Jessie waved her off. "Wait a minute, maybe I do want to know. What are you up to?" Jessie scowled at her.

"I'm giving you a little nudge, my friend. Although, with Matt here it's quite possible I'll be nudging him." Katie smiled at her expression. "Be nice. I am your best friend after all. I want to get married, but I don't want to wait for years for you to do the same. My kids could graduate from high school before you get around to it."

"Katie, I've told you, no matchmaking. What more do I have to say?" She frowned, pursing her lips.

"You know, I never pay attention to the word *no*. No is exactly the word that says *do*, to me. I do what's best in any given situation. Besides, you love me." Katie smiled, clapping her hands. "You know you do."

Jessie didn't soften her glare. "That doesn't mean there aren't times I wouldn't dearly love to strangle you."

"Now, Jess, you know murder is against the law. I just heard you threaten another citizen." Jessie jumped at the sound of Matt's deep voice. He winked at her as he reached out to steady her.

Katie grabbed Matt's arm. "See?" Katie stuck her tongue out at Jessie. "He's on my side." Her eyes sparkled playfully. "Let's eat, before it gets cold."

Jessie figured out Katie's plan the minute she was seated next to a tall, attractive, dark-haired man. "Jessie, this is Steve Murphy from New York. He's in the area on business." Katie beamed at him. "Steve, this is my best friend Jessie Reynolds. Why don't you two get acquainted?"

"It's nice to meet you, Jessie." Steve stared at her, his mouth open. "Katie has been telling me all kinds of stories about you."

"I just bet she has." Jessie turned a quick glare on Katie. "Steve, this is my friend Matt Parker." Steve shook hands with Matt. Jessie tried listening to Steve, but Katie's whispering in Matt's ear distracted her. Frustrated, all she could hear was his reply.

"The thing is, Katie, I don't need any help. I'm a big boy and I can do it on my own."

Darn her, she was still at it! Steve was charming but a little self-absorbed. Jessie listened to him drone on for a while, feeling uncomfortable with him. Finally, she excused herself to carry her plate and silverware into the kitchen.

Matt followed her out. "Shall we call it a night?"

"Oh, please," she pleaded with him, her hands wet from rinsing her dishes. "I need to get out of here. Katie means well, but she is driving me crazy with this whole marriage thing." She rinsed the plate he handed to her.

"Besides, there is something about that guy that bugs me."

"Didn't you think the same thing about me when we first met?" He gave her playful swat with the towel.

She laughed at him, shaking her head. "Sure enough did, but you treated me with equal disdain." She closed the dishwasher door. "He was telling me about all his cars, money, and property holdings. I just met the man." She frowned. "I feel like I did the first time I met Pastor Rick."

"Which was?" He was watching her closely.

"He's slick, not quite real, and has a false charm. There's an edge to him. You wouldn't want to cross him. You know, a veiled anger running beneath the surface."

"Let's thank Katie and get out of here." He walked with her back to the cottage after they said their goodbyes. "I trust your instinct. There's a reason you feel that way about him, and you need to check him out." Matt's hand brushed her hand as they walked. He grinned, moving closer to her. "Personally, I wanted to punch him for hitting on my girl."

She glanced at him, moving over on the path. "Could you be serious?"

"I am, and damn if Katie didn't know I wanted to hit the guy. She was smirking at me every time I looked at her." He studied her profile, moving closer to her again. "What are you thinking?"

"I hope I don't become suspicious of everyone I meet. I really do like people. I might be a little jaded after the last case, though."

"I don't think that's possible." He sounded serious. "You're a sweetheart, but you read people. You know if they're being real with you or not. The last time you talked yourself out of the warning you felt, you almost died. Go with your instinct."

"You're right. I think I may have to check up on one Steve Murphy." She smiled, picking up her pace. "Do you want to come in?"

"Let me grab the files. I'll be right with you." She watched him veer off toward his car. She unlocked the door, flipping on the porch light. She slipped her shoes off and walked into the kitchen for a glass of water. Jessie's gaze drifted several times to Matt when he walked in the door. He headed toward his favorite chair, sat down, pulled a pair of black reading glasses from his pocket, and began poring over the files.

"I didn't know you wore glasses." She scrutinized his face. They tamed him somehow.

"They're a new feature, you know, for reading. Too much strain on my eyes." He bent his head to study the file again.

"You look good in them." He looked more approachable. The familiar heat crept up her neck warming her cheeks. "Can I get you anything?" He glanced at her, shaking his head no. Did he know how nervous he made her feel?

She walked past him to get to her computer.

"Jess…" He grabbed her hand and held it for a brief moment. "Are you ever going to be comfortable around me?"

Her eyes narrowed. "Probably…" She grinned, freeing her hand. "You're like a caged wild animal."

"Is that right?" He raised his brows.

"I don't mean that in a bad way, but you're not like my dad," she blurted out.

"I sure as hell hope not." He grinned to lighten his testy response.

"I mean," she stammered, "you have a wild energy about you, an almost unbridled energy. I'm not used to it, that's all."

"At this point I'll take anything you give me. Wild is good."

She frowned at him, marched over to her computer, and turned it on. She started browsing. "Where did you see the white car?"

"It was sitting on one of the side streets as we left the station. No one was in it, or I would have stopped." He opened another file. "I have to be observant. You're learning to be." He watched her scroll down the page.

"Did you know Steve was here to donate money to Blue Cove Hospital to help enlarge the pediatric wing? I find that interesting, don't you?" She lifted her eyes from the screen.

"Not particularly. The hospital's annual charity ball is coming up. I'm sure there are a few more like Steve in town. What else did you find?" He smiled at her.

"There doesn't seem to be anything negative about him. He's a philanthropist, has a great reputation, and is known for being extremely generous to childhood causes." Her eyes scanned through the information on the screen.

"After our last case, a model citizen with a great reputation doesn't mean anything. He's worth checking into." He glanced up from his file again.

"Believe me, I'm going to leave no stone unturned. There was something going on. I could see it in his eyes." She tapped her finger against her check.

"Yeah, it was lust; he couldn't take his eyes off

you." Matt's smile faded, replaced by a scowl.

"No, I was thinking it was more along the lines he was angry at me for something, which of course doesn't make sense. I've never met him before." She glared at the computer screen.

"I still think it was lust, but you can keep digging, maybe you'll prove me wrong." He folded his arms across his chest.

"Did Dave identify the murder victims?"

"Two of them. I want you to investigate them as if you were doing a story on our kidnappers." He walked over to the computer, handing her a piece of paper with both names on it. "There are a few people who would have gladly pulled the trigger on Eddie Lutz. Karl Hampton, I don't know much about yet."

"You wonder what made them get into this line of work. It obviously didn't work out too well for either of them." She looked at the names on the paper.

"I want to run a few things by you before I leave." He went back and sat down. She followed him and sat on the couch with her notepad and pencil. She took notes as fast as he spoke. When he finished, he jumped up, gave her a quick kiss on the cheek, and was out the door. "Don't forget to lock up nice and tight." She watched him walk to his car.

Where was the white car now? She peered into the darkness. Had he found out where she lived? She wasn't sure what was worse, someone tailing her or the person sleeping in the Inn who seemed to be angry with her.

Chapter 18

One of these times, she would surprise him and kiss him breathless. Jessie smiled, feeling warm at the thought, turned off the light, and crawled into bed. She wished shutting off her mind could be so easy. It would be cool if she could just flip a switch to an instantly quiet mind. While she imagined that switch, maybe she should design it to flip the other way and keep Katie out of her romantic life. What romantic life? She sighed. If she were honest, she had been running from men ever since the day her dad had made it his mission to protect her from life. She looked around the dark room folding her hands behind her head. Dad was great, but he was crazy when it came to her.

Love made people act strangely, a little out of control. She smiled as she rolled onto her side and propped her head up with her arm. Some of the boys who had pledged their love to her over the years had been downright bizarre. Like Bobby Angel, whose love manifested itself in an endless round of torment and teasing. Then there was Jake Perry, she'd found herself tripping over him every time she turned around. He was always underfoot, trying to do everything that she could do for herself. She had to break up with him, in order to find enough space to breathe.

She had watched more than one of her girlfriends get a little goofy when they got serious about someone.

Katie was an excellent case in point. Any man she went out with might be her future husband. Jessie had lost count of the times Katie had said, "This could be the one." She smiled and shook her head. So how had others seen her actions? Maybe she really was the ice princess. She sighed.

She had to admit Matt intrigued her. Nothing seemed to faze him. She enjoyed his humor and his professionalism. When it came to men, Jessie wished this time she could be more like Katie. She stretched out on her back. Then maybe she could approach the whole idea of a relationship with a man with a little less intensity. Just once, she thought, she'd like to stop over-analyzing it, throw caution to the wind, and enjoy the ride. She smiled. It could be fun to experience being with a person just for the sake of being with that person. Especially, when he was as good-looking as Matt was. She exhaled a long slow breath. Oh, well, she was her father's daughter, and the apple doesn't fall far from the tree. Yet, there was a little something of Grams in her too. Her mind churned with the possibilities. Finally, she rolled over, closed her eyes, and fell asleep.

****

Jessie crashed through the trees in a panic. A low-lying tree limb smacked her cheek with a sting. Her heart beat so fast it felt as though it would explode in her chest. The pounding increased at the sound of the car closing in fast. Fear sucked the air from her lungs and her breath came in short gasps; she scanned the woods for a place to hide. Any place, please. *Panting, she ran on. Suddenly, she found herself out of the trees in a wide-open clearing. The car stopped behind her. No place to hide! Her sides ached. Her lungs felt on fire. She was cornered, defeated, and stood frozen to the spot; paralyzed, like a deer caught in the headlights on a dark night.*

"Get the damn kid!" She heard someone yell. Big hands yanked her to the ground from behind and a large foot kicked into her side. She rolled just in time to miss the next blow. On all fours, she tried to crawl away only to be pulled back by her legs. She kicked and clawed at her captor's arms hearing his curses until she was too weary to fight anymore. Instinctively she raised her hands to shield her face from his fists. The pain was beyond anything she had ever felt. One blow after another landed until she no longer could feel anything at all. A glorious numbness washed over her, and it was if she was floating above it all looking down on her body on the ground. Joshua lay motionless in the dirt, not her.

"Eddie, stop it, you're going to kill him." A smaller man grabbed at the big man's arm before he struck the boy again.

Eddie turned to a group of kids cowering by the vans and started cursing, threatening every child in the most vulgar way. "Now, every one of you little parasites knows what will happen to you if you try to run. Get this kid in the van and out of my sight before I kill him." His big fist doubled, and he slammed the side of the van. Terrified kids stared at the ground, too afraid to be caught looking. "Get in the damn van, now!" His eyes bulged in anger. They scrambled like mice scurrying into their holes at the sight of a big hungry cat. Jessie struggled to awaken, but fear gripped her and suspended her somewhere in between.

"We'll take care of him, just don't hit him again. If

he dies, we're gonna have to dump him," said one of the other two men. Eddie nodded at them. They lifted Josh and carried him away from the big man before he could change his mind. The two men rolled him into the van. A faint groan escaped from Josh's lips. She doubted they even heard him. They both kept eyeing the big man with a visible fear, whispering back and forth something she couldn't hear.

The atmosphere in the van was oppressive, heavy. The children tried unsuccessfully not to stare at Josh as he lay motionless. A girl with stringy, pale blonde hair and a thin face hugged a smaller redheaded girl who sobbed almost inaudibly against the blonde girl's shoulder. The blonde girl raised her head for a moment; her haunted blue eyes seemed to meet Jessie's. She looked at their faces, they were clearly terrified, and the silence in the air was punctuated only by a sniff or a quiet whimper. Tears rolled down her cheeks as she watched the faces of the traumatized children. Moving, the van was moving. The bumpy road tossed the children about, hitting one another. They tried hard not to hit Josh, holding on to each other. Jessie watched in horror when the door of the van opened and the two men rolled Josh's badly beaten body out. He hit the ground with a splat. She covered her eyes; she didn't want to see any more. They thought he was dead. Well, he almost was.

When she finally emerged from the dream, like a shroud, her blankets had wrapped themselves around her. "Please, let Josh live," she pleaded. "Let Josh live. Help us to find those precious children." Sleep eluded her as she repeated her plea again. She wanted desperately to find those children before they were scattered across the country and lost to their parents forever.

She got up and sat down at her computer. Words poured forth from her for the next few hours. NOT FOR SALE became the refrain beating in her heart and flowing through her fingers. No one, young or old, should have to live in slavery. She finished just as the sun was coming up, sending an email first to Sadie who checked her writing. Later, she would send a copy to Neil in New York, Max at the Blue Cove News, and maybe she'd let Matt read it, too.

****

The warm water rained over her body inviting her stiff, weary muscles to relax under its steady flow. She wanted to remain under its gentle spray until all the anger and fear she had felt in the dream went down the drain with the water. Josh's nightmare—even for that brief moment—was more than she could stand. He had suffered, so had all those who witnessed it.

She dressed for work and went through the motions of eating. Matt needed to hear this. She made a face, pushing her plate away. The fact was she desperately needed him to reassure her she wasn't losing her mind. She called her Grandma Sadie only to get her voice mail. She didn't leave a message. Honestly, she didn't know what to say. She was frustrated about hearing and seeing things no one else could. Yet, she was grateful at the same time. Talk about incoherent! She looked at her watch. She'd better get a move on if she wanted to hang out at Joe's for a while.

She passed the Inn without her usual honk or wave. Today, she would do it. She would talk to Pastor John. Her mind raced ahead with the idea that had come to her. A few minutes later, she pulled her car into Java Joe's.

"Hi, Jessie." Molly's friendly voice greeted her when she stepped through the door. "It looks like it's going to be another beautiful day."

"It sure does." Jessie glanced up at Molly as she grabbed her wallet from her purse.

"What can I get you?"

"I'll have my usual decaf and the scone of the day."

"Will that be for here or to go?" Molly took the money Jessie handed her.

"Here…" Jessie tossed her change into the tip jar. "I'm early today and have some time to enjoy it."

"Have a seat and I'll bring it right out to you." Molly smiled at her. Jessie nodded. She sat down at the table by the window where she could see the street and the door. She took out the article that she had written and began to read it over again, glancing up when Molly approached the table.

"Thanks, Molly. I bet you're getting excited about your wedding."

"I sure am." Molly beamed. "I can't wait for you girls to see my dress. I went for the final fitting. It's beautiful." Molly turned to look as the door opened. "I'd better get back to work. Refills are on the house."

Jessie tried to proofread her article, but her mind kept drifting to the dream or whatever it was that she had last night. Never had she felt anything so real in her life. Her scone was untouched, and her coffee was already cold by the time Molly stopped by the table again.

"Are you all right?"

"Yes, why?" Jessie looked up at her.

"You haven't touched your coffee or scone." Molly picked up her cup. "Let me heat this up for you."

"I guess I'm just daydreaming." She watched Molly carry her cup back to the kitchen and dump it out. Jessie thanked her when she brought back the fresh cup of coffee. "I'll drink this while it's hot." She took a sip, looking around.

Jessie noticed all the empty tables had filled up. Joe's was busy. She must have really been lost in thought. It was actually noisy. Why hadn't she noticed it? By the window, behind a grouping of leather chairs on the other side of the room, a lone man sat at a table. His paper hid his face. She noticed that his foot never stopped moving the whole time she watched him. His hair was dishwater blond, but that was all she could see of him. Her eyes traveled back to him, often. Wow, he had a lot of nervous energy.

The door opened again, Matt walked in. She watched him glance around the busy café, smiling when his eyes lighted on her. "Hi, Jess, you're just the person I wanted to see." He strode toward her.

"Oh yeah, why is that?" She smiled back, looking up through her lashes at him.

"No particular reason. I just wanted to see you. I like looking at you." He gave her a disarming grin. "It has become one of my favorite pastimes."

She shook her head. "If you'll be serious for a minute, I was actually going to call you later. I need to talk to you."

"Do you have time now?" He leaned on the chair.

"I have about thirty minutes which should give me enough time."

173

"I'll get some coffee. Don't disappear on me, I'll be right back."

She watched him walk to the counter. He was handsome, no doubt about it, so why was she so conflicted? Any girl in her right mind would love a man like him. Maybe she wasn't in her right mind. She smiled. At least that was the story she would stick too. She didn't know her own mind. Who could blame her? Since moving to Blue Cove, strange things had been happening to her. She really did wonder about her state of mind.

"What's up?" He sat down in the chair across from her.

She handed him the story to read. "You can read this after I leave. Let me know what you think. Remember it's a first draft, and I wrote it in the middle of the night. You'll understand more when I tell you what happened to me last night." She proceeded to tell him about her dream, watching the expression on his face.

"Wow. I guess that answers my question about whether Abigail was a onetime occurrence, or if you would have more." He lifted his coffee mug for a sip but never took one. The cup remained halfway to his mouth.

"Josh went through a living hell. It was awful. I can tell you one thing for sure; those kids will all need some help. They've been traumatized by this." She shivered. "Eddie Lutz was a terrible man. Everything you've heard about him is true." Matt was quiet. "I think Josh must be reliving the moment while he's unconscious. I got in on it somehow."

"Would you care to elaborate?" His brows rose.

"I would if I could. I felt suspended between being awake and asleep. At first, I thought I was the one running. It was happening to me until I saw Josh lying on the ground. I knew it was happening again. Do you think I'm crazy?" She scrutinized his face. "Sometimes I wonder if I need to move away from here. This stuff never happened to me before I got here."

"Like I'd ever let that happen. We'll figure this out together." He took a sip of coffee. He placed the mug on the table.

"I guess if my seeing Gina's ghost didn't deter you and this doesn't, then I think I can safely say you're going to stick around for a while."

"I'm not going anywhere, at least not without you." He reached across the table and took her hand.

She felt the tears well up in her eyes. "I need to get to work." She stood up abruptly and grabbed the keys from her purse. "I'll talk to you later." She made a quick exit.

****

He watched her walk away. He liked everything about her, even the weird unexplainable stuff. He didn't know how she held it together. Hell, he would have left when Gina showed up or had his head examined. She handled it all with grace. His feelings for her were growing, but it was too soon to spring anything on her. She had too much on her plate. He had never considered himself a patient man, but in this case, he would just have to try.

As he sipped his coffee, Matt received a text from Dave Lewis to give him a call as soon as possible. It was time to get back to the case he thought as he made the call. "Hey, Dave, this is Matt. What's up?" His fingers tapped on the table.

"I have another victim identified, and I thought you'd want to know right away. Does T.R. Booker AKA Travis Ray Booker ring a bell?"

"You mean the Booker on the FBI's most wanted list!" Matt's brows arched. "We're not talking about some petty criminal here. Booker is a major player in the crime world. Big money to hire him. He's been as elusive as hell for years." Matt ran his hand through his hair. "No one has seen him long enough to give an accurate description, but his calling card is well known."

"I have more if you can handle it."

"Sure, lay it on me."

"His counterpart was identified from fingerprints sent over from the hospital. He's Sammy Adelson, a thug with a rap sheet that goes back to when he was twelve years old."

"He's not in the same league as Booker. Maybe he's a hit man in training. Whew, I'm still processing the news that Booker was in the area. He doesn't come cheap." Matt's phone alerted him to an incoming call— Dylan. "Thanks, Dave. I'll get to work with this new information. I'll talk to you later." He took the incoming call.

"Matt, I spent some time talking to Karl Hampton's wife. It seems he traveled a lot for business. I don't think she had any idea about what her husband was up to. They have a couple of kids, and she was appalled to even think about him taking children." Matt could hear Dylan flip through his notepad. "I got the name of the third man that traveled with them. He's the one we're probably looking for. His name is Jed Johnson. His friends called him J. J. The three of them went to high school together in Evansville. I'm on my way to speak with his wife now."

"Good work, Dylan. Dave Lewis identified the last two men. You're not going to believe who one is, none other than T.R. Booker."

"The hit man, Booker?" Dylan gave a long slow whistle.

"One and the same." Matt drummed the ink pen on his notepad.

"Man, that's mind blowing. What are you thinking?" Dylan asked.

"I'm still processing it."

"I'll get back to you as soon as I talk to Mrs. Johnson. I just arrived at the house."

"Okay, I've got a lot to think about. We'll talk later." Matt ended the call.

Matt finished his coffee and picked up Jessie's article. It was powerful, thought provoking, and fed the passion he already felt for her. She had attached a note asking if he would be willing to teach some classes on the subject of human trafficking, or a class to teach parents how to keep their children safe from predators. Matt wasn't sure if he had enough knowledge on the subject, but he would check with Tom. She was right. They needed to educate people.

Matt's eyes strayed to the other side of the room. The man wasn't there anymore. Damn, when had he left? The man hadn't seemed right to him when he walked in. Was he the one following Jessie? He stood up to leave. For now, she was safe in the church.

"Thanks, Molly." Matt went to the counter to pay his check.

"Sure. I've wanted to ask how Kenny's working out on the desk."

"He's doing fine." Matt dropped a tip into the jar. "Did he tell you he got his letter of acceptance from the Police Academy?"

"I bet that's what he wanted to talk to me about, but I couldn't answer, we were too busy at the time. I'll give him a call back." She smiled. "Business has been booming lately.

"Act surprised. I'm sure he wanted to be the first to tell you. I went and ruined it." He grinned at her. "He'll make a good officer." Matt started for the door.

"See you tomorrow." Molly hurried to catch up with him at the door. "By the way, I think you and Jessie look real nice together." She smiled. "Is there something in your future?"

He smiled back. "That's for me to know and you to find out." He walked out the door and closed it behind him. Travis Ray Booker's long murderous career had ended in Blue Cove. Matt was having a hard time believing it. Wait until Tom heard this one. He made his way to his car mentally shaking his head all the way.

Chapter 19

Jessie knocked softly at John's office door. "Pastor, would it be possible to meet with you and Pastor Kevin for a few minutes sometime today?"

He looked up from his book and smiled at her. "I'm sure we can arrange it. What's up?" He bookmarked the page and closed his book.

"I have something to run by you. I'm hoping that both of you will see it as a worthwhile project for the church. Maybe even one that could include the other churches in town." She leaned against the doorframe.

"Let's see if Kevin is available now. I have to admit, I'm a little intrigued. Give me a few minutes to check with him." She looked at his phone and he chuckled. "Yes, I know we have an intercom. I need to get up and move every now and then." He smiled as he brushed past her and walked down the hall to Kevin's office.

She returned to her office when she heard the phone and caught it on the third ring. "First Community Church, may I help you?" She leaned her hip against the desk.

"Jessie, this is Steve Murphy. I hope you remember me. Katie gave me your number."

Jessie made a mental note to strangle Katie the next time she saw her. "Hello, Steve." Her chin edged up.

"I'll be in town until Saturday morning and I

wanted to ask you to be my date for the hospital's Autumn Ball on Friday night."

"I'm sorry, but I already have a dinner date for Friday. Maybe the next time you're in town." She shook her head. *That would never happen!*

"I can't entice you to break that date to go with me?"

She frowned. "No, this has been in the works for a while, but I appreciate the invitation."

"I'll take a rain-check then." He hung up before she could reply.

How rude! Her mind raced ahead. She hung up the phone with a bit more force than necessary. He hangs up when he doesn't get the answer he wants. What a child! Boy, oh boy, she was happy she had a date on Friday. She didn't have to lie to him, she smiled, but she didn't have to go with him either.

"We can meet now if you would like." Kevin's voice startled her.

"I'll be right in." She picked up her notebook and pencil from her desk.

Jessie walked into John's office and sat down in the open chair next to Pastor Kevin. She crossed her ankles, opened her notebook, and handed each of them a copy of the next in her series of articles, *Not for Sale*.

"I have some strange things to tell you." She shifted in the chair. "I also have something very important to ask you." She began by telling them about the unusual things that had happened to her since she had moved to Blue Cove. She almost laughed at the looks they exchanged when she talked about Gina, and what had happened with Abigail. When she told them about Josh's story, Pastor John got tears in his eyes.

Kevin cleared his throat. "You've never experienced anything like this before moving here?"

"No, and I would be happy if it never happened to me again." She shivered. "Except for the fact that Gina helped us to find the Harvest Club and the vision helped us to find Abigail. The vision also made us aware of the other kids who have been kidnapped." She shrugged her shoulders. "I both hate it and like it at the same time. It has interrupted my life on a regular basis with crazy visions, with threats, and gunshots. But, at the same time, lives have been saved." She paused and the room was completely silent. "So my first question is; why is this happening to me?"

Pastor John looked at her. "That's a loaded question and depending on who you asked, you could hear hundreds of different answers. There's a lot experiences in life for which we have no simple answers." He stroked his chin. "I have to be honest. I don't know why this is happening to you now, or why only since you moved here. I do know that Abigail is glad you heard her. Her life was saved." He looked down at the article she handed him earlier. "I bet some other kids will be glad, as well."

Kevin smiled, looking over his glasses at her. "No wonder you've been a little distracted lately. I think anyone in your shoes would be. Or maybe I should say in your head." He grinned at her, patting her hand. "Have you told anybody else?"

"Very few, and for the most part I've tried to downplay it. Of course, Chief Parker knows because I had to tell him to get him involved. Reba Thompson, on the other hand, knew about it before I told her." Jessie flipped the page on her notebook. "It's possible this may never happen to me again so I may have nothing to worry about." She uncrossed her ankles and folded her hands in her lap. "I did want you both to know. I feel normal but as you can imagine, occasionally I wonder. All this has turned my life turned upside down. If you see me being weird, let me know, will you?" She gave them a tight-lipped smile.

"I had no idea you were seeing Gina's ghost. I had heard a few others around the church talk about it, but I really never gave it much credence." John shook his head. "I have to admit, coming from you it sounds different than when Melinda told me she had seen a ghost. Her red hair was falling down as we spoke and her glasses were halfway down her nose. I'm not sure I paid any attention to what she said. I was distracted with wanting to push her glasses up and fix her hair so it wouldn't fall down in her face." He chuckled. "I sound like a pompous snob."

"I've had that same urge myself, sir. I guess we're both in trouble." Kevin chuckled.

"Make it the three of us." Jessie gave them a sheepish look. "My second question is, would you be open to offering a class to educate the church and others in town about human trafficking?" She looked at the open page in her notebook. "As you know, human trafficking is a major human rights issue. Millions of people are human slaves worldwide, and it's happening right here in our country, too." She gestured with her hands as she spoke.

"We have no clue yet why Abigail and the others were taken or where they were headed." She paused to take a breath. "Some of this case seems to have taken the authorities by surprise, breaking new ground. What is different about this case is normal-looking people from the community are the ones taking the children from their own neighborhoods. Josh was abducted right off his bike."

"That's a scary thought." John shook his head. "It sounds a tad too close to home for me."

"Please read the article and let me know what you think. There are organizations popping up all over who teach people what to look for. There are so many ways people can get involved."

"What are we looking at as far as a time commitment?" Kevin jotted some notes on the paper she handed him.

"As little or as much time as people want, basically. They train people to detect and report suspicious behavior. People disappear in this country every day. Some are forced to live as a slave in a house down the street." She looked at the two pastors. "I'm passionate about this subject, as you can tell. You know the town better than I do, whether this is a good topic for this congregation, or not. I think when people see how many kids disappear each year from the county they live in, they'll want to get involved." She shifted forward in her chair.

"Kevin, what do you think? Are you interested? You guys plan it, and I'll promote the class."

"I'm definitely interested." He looked at Jessie. "I think coming so close to Abigail's abduction and rescue would make it impactful."

"I believe it would too."

They talked a few more minutes, and then Jessie went back into her office and got to work.

****

Matt had dropped by the hospital on his way back to the station. Josh's parents were more upbeat this morning; his doctor had upgraded his condition. He was making steady progress.

The doctors were not as optimistic about Sammy Adelson who was still in critical condition with major internal injuries. Marsha Cane, the head ICU nurse, told Matt that Sammy's pregnant wife had been there most of the morning. She had just left to go rest. Matt left the hospital with her promise to call him the minute Mrs. Adelson was back at her husband's side. Matt trusted Marsha explicitly. The other nurses on the floor called her their drill sergeant. With her formidable manners and size, she appeared intimidating. She was harmless, and Matt loved to tease her. He knew she would call, so he could get to work.

Three murders was a lot to handle for his overtaxed unit. Matt looked at his watch. Tom Maxwell and his team would be there soon. He could use the extra hands and fresh minds. He twirled his pencil, staring out the window. If Booker came here to kill Karl and Jed, a person of influence had to be in the mix. How did Jed slip the noose and kill the hit man? Booker always got his man. Which one of them killed Lutz and more importantly, who had the kids? Were they still in the area? Booker's usual calling card wasn't there, which seemed a little strange for the elusive man. He was always meticulous about his hits. Matt needed answers. He stood, stretched, and walked out of his office. The walls were closing in on him. He walked into the kitchen, picked up a bottle of water, and unscrewed the lid. Why hadn't he thought of it before? He grabbed his phone and called Jessie.

"Hey, Jess." He grinned when he heard her groan.

"What's up?"

"About Friday night, I have a change of plans for you. We're going to mix a little business with pleasure if that's okay with you."

"Sounds intriguing, what do you have in mind?"

"I'm officially asking you to the hospital's Autumn Ball. It's a black tie event."

"Now that's odd, I just had someone else call and ask me to the ball. He even asked me to break my previous plans so I could go with him."

"I hope you set the record straight on that." He chuckled. "Do you have something to wear for the occasion? I know how you girls are about having the right dress."

"I think I can manage to pull something together. Oh, and by the way, I told him I'd think about it if I could come up with a good let-down so as not to hurt the other guy's feelings." He heard her muffled giggle.

"Now you're just being mean. There's no call for that, sweetheart." He walked back toward his office. "I hate these dressy affairs. If what I'm thinking pans out, though, we'll be watching for our guy to be there." He pictured her sitting at her desk. "I might even let you dance with him. It'll depend on how charitable I'm feeling. This was supposed to be our first date, and I'm not sure I want to share you with all the other boys."

"Who will we be looking for?"

"Let's leave it at *I don't know*."

"That will make it a little hard, don't you think? How do you know he'll even be there?"

"Oh, he'll be there all right. The kids are still in the area, my gut tells me. He'll be there out of curiosity.

His ego will tempt him to show his hand." Matt eased himself into his chair.

"So technically, it's work now and not a date."

He shook his head. He knew what she was up too. "It's a date, sweetheart. I'm going to give you a night you'll never forget." He looked up as Kenny popped his head in the door and gave him a thumbs-up. "I need to go; the cavalry has just arrived to help out. I'll stop by this evening to give you an update." His tone became serious. "Have you been to the shooting range?"

"Every day for the past week, scout's honor. Why?"

"I want you comfortable firing your weapon. You may need to! Find a way to carry it on you the night of the ball. I'll catch you later." He hung up the phone, leaving his office.

Matt walked into the reception area and shook hands with Tom. He introduced his officers and staff members to Tom. Tom did the same. The meeting room would be their place of operation for the next several days. Matt brought them up to speed. When they heard T.R. Booker was one of the victims, all of them had plenty of things to say.

"Booker has been on the most wanted list for years. He has flown so low under the radar I didn't think he'd ever be caught." Tom shook his head. "That changes this case considerably."

"It changes everything. You know somewhere there is someone with power, maybe a few people. What has me stumped though, he didn't use his calling card or his normal MO, which isn't like him." Matt looked around the room.

"Hell, that's the one constant when it comes to

him." Tom doodled on the edge of his notepad. "Are you sure it's him?"

"The DNA is still out, but the prints say it's him. Nothing is as it seems in this case, though. There is someone involved with impressive computer skills. They know the criminal background system well enough to tamper with records." Matt looked around the table. "Here's the case so far. We have three dead, two fighting for their lives, and one child rescued. Let's hear your theories on what we're dealing with." Matt sat down and listened.

They went back and forth from one theory to the next. Something one of the agents said triggered a thought in Matt's head. He stood, excused himself, and asked them to continue with what they were doing. He walked back to his office, sat down, and opened the file, studying his notations. He wrote a new name on the top of one of the pages with a question mark beside it.

Kenny interrupted his thoughts. "Matt." He looked up from his file. "Dylan is on line one. I would have put him through, but I thought you were in the meeting room."

"Thanks, I just got back here. I'll take it."

"What do you have for me, Dylan?" Matt picked up his pencil to write.

"I talked with Jed's wife Barbara today. She's still in a state of shock. She said she knew he was involved when she saw the mug shots. She quit taking his calls after that. Jed is a father with three kids."

"Was she suspicious of him at all?"

"Not really. She had an interesting bit of information that she passed on to me. He still hangs out with a group of friends from high school. They were the jocks from wealthy families, with some big plans. They had dreams of becoming rich. After high school, some of them moved on, but some stayed in Evansville. A few made it to the millionaire's club. About five or six years ago, they recruited Jed, Karl, and Eddie to be a part of their business. The three of them traveled a lot. She got out his old yearbook and showed me pictures of some of them in high school. I marked them and I'll bring it back with me."

We'll check out the yearbook when you get back." Matt took notes.

"She also mentioned Jed knew all the places to hide in the area. They used to have keg parties in high school. They were always one step ahead of the local police and love to brag about how they gave them the slip."

"Interesting, things are starting to add up. Is there anything else?"

"Only that Jed has been living pretty high. So was Karl. If Eddie has money, I don't know what he's doing with it. What they made was peanuts compared to a couple of other men in the group. They're very well-off according to Barbara."

"Good work, we'll talk more when you get back."

If Matt were a betting man, he would put money that the name he had just written down would be one of the people in that high school group. He wanted to get Jessie involved in this part of it sooner rather than later.

Chapter 20

Dylan arrived back from Evansville shortly before Matt was ready to leave. He opened the yearbook and showed Matt the photos of a few of the jock club members, Jed Johnson, Karl Hampton, Eddie Lutz, Robert Drunner, Mike Pearson, and Larry Thompson. "Barbara told me they all played football together. They were on the team the year Evansville took state. They were a close group, drove fast cars, had lots of girls, and they liked to party. Somehow, they managed to have good grades and stay out of trouble with the law. All except for Eddie Lutz, he had a few things on his juvenile record."

"I guess every high school has a version of that group."

Dylan nodded, opening his file. "Eddie had a drinking problem, even in high school. He was arrested a couple of times, but Daddy always bailed him out. He married his second year in college. His dad was angry. He didn't like the girl and cut Eddie off. One night while he was in a drunken fit, Eddie beat her up bad. She divorced him, which Barbara said started his downward spiral. Sounded to me like it he'd been going that way for a while."

Matt nodded, jotting something on the file in front of him. "That's only six. Are there any more?" Matt didn't see the name he was looking for.

"Barbara said that a few of them came in from a different school and she didn't know their names. She didn't meet Jed until after high school." Dylan sat down in the chair. "But these six from Evansville still get together at least once a month." Dylan shuffled through the file. "She gave me a check stub from one of Jed's paychecks." He handed it to Matt. "I looked the company up online and it appears to be a legitimate business."

"It could be their cover in the community. They might launder money through it." He looked at it and smirked. "It's a little ironic don't you think?"

"You mean the name of the company, Tot's Togs & Toys?" Dylan grinned.

"I'm talking about their slogan: *Your kids—are our business*." Matt clicked his pen on and off.

"A little too honest if you ask me." Dylan stretched his legs.

"We'll need search warrants for all three homes. I'll get in touch with Judge Sanders." Matt scribbled a few notes on his file. "I think I'll have Jessie look into the store."

"Barbara told me she orders things from the store for her kids all the time. Being a wife of an employee, she gets a nice discount. She was never suspicious and neither was Karl's wife. I got the impression from both ladies that Karl was a little bit of a follower, a nice guy." Dylan stood up to leave.

"Maybe not as nice as everyone thinks!" Matt frowned. "I guess we'll never know."

When Dylan walked out, Matt gathered up his stuff and left his office. He stopped to fill Tom in on the high school jock club. He needed to get to the hospital.

Marsha had called to let him know Mrs. Adelson was back in the room with her husband.

****

He walked into the room and found her sitting by the bed. So young, was his first thought. Her dark hair covered her Madonna-like face. She was very pregnant and looked to him as if she was ready to deliver. He caught the strain that clearly showed on her face when she turned her dark velvety eyes on him. Her small hand stroking Sammy's cheek suddenly paused.

"May I help you?" Her voice was barely above a whisper.

"Mrs. Adelson, I'm Chief Parker with the Blue Cove Police Department. I need to ask you some questions. Is this a good time for you?"

"I've been expecting someone to come and question me, seeing as there's a policeman outside of the door. Please be seated." She motioned toward a chair. "My name is Lindsey, by the way." She smiled.

"How's he doing?" Matt sat in the chair.

"He's holding his own." She turned her chair to face Matt as he sat down. "I am as surprised as anyone that Sammy is here. He had a lot of problems growing up, but none lately. We met a few years ago. You know the story, we fell in love and got married. The last several years, Sammy has stayed out of trouble. A few weeks ago, an old friend called him with a great job opportunity. He was so excited because it was great money, and with the baby coming, well, you can imagine how happy he was." She placed her hand on her stomach when the baby suddenly kicked.

"Was it from a company called Tot's Togs & Toys?"

She nodded. "How'd you know?" Her eyes questioned him briefly. She straightened in the chair and shifted again. "Sammy brought me a catalog, filled with everything you could want for your child. He told me to get everything I needed for the baby. He had received a bonus when he went to work for them plus an employee discount." She scrutinized Sammy's quiet face. "What did he get himself into, Officer?" She turned her eyes to Matt.

"He was found shot beside a notorious hit man. Do you know the name of the friend who called him?" He sat forward in the chair.

"I know that Sammy had gone to high school with him. They grew up together in Rocky Pointe. Sammy said he hadn't seen or heard from him in years. His name was Travis something." She looked at Matt. "He couldn't possibly be your hit man, could he?"

"If his name was Travis Booker then, yes, ma'am, he could be." He watched emotions play across her face.

"Booker, hmmm, yes, that's the name. I remember Sammy telling me they hung out during their senior year. A couple of other boys took them once or twice to a group that Sammy had called the jock club. They were all athletes, good students, and dreamers. Travis and Sammy were misfits. The jocks in that group bullied them. Sammy was surprised when one of them called him about the job. Travis called right after."

"Do you remember the name of the guy who called?"

"No, I don't. We didn't get much of a chance to talk because he came home after the interview and packed. He told me he had to leave to go on a business trip." She wiped the tears running down her cheeks. "He handed me fifteen thousand dollars and told me to get the baby's room ready; he'd be home in a few days. He called every night until the day I got the call to come here." She looked at Sammy's deathly pale form. "They aren't holding out much hope for him, but he's hung in longer than they thought he would already. I hope he lives so he can give you all the names. Maybe he can make it all right somehow."

"I hope he does too, ma'am. I hope he lives to see his child." Matt talked to her for a few minutes more. He stood up to leave. "Lindsey, do you need anything?" She shook her head no. Matt left the hospital thinking he should bring Jessie by to meet her. Lindsey looked so young and alone.

****

Jessie went to target practice and then for a run after work. When she got back to her house, she found Matt sitting on the bench out front. "What are you doing here?" She smiled at him unlocking her door. "I'm not dressed for company, obviously."

"I'm waiting for you. Do you think it's wise to be running alone with Jed out there? I mean they've already tried to kill you once." He glowered at her. "Why not put a target on your back?"

"Okay, I get it. You're upset that you had to wait, but what's this really all about?" She opened the door and motioned him in. "Sit down, get something to drink, and I'll be out in a minute. I need to change my clothes." She walked out of the room before he could say anything.

"Look, Jess, I'm sorry I snapped at you." He looked almost penitent by the time she returned, dressed in a long sleeve t-shirt and clean jeans. "I really don't have a good excuse, so I won't make one. I know you didn't have any idea of when I was coming. Sometimes I find it hard to stay away. You're beautiful scenery to me."

She waved his comment off. "Surly is how I know you best. What's up?" She sat down on the couch and tucked her legs under her, noticing how tired he looked.

He brought her up to speed on all the details that had unfolded so far and gave her the names of the six men from Evansville. "You can look them up and see what you find on all of them." He told her about Lindsey, the conversation they had about Sammy and Travis. "She looked so young and scared. I don't know why a guy would do something so stupid with a wife and a kid on the way."

"He was probably worried about money. We tend to focus on the wrong things when we're under pressure." She sighed, feeling sad. Poor woman, what would she do now? Money can suck people in pretty fast. "I hope for her sake he does wake up."

"While you're at it, look into Tot's Togs & Toys. I know it's a front, but it may be hard to prove." He took his glasses out of his shirt pocket and put them on.

"I can do that." She leaned forward on the couch. "Do you want something to eat? I was just about to make dinner." She stood up.

"I ordered a pizza while I was waiting. It should be here in a few minutes. I was hoping we could eat together if you didn't already have plans." He looked thoughtful, shrugging his shoulders. "You don't already have plans, do you? I guess I should call before I drop by. But I did tell you earlier I'd be by later."

"No, I don't, and yes, you should." She pointed her finger at him. "But since you told me you were coming by, I'll let you off the hook."

"You relax, and I'll get things ready. I even ordered a salad." He went into the kitchen and took the plates and glasses out of the cupboard.

"Pastor Kevin is willing to organize classes for the community if we bring in the instructor. I thought I should mention it so you can talk to Tom about it." She walked into the kitchen to watch him as he filled the glasses with ice.

"That sounds good. Maybe we can prevent it from happening again. The community can often be our best witnesses once they know what to look for." He filled the two glasses with iced tea and went to answer the knock at the door. "Pizza is here."

"You do know a girl could get used to a man bringing dinner."

"I sincerely hope so." He gave her one of his lopsided grins.

The rest of the evening was quiet. Every time her eyes strayed from the computer screen, Matt was working on his files. She talked to Jeremy a few times. She chased a few leads when she finally stumbled on one.

"Bingo, I think I found something." She tapped her screen lightly. "The store is a partnership. The owners went to high school together. I bet you can't guess where."

"Rocky Pointe?" He walked over to stand beside her.

"Yes." She nodded. "It doesn't mention the owners' names, but the managing CEO is Steve

Murphy." She scowled. "At least now I know why he looked so angry the other day. I was messing with his operations." She grinned up at him. "Maybe I should go on that date with him on Friday and use my womanly wiles to get him to talk." She bit her lip.

"Like I would ever let that happen. You're going with me." He frowned and she giggled. "Although, I might let you dance with him while I watch closely." He smiled, one eyebrow raised. "Keep digging. We have to be able to tie all of them together. So far, all we have are a lot of loose ends." He collected his files, placing his glasses in his shirt pocket.

"I'll stop by the hospital to meet Lindsey tomorrow." She stood up, walking over to him.

"I knew I could count on you. Take care." She could tell he was preoccupied with other things. Feeling a little disappointed she closed the door behind him.

She was in the kitchen loading the last dishes into the dishwasher when she heard a light tapping sound at the door. She opened it to find Matt standing there. "I can't believe I forgot this." He gave her a quick kiss and left her standing with her mouth open. "Jess, you make it so easy."

She heard him laugh on the way to his car. She stood at the closed door smiling until she heard his car pull away. Jessie closed up, turned off the lights, and headed for her bedroom. She snuggled into her bed, reaching up to shut off the light. What was that noise? Where was it coming from? She peered into the dark, straining to hear.

****

She heard their voices before their faces came into view and paraded in front of her like a ghostly nightmare. Their ashen skin and corpselike desolate eyes made her wonder if she was seeing the living or the dead. One faded from view, soon replaced by another. Tall, small, and sizes in between, they drifted in one after another, calling her name and crying for help. She found herself reaching for one child only to see that face melt and another take its place.

Her heart raced, she covered her face with the blanket, but they were still there. Tears ran down her cheeks as she fought a fear that gripped her so powerfully that she no longer knew what was real or if she was going mad. She was near the edge of a precipice that threatened to swallow her up. "I want to help you. All of you!" She heard her own voice calling out to them. Suddenly they were all looking at her, thousands of little faces, from different backgrounds, with a look of hope and wonder in their eyes.

Jessie sat up in bed, turned on the light, and wiped the tears from her eyes. This had happened when she was awake again. Shaken, she drew a deep breath. At least she thought she was awake. She went to her computer and wrote another in the series of "Not for Sale." The sadness of children's faces came through in the words on the paper. *We cannot buy and sell the next generation,* she typed, *for they are our future.* The sun was a few hours from rising when she finally finished, setting the manuscript aside to be proofed. She stretched, turned off the light, and went to bed.

Chapter 21

Jessie's phone and alarm went off at the same time. She rolled over, turned off the alarm, and fumbled with her phone on the nightstand.

"Hello." She winced, her voice sounded groggy.

"Jessie, is that you? Are you awake yet, girl?"

"Barely, Grams, I had a late night." Jessie sat up, rubbing her eyes.

"I gathered that from an email I received in the middle of the night. Of course, I didn't see it until this morning. Your words touched me, honey. That was one enlightening article. It makes me want to do something to help those kids whatever nation they're in." She paused. "Are you still there? I know you're there because I can hear you breathing. Jessie, you're so like me in so many ways. How are you holding up?"

"I'll live, but I was a little scared last night." Jessie took a deep breath. She could still see the faces in her mind. "The one hope I've had since I was little was to be like you. It makes me happy to hear you say that I am." She smiled to herself.

"You know, don't you, or maybe I've never told you." Her grandmother paused. "I might not have told you, because your dad might have gotten wind of it and had me committed. I had similar experiences. They happened when I was working on important projects over the years. I don't know what you went through last night, but it must have been powerful because your article gripped me from the first word." She cleared her throat. "So you see, you're more like me than you'll ever know. When I come at Thanksgiving, you and I are going to have an honest and upfront talk, just the two of us."

"Sounds good, I'd like that." Jessie got out of bed.

"I found a couple of corrections you need to make and sent it back to you. I'll let you get ready for work. I wanted to let you know how proud I am of you."

"Thanks, Grams." Jessie headed toward the shower. The warm water trickling down over her felt almost heavenly.

****

Jessie stopped by Joe's to get her morning coffee. She'd just made it to her car when her phone rang. "Hi, Jeremy, what's up?" She took a sip of her coffee.

"I've decided to come early. I'll be there tonight if that works for you."

"Of course, you're welcome anytime! I've got some research we can get started on."

"I was going to wait until Saturday, but I'm bored. I'm in need of a little motivation, and I figured you're just what the doctor ordered." She could hear the laughter in his voice.

"It's a little early for you to be up and about, isn't it?" She put her coffee in the cup holder.

"I know, but I'm excited to get going. See you in a few hours."

Jessie smiled. That was so unlike Jeremy. Not only was he not a morning person, he never got excited about much unless it had something to do with his work. She would have to invite Katie to stop by tonight.

Maybe she should try her hand at a little matchmaking and let Katie see how it felt. She smirked. It would probably just go over Katie's head! She'd get into the spirit of it and think of it as a great lark. Jessie giggled. Katie could make a party out of just about everything. She drove across the street, parking her car in the church lot. She went through the side door, walking down the hall toward the office.

"Hey, Blondie…" Melinda waved at her. "I opened your office for Reba. She's in there waiting for you."

Jessie stopped. "Did she happen to say what she wanted?"

"No." Melinda shook her head. "She just said she'd wait, when I told her you weren't here yet." Melinda's riotous red curls bounced up and down with her head motion.

"Thanks, Melinda. I'll check it out." Jessie headed down the hall, wondering what Reba wanted.

"Good morning, Reba." Jessie stepped into her office. Reba was sitting, with her ankles primly crossed, and her hair neatly coiffed. Her clear brown eyes twinkled, softening the smile lines at their corners.

"Hello, Jessie dear." She smiled. "I've come by to give you something." She took out a beautifully wrapped box and handed it to her. "You can open it now, dear. It will be perfect to wear with your new dress on Friday."

Jessie shook her head but didn't ask the questions she was dying to ask. She opened the box to find an oval sapphire surrounded by small diamond chips. She nearly gasped. "I can't accept this."

"Oh yes, you can, and you will. It was my mother's, and I had it reset just for you. I've come to think of you as the daughter I never had, sweet girl." She patted the chair beside her. "Sit, my dear. This will be stunning on you with your hair coloring and eyes."

"I really don't know what to say. Thank you, it's beautiful." Jessie felt her eyes filling.

"As are you, my dear." Reba smiled. "Now, let's get down to business, shall we?"

"What do you mean?" Jessie looked at her. "How'd you know I was going somewhere special on Friday?"

"Nothing magical about it! Matt told me he had a date for the hospital's Autumn Ball, and you are the only one he would ask. It was an easy deduction to make, my dear."

"He told you he had a date?"

"He sure did, and may I add, he smiled the whole time he talked about it." Reba frowned suddenly. "I've come to warn you that life can change in a moment. Be careful and on guard. It's your turn to watch over your friends. You'll find the strength within you to do it."

"Are you sure about that?" Jessie felt uneasy.

"I only know what I felt. I can tell you that you will be strong enough when the moment arises, dear." She started to stand. "If you haven't got the new dress yet, it's got to be a rich blue color. You'll look beautiful in it."

Jessie stood up with her, and Reba wrapped her in a big hug. "You are a remarkable girl. Blue Cove is lucky you're here. Have a wonderful first date, young lady. I'm not so old I can't remember the first stirrings of love in the air."

"Thank you again," Jessie called after her as she walked out the door. Reba smiled and waved at her.

Jessie looked at the beautiful necklace in the box. It

was exquisite. Once again her eyes burned. What a dear friend! The rest of Reba's words left her troubled, however. How would she know who needed her help? Was she up to it? She definitely needed more practice time at the shooting range. She didn't want any of her friends to be a potential victim.

She sent a text to Matt letting him know Jeremy would be there this evening. Maybe she could get Jeremy to ask Katie to the ball. That way Katie would have to take a trip into the city to shop for dresses with her. She did a quick check of her favorite store online. She knew exactly what she was looking for. The perfect dress in the exact color she wanted, and they had her size, too. She called and asked them to set it aside. She couldn't wait to see how it looked on her.

She forced herself to get into her day. If she worked steadily, time would go faster, right? The clock, however, would not oblige her today. It seemed to be moving at a snail's pace. More than once, she glanced at it hoping for a different result. She chalked it up to her excitement at seeing Jeremy. Finally, noon arrived—lunch—and at least she could think about something else.

She grabbed her phone and called Katie.

"What's up?" Katie's cheery voice answered.

"Do you want to go into the city on Thursday? I have a personal day." Jessie glanced again at the clock.

"Why are you going?"

"I saw a dress and asked them to set it aside for me. I need to try it on and see if it suits me. I'm going on a date." Jessie held the phone away from her ear as Katie shrieked.

"I can't believe it, are you kidding me? You

wouldn't tease me, would you?"

"No, I'm serious. It's a mixture of business and pleasure, as I was told." Jessie giggled, tilting her head back against the chair.

"Okay, don't hold back on the details. Who is the guy and where are you going?"

"I'm going with Matt to the hospital's Autumn Ball, and I'm thinking that I have a date for you, too." Jessie smiled as Katie squealed again.

"First of all, Matt and you on a date is way too cool! Where did you get the idea I need or even want one? I'm pretty good at taking care of myself."

"Hmm, seems I've said the same thing to you, but it didn't stop you. Now did it?" Jessie laughed. "You would be doing me a favor. My friend is coming in from New York tonight, and I didn't want to leave him alone on Friday night. Don't you remember, I told you about Jeremy?"

"I vaguely remember you telling me about him. Of course, if he asks, I'd go out as a favor to you."

"Why don't you stop by tonight at about eight and you can check him out?" Jessie managed to keep a straight face.

"I can do that." Katie laughed. "We'll shop! And just so you know, my nudge must have worked. I'm really good at this stuff." Katie hung up. Jessie smiled. She would have to give Katie her comeback later. It was Matt who had sold the date to her, not Katie.

Chapter 22

Jessie arrived home just before Jeremy was due to arrive and scurried around doing a bit of last minute straightening up. Thirty minutes later, a loud knock sent her dashing to the door and straight into his arms. "Jeremy, you look so great!" She beamed up at him. He really was handsome, a real looker as all her friends told her often enough. His wire-rimmed glasses couldn't hide his amazing chocolate colored eyes with small gold flecks that made them interesting. His sandy-blond curly hair, which was always slightly messy, gave him his boyish good looks. It was his brain that Jessie found the most fascinating. He was so intelligent. The conversations and debates they'd had over the years had been stimulating, to say the least. Sometimes she'd wished there had been some kind of chemistry between them, but he was the wonderful big brother she'd never had and that was all he'd ever been.

"Hey, sweetheart, I've been looking forward to seeing you, too!" He laughed when she stepped back out of the hug. "Nice greeting by the way. I'll stay away again so you can greet me any day."

She made a strange face, nudging him playfully. "It's only been a few months, but it seems like forever. I've gone through so many crazy things since moving here. You remind me of when my life was actually sane." She motioned for him to come in. "It's really good to see you."

"Nice place you've got here." He looked around, smiling as he walked to the front window. "Wow, would you look at that view. I understand why you're here now." He turned to look at her. "A man could get used to this."

"I love the view from there. You should see this place in the summer. The gardens are great." She smiled and plotted. "You know my friend Katie owns the Inn and this cottage. She's stopping by later." She trailed off. "We'll have to eat at the Inn one of the nights during your stay. She's an incredible cook."

He brought his things into the house and settled into the guest bedroom. They ate a quiet dinner as they talked over her current case. She also mentioned her date on Friday with Matt and got him to offer to take Katie. Katie would be proud and maybe even a little envious of the way she had maneuvered him into thinking it was his own idea. She hid a smile as she carried dishes into the kitchen. She made short work of cleaning up and sat down at the computer. He pulled his chair up close and set up his laptop.

****

Matt heard her laughter as he lifted his hand to knock on the door. He knocked and walked in to find them sitting side by side.

"Hi!" She looked up from the computer at him for a brief moment. "Matt, this is Jeremy. Jeremy, Matt." Her fingers went right back to work, flying over the keyboard.

"It's great to finally put a face with a name." Jeremy stood up to shake Matt's hand.

"What are you two up to?" Matt was irritated.

Jessie was laid-back with Jeremy. She was never relaxed with him.

"We're doing a little research. Jeremy is helping me to do a little behind-the-scene sleuth work. I'm learning to fly under the radar, but only when he tells me at each step what to do." Her blue eyes sparkled.

He watched them for about ten minutes. Jealous, he felt the green-eyed monster nipping at his thoughts. It bugged the hell out of him, too. It wasn't as if he was still in high school. Jealous! Damn, he didn't like the feeling. When it came to Jessie, nothing was clear. He felt downright possessive. Matt was happy when Katie showed up and Jessie introduced her to Jeremy. Katie took charge, bless her. Matt had noticed the way Jeremy looked at Jessie, which hadn't helped. Jessie might be detached, but Jeremy wasn't. He was smitten; Matt saw it in his eyes. Oh, he knew that look all too well. Dylan had it, along with Kip and Tom. Jessie walked over and sat down next to him. "You're scowling, mister. Did you have a bad day?"

"Not at all, I'm just thinking." He grabbed her hand, rubbing his thumb across her palm. "You look pretty tonight."

"Thanks." Her cheeks took on a rosy glow. "And that made you scowl?"

"Are you ready for our date Friday?" He leaned in close to her to whisper it.

"Almost…" She smiled at him. "First I have a little trip to take to the city. On Thursday," she whispered back. "I think Jeremy is going to ask Katie to the ball. I didn't want him to be here alone. Reba told me she could get them some tickets. I think I maneuvered this pretty well." She grinned. "I'll give Katie a little taste of her own medicine."

"Aren't you the little schemer?" He hid his grin. "I didn't know you had it in you."

"There's a lot about me you don't know." She chuckled, hitting him playfully with the pillow.

"I've got the time and determination to discover it, sweetheart."

"Is that right?" Her eyebrows rose in challenge.

"Yes, ma'am, this is one challenge I'm going to win and you're going to be mighty thankful."

"Thankful indeed…" Her lips tightened, trying not to smile. "Next thing, you'll be going rogue caveman on me and carrying me over your shoulder." Her smile widened and she giggled.

"Believe me, I've thought about it."

"No, you haven't." She shook her head.

"Au contraire, you have no idea what I've imagined doing to you." He laughed as she jumped up and went over to the computer. "Coward!" he mouthed at her when she looked at him.

"Behave," she mouthed back at him. She scrolled through the information on the screen and noticed something happening on the site. "Jeremy, look at this. I don't think I'm flying under the radar anymore."

He walked over and stood beside her. "Someone's tracking your computer and trying to hack it. Here let me handle this." She stood up; he took her seat and got to work. His fingers flew across the keys.

Matt came and stood beside Jessie. "What are you doing?" He directed the question to Jeremy.

"I'm having a little talk with her computer, so we can keep this person out of Jessie's personal files. Maybe in the process I'll find out who is doing it and try a little hacking myself."

Katie got bored watching the three of them and left. Matt was fascinated watching Jeremy at work. It was like a complex chess match. They volleyed back and forth. It took a while, but Jeremy was able to secure her computer. In the process, he traced the hacker's IP address. He did some maneuvering and handed Matt the address of the New York building where the hack had originated. Matt was stunned when he looked at the information that he had just been handed. Nothing was ever what it seemed.

"I've got some things to think about, you two. I'll catch you tomorrow." Matt gathered his things. "Jeremy, when Jess is at work, stop by the station. I'd like to investigate this further. I want you to show my tech guy how you did that."

"Sure thing. I'll stop by." Jeremy went back to work on her computer.

Jessie walked with Matt to the door. "Good night." She stepped outside with him.

"Jess, I'm not a real patient man, but I'm willing to wait. What I'm not willing to do is become another one on your long list of guy friends." He lifted her chin up to gaze into her eyes. "I'm serious about us and I'm working full time to prove it to you." His finger traced her lips. "So sleep on this, sweetheart." He pulled her into his arms and kissed her thoroughly.

She responded.

"Sweet dreams." He stepped back and smiled at the bemused look on her face. He headed toward the car. When he turned to see her still standing there, he grinned. "Goodnight, Jess."

Chapter 23

Wednesday went by in a blur. Jeremy worked with the FBI at the station all day while Jessie was at the church. He was on a mission to find out who the partners were. Matt had also given him some kind of special assignment, but Jeremy told her he couldn't say what it was.

Tom talked with Pastor Kevin about the trafficking classes, and they scheduled meetings for the community at the church. Kevin had already notified the other churches and the schools in the area.

Jessie closed down the office at five, went to the shooting range, and then stopped by the hospital to see Lindsey Adelson.

Lindsey smiled at her when she walked in the room. "Guess what happened today?"

"Did he wake up?" Jessie walked over to the chair beside her.

She nodded with a smile. "He was awake for a few minutes, which was more than they expected. He responded to my voice by squeezing my hand." She gently pushed his hair off his face as he slept. "Maybe he'll be able to talk to the police soon. I hope so." She sighed. "That would mean he might actually recover."

"That's a cause for hope and a minor celebration." Jessie pulled a gift bag out of the paper bag she was carrying and handed it to her. "Please open it."

Lindsey's face lit up as she pulled out a shower gel, lotion, scented soaps, and a vanilla body spray. "Thank you. It was nice of you to think of me."

"How are you holding up?" Jessie sat down in the chair next to her.

"I'm okay. I get awful tired now, but at least when I leave here I finally sleep through the night. The staff has been very kind to me. I wasn't sure if they would after all Sammy was involved in." Lindsey rubbed her belly. "I hope he gets to see the baby. I was keeping it as a surprise, but I found out it's a little girl. I know he would love a daughter."

"I'm sure he would love a daughter. They all talk about wanting a son, but they turn to mush when they have a little girl to look after." Jessie smiled at her.

"I got most of her room done before I left home. It's pink of course, with butterflies. It's such a happy room. I smile every time I walked in there." Tears trickled down her cheeks and Lindsey dabbed at her eyes with a tissue. "It will never be the same now. I know it can't be. He'll go to prison, and I'll be raising her alone."

Jessie touched her shoulder gently, feeling her sadness. It would be a hard road ahead for her. Next Jessie went to Joshua's room where she found out Josh was making steady improvement. His doctor had taken him off the meds and was waiting for him to wake up on his own. She offered to sit by his side so Colin and Martha could eat dinner away from the hospital for a change.

"Josh, I don't know if you can hear me but keep fighting. Your parents want it so badly and so do your sisters." She squeezed his hand. "I know what you've been through; you showed me all of it in a dream. You're braver and stronger than you realize. I don't know how you had the courage to escape or the ability to fight as long as you did. You are my hero. I hope you can hear me, Josh. I'm praying for you to live a long and healthy life." She felt his hand move in her hand.

Jessie pushed the call button on the bed. The nurse walked through the door. "Did you need something?"

"I felt his hand move in mine when I was talking to him. I was wondering if he might have heard me." The nurse took his hand and talked to him. His thumb pressed her hand.

"I'll be right back. I'm going to put a call in to his doctor. Keep talking to him, honey." She gave Jessie a hurried smile. "He must have liked what you were saying to him."

Jessie grabbed his hand and began talking to him. She rambled on about everything in the dream should could remember. She could see his eyelids flutter and her excitement built. His doctor, a distinguished looking man with silver gray hair, came through the door. He went to the sink to wash his hands, then pulled his stethoscope from around his neck and leaned over Josh. "Are you a family member?" He looked at her as Jessie stepped back out of his way so he could work.

"No, I'm a friend of his parents. I was sitting with him so his parents could have a break." She watched him listen to Josh's heart and check his pulse. "His eyes fluttered when I was talking to him just now."

The doctor nodded. "Josh, can you hear me? Squeeze my hand if you can hear me." He chuckled. "That was a nice firm squeeze, Josh." He wrote something on the chart. "I think you've been good medicine for our young patient. I can't say that I blame him." He gave some instructions to the nurse and turned to smile at her. "I'm Doctor Hathaway."

"Jessie Reynolds." She smiled as she shook his extended hand.

"Oh, of course. Now I know who you are. You've been writing some great articles for the town paper. Young lady, I'm going to leave him in your very capable hands. Don't stop talking to him. I'll be back to check on him in a while. If his eyes open, push the call button."

"I will." She watched them both walk out of the room. Jessie talked to Josh about Abigail. She told him about how Radar had searched for her and found her. It was thirty minutes later, right after she'd told him that the big man Eddie could never hurt him again, that Josh opened his eyes. He looked at her quizzically and she smiled. "I'm Jessie," she told him. "Your parents should be here in a few minutes." She pressed the call button. "You're in the hospital, Josh." She could feel those annoying tears starting to build.

He kept staring at her as she rambled on for what felt like an eternity to her, but in reality must have only been a minute or two. The nurse rushed into the room followed by Dr. Hathaway. Josh's parents followed the medical staff, alarm written on their faces as they saw all the activity in the room.

"Your son decided to wake up while this nice young lady was talking to him." Dr. Hathaway smiled at them. "I'm going to check him out and then let you have some time with your son." He took Josh's hand to monitor his pulse. "Welcome back, Josh." Dr. Hathaway shone a light into his eyes. "It's nice to see those eyes so clear, young man." He patted Josh's hand. He nodded to the parents, who rushed to the bedside and began talking to their son.

Jessie watched the happy scene unfold from the other side of the room. Smiling, she said her goodbyes and headed for her car. She called Matt on her way out of the hospital to let him know what had just happened. Once in her car, she breathed a sigh of relief and let the tears flow. "Thank you for allowing me to see him wake up," she whispered. After the horror of his nightmare, this was like a cleansing breath of fresh air.

****

Matt stopped by the hospital after dinner to check on Sammy and Josh. Sammy was sleeping, but the nurse told him it was a natural sleep. He could probably talk with him in the next day or two. Matt knew he would have to read Sammy his Miranda rights. The court would appoint an attorney before Matt could formally question him. He wanted just a few minutes to talk to Sammy alone, before the lawyers got involved. Maybe Sammy would give him that.

Josh was wide-awake when Matt arrived at his room. "Josh, you look better than the first time we met." He stood by the boy's bed and smiled at him. Matt noticed his puzzled expression. "You won't remember me from that day. You were hurt when we found you." Matt sat down in the chair beside Mrs. Harris. "His recovery is remarkable. He was barely hanging on the day we found him."

She nodded at Matt. "Remarkable is a good way to describe it. He's starting to recognize family, but he can't remember any of the days he was gone from us. He only knows what we tell him." Mrs. Harris talked softly to Matt so Josh couldn't hear. "Dr. Hathaway said it might all come back to him in time or he may have it locked so deep inside his subconscious, it's forgotten."

Matt chatted with her for a while. "I'll be back to see him again when he's a little stronger." He walked out of the room, stopped to talk to the officer standing watch outside the room, then headed back to his office.

Matt was waiting for Dylan's call. He was in Evansville at the police station. The police had questioned the remaining friends of Jed Johnson. The FBI was searching the homes of Jed, Karl, and Eddie today. He hoped their computers had some detailed records or emails that would shed light on why they had taken the kids. He knew they were all in it somehow, but he wasn't sure the level of their involvement. He sent an email to Jessie with all of their names. Matt wanted her to get busy investigating them from high school forward and to let him know if she stumbled onto something. He had covered all his bases.

Jeremy popped his head in the door. "I showed Gary how I set up a heavy-duty firewall for Jessie's computer. He's working to make sure none of yours are being hacked."

"Come in and close the door." Matt motioned to a chair. "What have you found out?"

"I'm still trying to break through. Whoever it is, he obviously knows his way around a computer." Jeremy rubbed at his chin.

"Damn, I was afraid of that." Matt frowned. "I don't want to open this can of worms unless we have plenty of evidence."

"I'll keep working at it. People always think

they're so damn clever, then they get careless. They always leave some little footprint. I'm good at finding them. It takes time, but if it's there I'll find it." Jeremy smiled. "I'll work at it tonight after dinner. I'm taking Jessie and Katie out so we can become better acquainted. Actually, I think Jessie outmaneuvered me there." Jeremy frowned, followed by a grin. He ran his hand through his hair, tousling the curls.

"It's those damn blue eyes." They had sure taken him in more than once.

"You've got that right." Jeremy nodded, chuckling. "They've gotten me to do things I didn't want to do over the last few years." He stood up to leave.

"You know you're free to work here anytime you want over the next few days."

"Thanks. Jessie and Katie are going into New York tomorrow, so I might take you up on that."

Jeremy had just left the office when Dylan called.

"Matt, they're all involved in the same company. Salesmen with dark secrets about how they make their living. Isn't that something? I think you're going to want to drive over here and question them, too."

"Set it up with the authorities for tomorrow. We'll take turns at interrogating them. Tell them the FBI may want to question them at some point too." Matt could hear Dylan talking to someone in the background.

"Is ten o'clock tomorrow okay for you, Chief?"

Matt looked at his schedule. "That's fine."

On his was out of the office, Matt stopped to talk to Tom. "The plan is to question them tomorrow."

"I'll send a couple of agents with you. I'll schedule a follow-up for the next day with the FBI doing the questioning to keep the heat on them."

"Sounds like a good idea. I'm calling it a day, Tom. I'll see you tomorrow."

"I'm about to do the same. Say, before you go, we were able to trace the VIN on the van, and I have someone in the area checking out the records to find out who originally bought it."

"Great. Let me know when you find out," Matt said as he headed out of the station to his truck. He already had questions lined up he wanted to ask them in the morning. What he wanted now was down time.

****

Jessie stopped by the Inn early to pick up Katie. She came out smiling, pushing her purse strap back up onto her shoulder. "Coffee, I need coffee." Katie fastened her seatbelt and shut the car door.

"We can stop at Joe's on our way out of town." She looked at Katie and put her car in gear. "I'm just a little excited. I don't like living in the city, but I do love shopping there."

"What stores do you have in mind?"

"I'm going to my favorite place. They're holding a dress for me, but other than that, we can go anywhere you want."

"How did you know what you wanted without trying on hundreds?" Katie looked shocked. "It has to be formal, after all."

"I saw it the last time we were there. It'll be perfect with what's inside the box in my purse." Jessie motioned toward her bag in the back seat.

Katie took out the box and squealed when she opened it. "Oh my gosh, this is beautiful. Where did you get it?" Katie held the necklace up so it could catch the light.

"Reba Thompson gave it to me." Jessie smiled at the memory. "I told her I couldn't take it, but she insisted." She felt herself tear up. "She told me I was the daughter she never had."

"Wow, she's something. This is beautiful." Katie placed it carefully back in the box. "Obviously your dress has to go with this, right?"

"Right! I found a Marchesa gown in a blue silk. It's form fitting with a V-neck that will be perfect with the necklace." Jessie pulled into a space near Joe's. "As long as it fits, the dress will be coming home with me."

"Sounds divine." Katie whistled. "I think that shop is my favorite anyway, so I hope there's something there for me." They went into Joe's and got coffee to go.

The girls had a terrific day shopping. Jessie's dress fit perfectly. The design was her style all the way. She loved it. Katie found a Kay Unger gold satin, cowl neck, sleeveless number with the back cut out in an exquisite pattern. The gold was perfect on Katie. Her red hair and green eyes looked gorgeous. After they had finished shopping for shoes, the two of them sat down for lunch, oblivious to the admiring glances turned their way.

"I can't believe I found that dress on sale. I was so happy to get it at that price." Katie smiled. "I love it."

"The back is jaw-dropping gorgeous, and the color is perfect on you." Jessie took a quick look at the menu as the waiter approached. "I'll have the Oriental chicken salad."

"I'll have the same." Katie handed him the menu. "I'd also like an iced tea." Jessie nodded when he asked if she would like tea also.

"What do you think of Jeremy?" Jessie felt she had waited long enough to ask her.

"You could have told me he was drop dead gorgeous." Katie glared at her. "I think that was the first time in my life I felt tongue-tied with a guy."

"That is odd for you. You can take charge of any situation or guy." Jessie perked up.

"I know, but he's different." Katie looked thoughtful. "I don't want to mess this up being my crazy aggressive self." Katie paused. "Did Jeremy and you ever date?"

"He asked me out a couple of times, but honestly there is no chemistry between us. We really are just friends."

"I find that hard to believe. I mean you're you." Katie waved a hand. "And he's well, you know, really a looker. How could you not be gone on each other?"

"We aren't, you'll just have to trust me on that." Jessie thanked the waiter when he put her salad in front of her.

"Jessie, sometimes you're oblivious to how a guy feels about you. Are you sure? I mean, I don't want to step across the line."

"We're really just friends. To me, he's like the brother I never had." Katie's actions puzzled Jessie. She had never seen Katie this uncertain.

"What do you really think about Matt?" Katie grinned.

"Matt is an entirely different story. He isn't very brotherly at all. He intrigues me and scares me at the same time." She frowned and poked at a piece of chicken in her salad. "I think with him it might be easy to lose control."

"This sounds interesting." Katie leaned her chin in her palm, her salad forgotten. "Tell me more! I've never heard you like this before."

They finished lunch giggling and talking about men. The conversation continued on the drive home. Jessie dropped Katie off at the Inn. *What a great day.* She smiled. Jessie grabbed her packages out of the car, she was happy to be home. She had her dress, she had her shoes, and she had her date. He was some date. She leaned against the door and sighed.

Chapter 24

Matt drove home from Evansville frustrated. With pricey lawyers by their sides, the suspects had stopped talking. "Damn, I hate when they clam up like that. The only thing worse is when they spout the same stuff. You know they were schooled by the lawyers."

"They were a little more talkative yesterday and cocky." Dylan shoved his file in his briefcase.

"This was a complete waste of time. Maybe a family member or wife will say something." Matt ran his free hand through his hair.

"I thought if I heard one more time that they all knew Johnson, Hampton, and Lutz as friends, but nothing other than that one more time, I would punch somebody."

"I almost had Mike Pearson talking, but at the last moment, he clammed up. I gave his lawyer a lot of incentive to talk Mike into testifying for the state. He didn't bite." Matt frowned, his knuckles turning white as he gripped the steering wheel.

"We've had bad days before. Why has this got you so upset?" Dylan looked his way.

"I was hoping for something, and they gave us nothing. Those kids are in someone's hands. We need to find them soon, or we could lose them for good." He raked his free hand through his hair. "I hate wasting time. This is the part of a case that drives me nuts."

"You know how these things go." Dylan shrugged. "We'll nail them. It's only a matter of time. We might find stuff on their computers or from the search."

"If it was just about solving the murders, that would be one thing, but it's the kids." Matt pounded his fist on the steering wheel. "Every day we don't find them, we're one day closer to seeing those kids being moved. This case is breaking ground in a new area." He signaled and changed lanes. "We've got to find those kids. Somebody had better start talking soon."

"Maybe Maxwell will have better luck. The FBI is a little more intimidating than us small town cops." Dylan's tone was sarcastic.

"It wasn't working today, but maybe tomorrow. At this point I don't care who gets the information, just so we get it." Matt turned off the highway and headed toward Blue Cove.

"Not to change the subject, but I heard you're taking Jessie to the Autumn Ball tomorrow night." Dylan turned to look out the side window with a grin on his face.

"Do you have a problem with that?" Matt's eyebrows rose.

"Who, me?" Dylan chuckled. "Nope, I was just thinking that it was about time, that's all."

"I asked her on a date for Friday, but not to the ball. You know how I hate those things. When I found a little bit of information about some of the folks attending I decided we needed to combine business with our date." He pulled the patrol car into the station parking lot. "It's probably not the best way to ask a girl out for your first date, but I guess it comes with the job."

Dylan laughed outright. "You two have fought each other from the moment you met. Those of us watching from the sidelines had to give up pretty early on. We all knew from the start it was you. It's been fun to watch though."

"Why don't you tell *her* that?" he grumbled. "*She* still doesn't know it."

"Yeah, but she will. I think she's already started to."

"What makes you think that?" Matt shut off the engine.

"The way she looks at you when she thinks no one is looking." Dylan smiled.

"And how would that be?"

"All soft, I guess." He shook his head. "Damn, I don't know how to explain it, interested I guess. I'm not good at this feeling stuff. But hell, I can say for sure, she doesn't look at the rest of us like that."

"That's good to know." Matt felt his mood brightening as he walked into the station.

Jeremy followed Matt into his office. "How'd it go today?"

"It didn't." Matt frowned.

"Maybe I have something that will help." Jeremy handed him a spreadsheet. "Those six guys have been getting a whole lot of money paid into some offshore accounts." Jeremy pointed to the numbers. "If you notice, the payments come at different times. It's like these three are a team because they get paid at the same time and these three are a team." He pointed. "You notice there is a lapse in time between payouts for each team." He had circled the dates. "It's like they were being used in rotation."

"Did you find out who was paying them?" Matt leaned his elbow on the desk.

"It's always a cash deposit, never a check." Jeremy adjusted his glasses. "But Steve Murphy also has an offshore account and makes large cash withdrawals equal to their cash deposits, which I find interesting." He ran his hand through his tousled hair.

"Nice work. Anything else?"

"I'm getting close on the other and I'll let you know as soon as I find anything." He stood up. "I'm out of here. I'm headed for dinner at the Inn."

Matt nodded and Jeremy left. He laid out Jeremy's spreadsheet next to the timelines he'd drawn of abductions in the surrounding areas. The two sheets told the story. The payouts came a few weeks after each round of abductions. Apparently, it took an average of four weeks from when the last of the kids disappeared in the area before the payoffs would start. Steve's account first received a huge amount and then the members of one of the two groups would get a deposit not long afterwards. Matt frowned. It seemed that if the operation went smoothly the kids would be out of the area within three weeks of the final abduction. Meaning they needed to hurry up and find those kids.

It was about two weeks ago when the kids in New York were abducted. Things were a little messier this time, but still he figured they had a week or two tops, and then it would be too late.

Tom popped his head in the door. "Hey, we're back." He leaned against the doorframe. "One thing my team learned in talking to the wives was that these guys were a whole lot chummier than they were letting on to us. They traveled together, and the families even vacationed together from time to time. Last year, they all traveled to Disney World together and stayed in the same hotel. Even though the wives were friends, they weren't as close as the men were. Not one of them seemed to have a clue that their husbands might be involved in something illegal."

"It always amazes me how men can keep one whole side of their lives so secret that their wife never picks up on it. We saw that in the last case as well, with the Harvest Club." Matt doodled on the edge of the paper. "The thing about this case that makes me so mad is that there are a lot of innocent kids and families involved."

"I know and I can feel it breathing down my neck. If we don't find them soon they will be relocated." Tom pushed away from the door. "We'll just have to do better, that's all."

"That's how I feel." Matt's phone rang. "I need to take this."

The hospital was on the line to let him know Sammy Adelson was awake and wanted to talk to him. Matt gathered up his stuff, including a small tape recorder, and headed toward the hospital. When Matt walked in the room, the first thing he saw was Sammy sitting up in bed. His face was white as the bed sheet, but he was very much alive. Lindsey was by his side, holding his hand.

"Chief Parker, this is my husband Sammy." She smiled.

Matt nodded to her, turning his gaze on Sammy. "I was told that you wanted to talk to me."

"Yes, sir, I do." He shifted in the bed and grimaced with pain. "My wife has been telling me how nice you've been to her. I appreciate it. I know you're going to have to arrest me, but I wanted to talk to you before any of that happens."

"We need to do this formally. You have the right to remain silent..." He recited the Miranda rights, praying that this man would decide to come clean, give them the break they needed here, and not hide behind an attorney as the others were doing. When he finished, Sammy simply shrugged. His chest tightened with hope. "Do you mind if I record this?" He shook his head no. "Will you please repeat what you just said for the record?" He nodded.

Matt turned on his recorder and Sammy repeated what he said and then began to tell his story. "First I was surprised by a call from Jed Johnson. He told me about how he had become a big executive with a company selling children's clothing and stuff. He wanted me to get in on the action." Sammy sipped some water. "I never ran with Jed's crowd." He grimaced. "I was nothing much, and he was a jock, you know what I mean. I was a little skeptical and didn't want to commit to anything. A few days later, I got a call from an old friend I hadn't heard from since high school. We had gotten into a lot of trouble together, Travis and I. I have to admit I was surprised to hear from him. He asked me if I was working, and I told him I had been looking. He told me about a high paying job he knew of, and he wanted to take me to meet the boss. I went and he hired me, for what I wasn't sure. He mentioned something about kids' stuff and being on the road for sales and demos. Now that I think about it, there was a lot of double-talk. None of it made very much sense. He offered me a fifteen thousand dollar signing bonus and a huge discount at his store. I knew my wife would be happy to fix up the baby's room, so I took it." He paused, looking perplexed. "I should mention before I go on that something seemed a little off about Travis."

"What do you mean?" Matt quizzed him.

"He seemed like a whole different person. He didn't remember some of things Travis should have known. I chalked it up to the years that had gone by." Sammy's color faded when he tried to move. "Anyway, when Travis brought me home, he told me to pack my bag. We were headed out of town on business. I gave my wife the money, told her to fix up the nursery, and to order everything from the store. I left in a company car, following Travis. At lunch on our way here, he told me what he did for a living." Sammy looked away. "Then he told me what we had been sent here to do. He was going to kill three men, and all I was supposed to do was shoot the gun he gave me, but not at anybody. I am guessing now I was meant to take the fall so no one would ever know he was involved." His face twisted. "I mean why else would anyone take along a guy like me, tell me I was just to shoot, but not at anyone." Sammy's face looked pinched. "My record would convict me." Lindsey held the straw to his lips. He took a sip.

Matt pushed the pause button on the recorder for a moment. "Do you want to rest?"

"I need to tell you." His voice had weakened. "We went out on Homestead Road and hid our cars. We set up about 150 yards from the road, on the hill, hidden in the trees. Then we waited. Travis was quiet. He kept looking through his high power scope on the rifle. After we sat there for about fifteen minutes, a black SUV came down the road and stopped. The passenger door opened and this man started to get out. That's when Travis fired, and the man went down. He told me to start shooting. I did." Sammy shifted weakly, trying to find a more comfortable position. Lindsey adjusted his pillows behind his back and head. "He missed the second man who drove away. Travis was mad as hell. He told me to get in my car quick. We had to get him. We stopped before turning onto the highway. Travis said he wanted to talk to me. The last thing I remember was a gunshot and watching Travis fall. I tried to get back to the car but Jed Johnson saw me and shot me. I'm not sure if he shot Travis. I knew there had to be a connection with that kids' stuff and this job." Drained, Sammy closed his eyes and quickly fell asleep.

"I'm sure he can give you more details when he's not under so many pain meds." Lindsey's eyes glistened as she looked up at Matt. "He wanted to talk to you today before others start getting involved. He wouldn't take no for an answer. So I hoped this would help you in some way."

"Yes, Lindsey, it has." Matt smiled at her. "Are you going to be okay?"

She looked back at Sammy, her face tender and full of sorrow. "He'll probably sleep for a while. I'll go back to the hotel to rest. Thank you for coming so quickly."

Matt walked out of the hospital, happy that another piece of the puzzle had fallen into place. He would have to wait for another day to ask him if he knew why they wanted the men killed, or if he knew anything about the kids. Matt had his doubts. If they had hired Sammy as the fall guy, he would have very little real information.

Matt wanted the name of the man who'd interviewed him.

He got in his car and gave Jessie a quick call. "Are you at home?"

"Yes, why?"

"Is Jeremy there?"

"No, he's not here, why?"

"Can I stop by for a while?"

"Sure, but why?"

"Just because I want to, Jess." He could almost hear her reaction. He grinned. "I'll be there in a few."

It took all of ten minutes to get to her house, but he felt relief at the sight of her. She had a way of stirring his blood and calming him at the same time. She smiled at him when he walked through the door. She was sitting at her computer. He loved watching her there. "What's up?"

"I was just up with Sammy. He told me quite a bit before he faded." He walked over to stand beside her and filled in what he had learned so far. "Did you learn anything more about the store or the owners?"

"Not yet, but between Jeremy's and my research, we're getting close."

"Keep working. I'll sit here and do my paperwork." He walked over to the chair and sat down, stretching his legs out and balancing a file on the arm of the chair. He felt a lot better after what Dylan had told him earlier. He was hoping to catch that look for himself. He hid a smile, got busy. He realized when Jeremy walked through the door that he hadn't watched her at all. *What is next, Matt?* He did an internal eye roll. *You'll be falling asleep in this chair.* He liked the peace of being in her world.

"How's it going?" Jeremy leaned over Jessie's shoulder. Matt found himself watching their interaction.

"Look at this." She pointed to something on the screen.

"Move over, sweetheart, and let me take it for a minute." Jeremy sat down as she slid out of the chair.

Jeremy's fingers moved rapidly over the keys and then stopped suddenly, pointing something out to her. "Look, what do we have here?"

"Matt, I think we've found something that can tie all these guys together." She looked up excitedly as he walked over.

"Explain to me what I'm looking at."

"I've been able to get into the sent emails for the company and there have been a lot of them to guys on this list. I'll print out a few of them for you, see if anything looks useful."

"Bring them with you tomorrow if you come in; otherwise just give them to Jess to give to me. I appreciate it, man." Jeremy nodded without looking away from the screen. Matt picked up his files. "I'll be by to pick you up tomorrow at six." He looked at Jessie as she got to her feet.

"I'll be ready." She smiled. "Badge and gun will be present and accounted for."

"That's nice to know." He grabbed her hand, giving it a squeeze. "See you tomorrow, all dolled up and looking like a girl." She closed the door behind him.

Chapter 25

Jessie looked up at the clock. Only eleven-forty, it was not time to go. There was no way she could concentrate! She had already made so many typing errors. She frowned at the page. At this rate, this paragraph could take fifteen minutes. She turned her chair away from her desk and then turned back around again. Excitement and apprehension both licked at the edges of her mind every time she thought about the ball. She shut off her computer. Matt was definitely the reason for the excitement. Maybe dating him wouldn't be so bad after all. She smiled and fanned herself. He was nothing if not persistent. Darn Reba and her dire warning! Jessie would have loved to enjoy being with him without the stress of the case. At this point, not possible. Reba had called again this morning, warning her to be on guard. It didn't sound like a very promising evening to Jessie. Reba was never wrong.

She had spent most of last night trying to figure out where she'd carry her gun. The dress was silk and flowed over the curves of her body. No matter where she strapped it, the bulge showed. She had tried strapping it to her thigh and near her ankle on her calf, but it wasn't going to happen. No way, she couldn't wear it under this dress. Everyone would know she was packing! She giggled. No doubt about it, she would have to put the gun in her evening bag and keep it close by at all times.

She had practiced most of the night, pulling the gun from the bag repeatedly. Matt would have teased her if he had seen her. Now she had the action down and was getting faster. Of course, this was without any of the pressure of trying to save someone's life, or shooting at a real person instead of a target. She frowned, looking at the clock again.

"Earth to Blondie, are you in there?" Melinda was peering from the doorway with a puzzled look on her face. "You didn't even hear me walk in. What's got you looking all dreamy? Maybe it's that hunky chief of police, eh?" She cackled and the corners of her eyes crinkled.

Jessie smiled as she got a good look at Melinda. Her red hair was standing on end where she had just tousled it with her hands. "Actually, I wasn't thinking about him at all. I was thinking about something Reba said earlier."

"Forget Reba. If I were you, I would be thinking about Matt. He's a hottie!" Melinda plopped down in the chair. "Pastor said you were leaving early so I thought I'd tidy up in here, if that's okay with you."

Jessie bit her lip. "I have few minutes before I leave, but I don't mind you starting before I do. I would enjoy the company."

"The rumor around town is Matt's sweet on you. No one can blame him. I mean what's not to like about you. Unless of course, if you're another woman sweet on Matt, I suppose that would change it a little bit." Melinda slapped her leg, laughing at what she'd said. "I get such a kick out of me."

"Matt and I are good friends. I don't think women

in town need to be worried yet."

"That's not how I heard it." She moved the magazines on the lamp table to dust. "It must be true because, Blondie, your face is as red as my hair." She grinned.

Jessie wished above all things she didn't blush so easily. Melinda's chattering calmed her mind. She relaxed, laughed, and bantered back and forth until it was time to leave.

She walked out of the church without seeing the white car in front of Patterson's. Once out of the church her anxiety returned. She had no control over too many variables. There were the unknown factors of when, how, and by whom. She was excited to go and mingle with the elite of Blue Cove, but who would be the target? What would the case look like by the end of the evening? Seeing Matt all dressed up appealed to her, and yet she was afraid where this evening might take them. She scrunched her face in thought. Melinda had spoken wisely. "He's a hottie." Jessie grinned.

After getting her nails done, Jessie got home in time to walk in with Jeremy who was carrying his tux. "Where did you find one?"

"Matt hooked me up." He matched her step for step. "You know your friend, she's a little intense, but she's fun. I think we'll have a good time tonight."

"That makes me happy. You are two of my favorite people."

"Don't be getting any ideas on trying to fix me up with her. I'm doing this as a favor to you. I like her, but that's all for now." He smiled at her. "Do you get my drift?"

"I fully understand. She drives me crazy trying to

match me up with every man that comes along. I might bug her, but I'll leave you out of it. I promise!" She did a pinky swear with him. "You're my friend and I know you can figure it out on your own. You have to admit she's pretty."

"I'm not going there with you." He smiled as he placed the tuxedo on the back of the chair. "You girls just can't help yourselves, can you?'

She shrugged and smiled. "See you in a while. I have to start getting ready." She headed toward her room.

"Why? You still have a couple of hours."

"Jeremy, Jeremy." She sighed. "You obviously don't know much about girls. We like to take our time to look extra nice on special occasions." She paused at her bedroom doorway. "Make yourself comfortable and whatever is in the refrigerator, you're welcome to it."

She was happy to have some leisure moments to shower and do her hair without having to rush. She wanted it to be perfect. *Please let it be a good hair day!* She made faces at herself in the mirror as she held the blow dryer with one hand and her brush in the other, tackling the project with a single purpose in mind. It was a time-consuming pain to blow her hair dry, but today she wanted to wear it down. Turning curls into long soft waves took a lot of work. Determined, she smiled as she rolled a long strand around the brush and moved the dryer back and forth. It took every minute of those couple of hours to accomplish it all.

****

Matt felt like it was the night of his senior prom as he walked down the path to the cottage. He was definitely just as nervous. He pulled and tugged at the bow tie and collar of his shirt. He hoped to give himself a little more room for comfort. "Why did they make these dumb collars so tight?" he swore under his breath. He wanted to rip the bow tie off and open the first couple of buttons on his shirt. *Who was the idiot who invented the tux anyway? How did he convince men that they needed to look like penguins to dress up? It must have been a woman who was angry with her husband. Yep, the prom was a piece of cake compared to this.* He gave up on the bow tie. He had a lot riding on this night, and he didn't want to mess it up. He frowned. Why did everything have to be so damn complicated?

Jeremy answered Matt's knock at the door. "Hey, man, you look just as uncomfortable as me. I'm glad." He smirked at Matt.

"Misery loves company, they say." Matt walked in and looked around. "Where is she?"

"She went into her room a couple of hours ago and has yet to emerge. I can't imagine what torture they must put themselves through to spend two hours getting dressed." Jeremy ran his hand through his hair, messing it up.

Matt heard her bedroom door open. "I think we're about to find out. It might be hard to improve on perfection." Matt stood with his feet apart and waited.

Close your mouth, Matt, and quit gawking like a schoolboy. She was beautiful, and he was stunned. Her dress fit entirely too well, showing off the curves of her body. From the moment he saw her, he wanted to run his hands through the shiny softness of her hair, feeling it flow across the tips of fingers. This was going to be one long night. He silently groaned.

From the looks of it, Jeremy wasn't faring much better, which made Matt want to punch him. Matt resisted and stepped toward her.

"Did it work?" She smiled sweetly at him. "Do I look like a girl?"

He nodded at her, his mouth going dry. "Are you ready?" Before she could answer, he bent down close to her face and whispered in her ear. "You don't look like any girl I've ever known." His eyes traveled slowly over her. "Every inch of you is a beautiful woman."

"Why, thank you, sir. I'll take your compliment as your approval." She smiled up at him. "I think you look very fine yourself, Mr. Parker."

"Do you have a coat? It's a little chilly out there."

She handed him her evening jacket. He held it as she slipped it on. "You look very handsome, Jeremy." Jessie smiled after she noticed him leaning against the door.

"Thanks. I'll see you guys in a few." He opened the door and left ahead of them.

"Do you have your gun and badge? The way that dress fits, it's obviously not on your person."

"No, but you wouldn't want me to hit you in the head with my purse." She swung her evening bag back and forth. "We girls can be pretty resourceful when the need arises. It's attached to my wrist." She flexed her muscles. "We just can't mess with the look of the dress." She winked at him.

Matt held the door open for her, then closed the door behind them and made sure it locked. Grabbing her hand, he walked with her up the path to the car. The gun in her purse made him smile. "How fast can you get that out of your purse if you need to?"

"Pretty fast. I practiced most of the night. Do you want to see?" Before he answered, she had whipped it out.

"I declare, ma'am, you're fast on the draw," he drawled as he opened the car door for her. He was still smiling as he got in the driver's side and closed the door. He really hoped nothing would spoil this evening for them. He had this feeling. It was just a gut feeling that someone was going to try something. He really wanted to be wrong.

****

The Yacht Club's ballroom was the site of the night's gala. Jessie's eyes traveled around the room taking in the panoramic view through the windows to the cove beyond. The sun had already set, but lights from the surrounding buildings reflected on the water, making it glow. A beautiful full moon peeked above the distant horizon as it made its ascent into the starry sky. Matt checked her coat. She walked toward the windows in the ballroom. Autumn colors filled the room. Oranges, browns and gold, repeated again in the table candles and floral arrangements. She stopped when she got to the windows and looked out at the shimmering glow of the moon on the water. Boats rocked gently in the water near the docks and in the cove where their owners had secured them. She could see a rather large boat just entering the cove, probably on its way home. Was someone on it signaling to shore? No, it had to be her imagination. She fixed her eyes on the large boat to see if happened again.

"A penny for your thoughts." Katie tapped her on the shoulder and startled her. Jessie turned to look at her. "Wow, you look sensational. The dress is killer, and the necklace is perfect." Katie turned slowly around in front of her. "What do you think?"

"You're a knockout." Jessie smiled at her. "The back of the dress is a piece of artwork."

"I do look pretty good, don't I?" Katie made a pouty face. "But, alas, not as pretty as my gorgeous, hunky date." She fluttered her lashes and growled. "He looks good enough to eat."

"Speaking of your hunky date, I see him weaving his way here with Matt." Katie looked where Jessie was pointing.

"I think Matt cleans up well. So does the rest of your following." Katie waved at Dylan and Kip who each had a date beside them.

"They're not my following." Jessie rolled her eyes at Katie.

"Yeah, sure, whatever you say. They never take their eyes off you. They look like your groupies whenever they're near you." Katie giggled, her green eyes lighting up.

Jessie pinched Katie's arm. "Oh no, you don't. You're not going to start that again." Katie rubbed the spot.

"Start what?" Matt looked at Jessie quizzically.

"Only a few of Katie's crazy theories, not based in reality, and she's trying to hang them on me. I won't let her."

Katie gave her a wounded expression, putting her hand to her heart. "You just watch, you'll see."

"I'm not going to do any such thing. Behave yourself." Their eyes met and they started giggling.

Matt placed her hand on his arm. "I think we should mingle and make our way to the table."

Matt introduced her to people along the way. She would never remember all of the names. She let her mind free to admire all the beautiful dresses and sparkling jewelry. It was a veritable feast for the eyes. Their table was at the back of the room close to the dance floor. She wondered if Matt would ask her to dance. Would it be safe? Whom did she need to be watching for? Was he here now in this room watching them?

Chapter 26

Their seats were right where Matt had requested them. A table at the back of the room, near the dance floor with a wall behind them. From here, he could see the whole room. He pulled out Jessie's chair for her. It would be hard enough to concentrate on what was happening in the room with her next to him. He didn't need any other distractions. As soon as the music started, the line would begin for a dance with her. He had seen how heads turned when she walked by. She was hot without even trying to be. She made classic look hot. He smiled. He'd heard her tell Katie how beautiful everyone looked. It was time for him to launch his charm campaign.

He whispered in her ear as he pushed her chair in. "Sweetheart, no one compares to you in this room."

He listened to the conversation at the table halfheartedly while trying to monitor Murphy, who was sitting next to Senator Brinkman and his wife. Tom Maxwell and one of his team were at the table. Dylan and his date were sitting by another person of interest in Matt's mind, Jason Fredrick, the hospital director. He was an unknown equation in all of this. Would Jed make a move tonight? Was he angry enough at being set up to risk exposure? Matt had a nagging gut feeling that something was off, but nothing concrete.

Once dinner was finished, Katie and Jessie excused

themselves to freshen up before the guest speaker and dancing began.

"You've been quiet." Jeremy looked at Matt.

"I'm trying to pay attention to what's happening around me. It's a major challenge with Jessie sitting next to me. I'm glad Katie is keeping her entertained, I probably won't get a very high rating for our first date." He leaned back in his chair and tugged at his collar. "If I don't do well, I might not get a second chance."

"Man, I can put your mind at ease. I think you'll come out okay. I've never seen Jessie behave with anyone the way she does with you. I saw your little scene at the house. She's into you. She's never looked at me that way, I'm sad to say."

"It must be tough."

"Not anymore, but it used to be hell. Jessie's a beauty and a real sweetheart which makes her lethal." Jeremy twirled the stem of his wine glass slowly. "I learned with time to move on. She saw me as a friend and nothing more."

"Speaking of friends, what do you think of her friend?"

"Katie is vivacious and fun to be with, but a little scary. She comes on strong for such a little package. Still, I find her interesting." He gave Matt a quick smile. "They're such opposites, yet they seem to get on. I enjoy watching them together."

"They have a great friendship. They're two equally strong, but very different women." Matt waved off the waiter offering more wine.

"It surprised me that Jessie learned to fire a gun. She never wanted to be around them. The last case really shook her." Jeremy frowned. "She told me being drugged and locked in the trunk of the car scared her. Nightmares still haunt her. She doesn't ever want to let someone have that much control over her again."

"Hell, it scared me. I thought she was a goner for sure." Matt noticed her the moment she entered the room, his eyes tracking her until she was beside him. He also noticed that Murphy and the senator were watching her.

She touched his shoulder as she walked by him to get to her chair and bent close. "Are you okay, Mr. Parker? You're so quiet I'm beginning to think you find me boring."

"You, boring? Not in a million years, sweetheart. I'm trying to keep an eye on a few of our friends without getting distracted looking at you. It's a little bit of a juggling act, even for me." He smiled at her. "How about you and I have a dance or two when the speeches are over? After that I'll think about sharing you with a couple of the boys, and then we'll blow this place." He gave her an engaging grin. "I need to start impressing you so we can move on to a second date where I don't have to share you with anyone."

"Impress away, that sounds intriguing to me." She gazed at him and then glanced away.

Matt's smile broadened. He reached over to slide his fingers gently down her cheek to her chin, lifting it up so he could see her eyes. "Duly noted. You have issued the challenge to impress you, and I'm going to give it my best shot." He noticed it, right there, in that moment. She gazed again into his eyes; it felt like a caress to him. He wished he wasn't in a crowded room. He wanted to be alone with her. Damn! Did he have to see it now! Here?

The checkbooks were out; the speakers were done, with the hospital as the happy recipient. The band took its place, and the music began. He wasn't about to let anyone else claim the first dance. It belonged to him. He saw them starting to make their way like vultures to the table as he stood up and took her hand. "You want to dance?" She stood up beside him, and they walked to the dance floor.

"Sorry, boys, this dance is mine." He forced a smile as he walked by them. Matt thanked his lucky stars it was a slow number as he pulled her in close to him. "Just so you know"—he looked into her big blue eyes—"I think you look beautiful tonight."

"I think you look pretty beautiful yourself." She held his gaze as their bodies swayed to the music. His arms tightened around her pulling her closer still.

Matt could see them out of the corner of his eyes waiting for the song to end. "It looks like I'm going to have to share you with the other boys. This is the dance you'll remember at the end of the night." He pressed a kiss on her neck as he whispered in her ear. "Oh, hell, let them wait another song, I'm not ready to give you up yet." The band was playing one of his favorites. He pulled her close, and she melted into his arms.

Suddenly her pliant body became stiff. He felt her try to pull out of his arms. "What is it, Jess? What's wrong?"

"We're being watched. I can feel it." He could hear the panic in her voice.

He pulled his head back to look at her. "Look at me, Jess." He needed her to focus. "Who's watching us?"

"I don't know, but I can feel we're being watched

and not in a good way. We need to walk off this dance floor now! It's about to break loose."

"Any quick action will alert them. Just play it cool." He danced on, guiding her to the other side of the room near the exit. They had almost reached the door when the first shot rang out smashing through a window, the bullet hitting the back wall near the table where they had been sitting. An explosion near the outside of the building, which overlooked the bay, followed that. The windows blew in and shrapnel and debris rained down on the guests.

Screams filled the air, people started running toward the exits, pushing so hard that those trying to get through the doors trampled those who fell. Others scrambled under the tables. "Please, someone help my wife, please," Matt heard a man yelling out. Then the second shot blasted a hole in the wall not far from Matt's head, and a woman not far from him fainted. He pushed Jessie, pressing against her, moving her forward, trying to protect her. Matt felt the blow, his arm going instantly numb as he pushed her to the floor and dived on top of her. The room was a chaotic scene of flying glass and drywall as more bullets punctured the walls, punctuated by screams, moans, and whimpers.

Several more shots split the night as they lay there. The sound was deafening and the smells, Matt knew he would never forget the smells: sulfur and blood filled his nostrils. He covered her ears with his hands and felt her shudder. Then it was silent, eerily quiet except for an occasional groan.

"Matt, you're crushing me, please, could you move?" Her voice was soft.

"I'm a little indisposed at the moment, but I'll try." Matt grimaced as he rolled aside, and she struggled out from under him. He groaned and she sucked in a quick breath. Blood!

"Oh, God, are you all right?" She touched his pale face and grabbed the phone he was fumbling with out of his hand. "Here let me do it." She called dispatch, asking for backup and several ambulances, repeating what he told her to say. She took his gun from the holster inside his jacket and sat beside him, holding his hand. Jeremy and Katie crawled toward them as more shots peppered the air from outside the building. They had been on the dance floor not far from them. Tom, and several with him, drew guns and ran out of the room.

"Trouble seems to follow you all the time." Katie looked accusingly at Jessie. "If my new dress is ruined, you'll have to buy me a new one." Jessie couldn't believe Katie had said it. Leave it to her to joke at an inopportune time.

"You're lucky you still have a dress on considering the force of the blast." Matt's voice sounded strained.

Katie's kidding stopped when she looked at Matt. "Do you realize that you're bleeding?" Her voice had a shrill pitch. He nodded and winced.

People peered out from under the tables. Dazed, some of them injured, they emerged from hiding as the club's staff went to work helping those who were hurt.

Matt saw Dylan coming toward them. "Where's Murphy?" Matt tried to support his arm while he struggled to sit up.

"He's dead." Dylan looked around the room. "What a mess. A bullet hit the senator's wife. It looks serious to me. Maxwell is outside, working the perimeter. So far, no sign of the shooter yet. The FBI is checking the grounds to make sure there are no more devices planted, and an explosives unit is on the way."

"Get out there and secure the perimeter." Matt pulled at his collar. "Help me get this damn thing off." Matt grabbed at his bow tie with his good arm. Dylan helped him out of his jacket. Matt swore under his breath while Dylan tore his shirtsleeve to see the damage the bullet had done.

"How bad is it?" Matt's brows furrowed.

"It's not pretty, but I think you'll live," Dylan said grimly. "It looks like it grazed you, but I'm no expert. There is no way I'll probe it to make sure. You would deck me. I'll let these guys take over." Dylan pointed at the paramedics who were rushing in.

The lobby of the club had become a makeshift triage area as a team of paramedics moved people into waiting ambulances. Matt gave orders to Kip and several others who had come rushing into the club as the pair of paramedics helped him out to the lobby. His vitals were steady. They cleaned and dressed his wound after he refused to go to the hospital. The young paramedic shook his head, put a sling on him, and told him to go to the ER when he was done at the crime scene.

"I think you'll need a couple of stitches." The paramedic looked over at Jessie. "Are you all right, ma'am? You have pretty big knot on the side of your head."

"I didn't even notice." She winced when she reached up and felt it.

He examined it. "Were you hit by something?"

"Yes!" She smiled at him. "I was hit by a falling chief of police and the ground that rose up to meet us."

"I can see that might be a problem." He chuckled. "I mean it, Chief; you need to have that arm looked at sooner rather than later."

"I'll make sure he does." Jessie smiled at the young man. "I'll wait here and take him myself."

"You'll do no such thing. I want you where you're safe." Matt was scowling. "This was meant for you. I just got in the way."

Her chin edged up. "I will take you there and you're going to have to live with it, Mr. Parker. This is my first date with you, and it will end when I say it will end."

He grinned at her and lifted his good arm. "All right. I give up. If it hadn't been for you, we'd both probably be dead."

"Why's that?" Dylan asked.

"She had one of those feelings. We moved out of the trajectory of the first bullet."

"That's our Jessie." Dylan smiled.

****

Jessie sat on a chair in the ballroom with her bag holding the gun in her lap. What an awful night this had turned out to be. Steve Murphy was dead, and Mrs. Brinkman was in serious condition. There had been numerous injuries from flying glass to people near the front windows. She had been standing there only a few hours earlier, looking out. Had he been out there then, watching her? A shiver ran down her back. What kind of monster would want to hurt so many people? At this point, no one knew the numbers or the condition of the injured. There were a couple of fatalities and that number could still grow through the night. She watched Matt work, scribbling notes on a napkin.

Matt was looking tired and pale. He was still barking out orders. It was time for her to intervene. With Dylan's help, Matt was convinced it was time for his arm to get attention. She held out her hands for his keys. "I'm driving you. You need to put your head back and relax."

"I can drive."

She shook her head no, and he dropped the keys into her hand. A few minutes later, she pulled into the ER at the hospital. There were many people in the waiting area still. The hospital was busy—so busy they'd had to call all their staff in. Several doctors from neighboring towns had come in voluntarily when they heard the news.

Jessie checked Matt in and went out to move her car. He was in with the doctor by the time she got back in the waiting room. It helps to be the chief of police! She read a few articles, watched the news showing the blast repeatedly on the TV in the waiting area. She stood up when he walked out, complete with six stitches, and a prescription for painkillers. A nurse followed on his heels with paperwork and instructions from the attending physician, which she handed to Jessie. Jessie breathed a sigh of relief. "Mr. Parker," the nurse called after him. "The doctor wants you to keep that sling on for a few days. Try to keep your arm somewhat immobile."

Jessie drove him to his house. She put it in park and turned to face him. "Here's the deal, Mr. Parker. If you want a second date with me, you are going to have to follow my instructions. We're here to get a few things. You'll stay at my house tonight so Jeremy can help you. I thought about it earlier while you were being stitched up. Jeremy already knows you're coming." She smiled sweetly at him. "That's my deal, take it or leave it."

"I just have to have a sleepover at your house to have a second date?" He grinned, which didn't quite erase the lines of pain around his eyes. "I think I can live with it. I hope you can, sweetheart."

"Tonight, I think I'm a little stronger than you. Yeah, I can live with it."

****

Jeremy helped Matt get his clothes off, and left the room, Jessie found him sitting up in her bed when she walked in with a glass of water for him. "I'm going to watch you take this pill." She handed it to him and sat down on the edge of the bed. "Even a tough guy needs rest and time to heal."

"Can I tell you what I need?" He pushed her hair away from the bump. "Sorry about this." He surprised her with his strength as he pulled her forward against his chest. He rested his chin on the top of her head. "I need you. I need you near me. I want to see your face smiling back at me. It makes feel like I can conquer anything. I want you, and I'm willing to wait a reasonable length of time for you to want me too." He kissed the top of her head. "Now, scoot before I forget that I'm willing to wait."

She gave him a quick kiss as she started to stand. "I'll say this for you, Mr. Parker, you promised me a first date I would never forget, and you delivered." She grinned to hide the sudden surge of confusing feelings that filled her and left the room.

The sun would be rising soon. Jessie made a bed on the couch. At least she didn't have to work today, unless of course, Matt needed her. Matt. What was she going to do with him? He was getting to her heart. She stretched out on the couch and closed her eyes.

Locked in her mind were the sights and the sounds of the night. It had been awful. Who was to blame for all of it? Could only one person have orchestrated all of this? She had her doubts. Who else was out there besides Jed? The next thought came several hours later as she struggled to wake up. Someone was watching her, and she could feel it. Matt was sitting in the chair across from her with his eyes fixed on her when she awakened.

"I was beginning to wonder if you were ever going to wake up." He studied her face. "Are you all right?"

"I'll tell you in minute after I see if everything is in working order." She groaned as she sat up. "You were like a dead weight falling on me."

"Sorry about that." He leaned forward in the chair.

She waved him off. "It's not your fault!"

"It bothers me that whoever is responsible is still out there. The bomb was crude, made to be a smoke screen for the sniper who was picking off people, but the placement of it was bad news. There were a lot of injuries from the glass."

"I keep thinking there's something important I'm forgetting to tell you." She thought for a minute. "Now I remember what it was. I saw a boat coming into the cove right before the evening began. It lined up with some of the other boats near the dock. I went out to look later on, and it was gone. So was a speedboat that had been at the dock. It could be coincidental, but I thought at one point the large boat was signaling someone on shore."

"Do you remember what the boat looked like?" He sat forward in the chair.

"It was too dark to see anything clearly, but I remember it had a little tower type thing on it. That's where I thought I had seen a signal, but maybe it was just a light on the boat. Then Katie came up to me and I stopped watching it." She scrunched her face.

"That tower would have been a great place to be sitting with a semi-automatic rifle fitted with a night scope. Between that and the bomb it sounds exactly like the calling card of one Travis Ray Booker, which has me wondering about something." He looked at her. "I'm going to step outside and make a call. Get dressed. I need you to do something for me."

Chapter 27

Matt made several calls and came in to find Jessie sitting in the kitchen with a cup of tea, eating a piece of toast. He handed her a short list of things he wanted her to check out for him.

"Could I have my keys? I need to get to the station." He filled a glass with water and swallowed a pill.

"I'll take you." She pulled his keys out of her purse. "Are you hurting today?"

"I've felt better, but I need to get to work. There's a lot going on. The senator's wife died in the night. We have lots of security footage to go through from the Yacht Club."

"I'm going to take you. The doctor told you to keep it immobile through the weekend. Normally, you wouldn't even be working today."

"I'll be fine." He shook his head. "You were up late last night, too. Besides, I want you to get on this for me." He drank the rest of the water and set the glass in the sink.

"I don't mind, and I'll work on this all day. I'm not taking no for an answer." Her chin nudged up, her lips pressed together. "You'll be putting in long hours and doing plenty without driving a car on top of it. I can be stubborn when I want to be."

"Okay." He raised his hand in surrender. "I'll let

you boss me around this time." He smiled at her, grabbing for the keys in her hand. She slapped at his hand. "How about we go for a quiet dinner tonight?" He followed her toward the door.

"Sounds good to me. I'll come ready when I pick you up. I have a feeling it'll be late." She held the door open for him.

"I'll call you when I'm free to leave. We have several press updates today." He scowled. "Not my favorite thing to do."

"You'll do fine." She smiled at him, unlocking the car door.

He turned in the seat toward her. "Thank you, Jess, for everything. I'm glad you stayed with me and made me go to the ER." He reached up and touched her cheek. "Hmm, so soft...and thanks for letting me stay here last night. It's nice to have someone who cares."

****

After Jessie got back home, she put a load of laundry in and poured herself a glass of iced tea. Then she sat down at her computer to research the questions that Matt had written down for her. She was learning some interesting things about Travis Booker. She wondered what Matt's line of thinking was. Maybe she had a good idea!

Halfway through the day, Katie knocked at the door. "Jessie, it's me, can I come in?"

"Of course you can!" Jessie opened the door for her.

"I needed to talk to someone. Last night freaked me out. It's all that everyone in town is talking about. Remind me never to go to the hospital's Autumn Ball again." She made her way to one of the chairs and sat down. "So many people were hurt. All that blood. I don't think I'll ever be able to close my eyes without seeing it." Tears filled her eyes.

"I know. It was awful." Jessie started to sit across from her. "Can I get you something?" She handed her the box of tissues.

"I'm fine for now." She shook her head. "What's happening to our town? I guess there is really no place that's completely safe, but I always felt Blue Cove was. Now..." She frowned. "I don't think I'll ever feel safe again."

"I know." Jessie stared out the window. "After the Harvest Club, I was afraid to close my eyes. And, now with the people talking in my head—well, let us just say I can have empathy for you. Believe me!" She paused. "You could talk to Dr. Gilbert. She's helped me to deal with the nightmares and the fear from the last case. I'm sure I'll be talking to her to get through this." Jessie grabbed Katie's hand. "I know she can help you too. I wouldn't have made it through the nightmares without her."

"I'll think about it. I think it's even harder because I talked to Steve Murphy's wife several times today. Someone is going to come and pick up all his stuff including a computer later today." Jessie stared at her. "I know, I know, weird, huh? I tried to set you up with a married man."

"He called at the church and asked me to go with him to the ball. Did you know that?" Katie shook her head no. "I should have left well enough alone."

"Yes, you should have!" Jessie noticed Katie's troubled look and softened her voice. "It doesn't matter now, besides, I told him no."

"His wife is in a state of shock, I feel bad for her. Men can be such jerks." Katie frowned.

"I know that he donated a lot of money to the hospital for the new pediatric ward." Jessie paused. "I just thought of something you said about them coming for his stuff. I'm sure the police will hold it as a part of the investigation. Let me give Matt a call." She talked to Matt for a minute. "Katie, what's Mrs. Murphy's number? They'll contact her." Jessie handed the phone to Katie.

When Katie finished, she handed the phone back to Jessie. "Gary is going to come by to collect Steve's things. He already has a search warrant." She stood up. "I guess I'd better be there when Gary gets here to pick it up. I don't want the guests more upset than they already are." Katie paused and looked back at Jessie with a frown. "I think after this I'm going to try not to interfere in your life. No more matchmaking for me. I learned my lesson with Steve. It would have been awful if you'd fallen for him." She shuddered. "I love you, friend." Katie gave her a big hug and headed back to the Inn.

Jessie couldn't believe that Steve had been married. Not that she had been in any danger of falling for him. Still she got mad when she thought about it. Marriage meant so little to some people; you had to wonder why they even bothered. She sat back down at her computer more determined than ever to find out a few answers. She wrote her findings out so she could go over them with Matt at dinner.

****

The station was bustling with activity. There was hardly a clear path to walk down the hall much less a place to think. Between the FBI and other agencies there to help, they used every available desk and table. There was enough red tape represented with all the agencies involved they could cover the whole town with it. Matt smiled. He had called a meeting for tomorrow morning. For the moment, he sat back in his chair enjoying the quiet of his office, turning his chair so he could look out the window. He hated having to stop work for all the news updates, but it came with the job. That darn bomb had changed everything, including the number of Federal agencies now involved. He wasn't complaining, he needed the help, but he was tired of tripping over them. After this evening's update, he was appointing Dylan as the local spokesperson.

Matt wondered what was going through Jed's mind now. Ballistics confirmed that Jed had an accomplice, and Matt was sure he knew who it was. Things were starting to come together in his mind. The only thing he wasn't sure of was whether the kids were still in his jurisdiction. After last night he had no clue where they were and with whom.

Dylan popped his head in the door. "I have the latest numbers for you." He set the paper on Matt's desk and sat down in the empty chair. "Besides Murphy and the senator's wife, a woman named Mary Wentworth died a few hours ago. She was near the front windows when they blew in. Twenty-five remain hospitalized, two in critical condition, three are serious, and the rest are in fair condition. Thirty were treated for minor injuries at the scene." Dylan shifted in the chair.

"How's Jason Fredrick?"

"He's on the critical list but making some headway." Dylan started to stand.

"After the four o'clock news update, you'll be the local spokesman for Blue Cove. I'll tell the reporters to direct questions to you."

"Ah geez, Matt, how can I ever thank you?" Dylan grinned and leaned against the doorframe.

"Just do a good job and keep them out of my hair. The pain in my arm has me feeling a little testy. I don't want to go off on some reporter. We need your finesse at the microphone. You will have to have a prepared summary of the case updates. You know the routine—what we'll take, what we won't…I'd like to turn it over to Maxwell as soon as possible."

"How long will they hang around, do you think?"

"The reporters?" Matt asked and Dylan nodded at him. "The fact that the senator's wife was killed may keep them interested a little longer. I'd say at least until the next big story comes along to draw them off." Matt picked up a pencil and scribbled a note.

"I'll take care of it, Matt. I'll run the updates by you before I do them."

"We'll work on it together. After today, I think one news conference should suffice. I'll run it by everyone, but I think we should announce that tonight." Dylan nodded and walked out of his office.

At a few minutes before four o'clock, representatives from the various agencies involved headed out to the parking lot where the microphones were ready.

Matt was the first to speak. "I would like to start by saying that this is our third and final update for the day. We'll be cutting back on the news updates to one a day so we can concentrate on our case. It will be at ten a.m. unless we have breaking news, in which case, we'll give you the heads-up and a thirty minute warning before we proceed." Matt paused. "We have a list prepared with the latest numbers, the names of the fatalities, and the hospitalized. The families have requested privacy at this challenging time." Matt reached for the paper Gary handed to him. "Dylan Mitchell will be the spokesman for the Blue Cove Police Department from now on. He will address all of the local concerns. I'll turn it over to Tom Maxwell, the head of the FBI unit working the case with us. He will fill you in on what happened at the Yacht Club and how it ties to a bigger on-going case. Pictures will be available as soon as he is finished."

Tom stepped to the microphone. He tied the two cases together. He paused and added, "We want to do all we can to keep these kids in front of the nation. We need the public to keep their eyes and ears open. Let's make it as hard as possible to transport these kids anywhere without someone noticing." Tom gave them a hotline number to call with tips. The various agencies involved closed it out by taking questions. Matt was glad that it was over and walked back into the station with the group of men. He had had to give a few press conferences on the Harvest Club case, and he had hated it then, too.

His arm was giving him fits. He was ready to call it a day. "I'll see you tomorrow, Tom." Matt headed to his office to grab his files, only to find Jeremy sitting in a chair waiting for him.

He handed Matt several emails that he had printed out. "There's a lot there tying them together. What's on this sheet, though, I think you'll find real interesting." He handed him another sheet of paper.

Matt read it. "I think we may have to open this can of worms after all. Great work, Jeremy. Tell me if I'm wrong. They were using customers' purchases, names, and addresses as a way to locate kids? Am I reading this right?"

"Yes. You can see from the other information, it backs up what you were thinking."

"Do you mind coming to the meeting tomorrow to share this?"

Jeremy ran his hands through his hair. "Not at all, dude."

"Are you headed back to Jessie's?"

"I'm going to the Inn for dinner. Did you need a ride?" He pushed away from the doorframe.

"No, Jessie is picking me up and we're going to dinner. I haven't had much of chance to see how she's holding up since last night."

"I know Katie is pretty shook up. You guys live a little dangerously."

"Not until Jessie got here—it was pretty tranquil."

"She has a way of messing things up with her writing. Now, with all this other stuff going on in her head, it's safe to say you'll probably have no peace for years to come." Jeremy chuckled. "Catch you later."

Matt picked up his phone and called her. "I'm ready anytime you are, Jess."

"That could be taken so many ways. I think you said it that way on purpose." She laughed.

"What do you mean?" He imagined the look she was giving him now.

"You know exactly what I mean. I should make you wait, but I'll be there in a few minutes."

Chapter 28

Jessie looked up from her computer when Jeremy walked in. "I thought you were going to the Inn for dinner."

"I am. I had to stop by and get something." He walked into the guest room.

"Before you go, look at this."

Jeremy glanced at the screen. "Stand up and let me have a look." Jeremy took over and pulled up more on the subject. "Hey, Jessie, weren't you suppose to pick up Matt?"

Jessie looked at her watch and jumped out of the chair, almost knocking it over. Fumbling with her phone, she raced for the door. "Thanks, Jeremy." Her phone was ringing when she grabbed for her coat.

"Where are you? I was starting to get concerned."

"I know. I'm sorry. I wasn't trying to make you wait. You'll think it was worth it once I tell you what I have found out though. I'll be there in a few minutes. I'm leaving my house now."

She couldn't believe what she had stumbled upon. When Jeremy walked in the door, he took over and they had found something with the potential to blow the case wide open. When she pulled into the parking lot, he was standing there with a frown on his face.

"I'm sorry, Matt," she blurted the minute he opened the door.

"No problem, once I knew you were okay it gave me time to get a little paperwork done." He smiled at her.

"You aren't mad? Why were you frowning?'

"Not at you. I have a nagging suspicion that I can't prove. It's bugging the hell out of me."

"Where are we going for dinner?"

"We missed our reservations, so how about we go for pizza or Patterson's." He watched her face. "Before you get too hard on yourself about it, I changed the reservations to next Friday night. You owe me a second date, and now I think a third for making me wait."

"You'll be glad you've been so nice when you hear what I have to tell you." She grinned.

"Park the car and let's hear it."

She pulled in next to one of the patrol cars. "I was in the middle of something when you called. I was going to stop to come pick you up, but I stumbled onto something about Travis Booker's family. Jeremy walked in, and he took over at that point." She paused. "You know how you said that it bothered you that Travis' normal MO wasn't present at the crime scene."

He nodded.

"I think I might know why."

"Why is that?"

"Travis has an identical twin brother which means they could have similar DNA but not necessarily exact. Their teen mother put Willie up for adoption at birth because she couldn't afford to raise them both. Recently, the two of them found each other. I talked to the woman who raised Willie and she told me they had been inseparable ever since."

"I had thought maybe he might have had a brother,

I even suggested it to Dave Lewis. I was convinced that the dead guy was not Booker, but his family ID'd him. We won't have DNA results for a few more weeks. The events of the last few days convinced me that Travis was still alive. I needed a way to prove it." He took her hand. "Thanks, sweetheart, this was worth the wait."

"You do know that Frank's dog can tell the difference between the twins even without the DNA results. Every person's body odor is the complex result of individual biochemistry. Radar will know."

"How come you're so smart?" He smiled at her.

"Frank told me about it. Science is just now catching up to all that dogs are capable of doing. They're even training dogs to find cancer in people."

"I might have to bring Frank back. What else can you tell me about Willie?"

"Here's the kicker. William, as his adopted mom called him, works in an office of a very powerful person."

"Let me guess," he interrupted her. "In Senator Brinkman's office?"

"Yes…You were already putting this together weren't you?" She smiled at him.

"I had theories; you've brought me the facts. Do you realize what an asset you are?" He eased his arm and grinned at her. "I think I'm going to have to keep you around permanently."

"May I ask how you plan on doing that? Never mind. I don't think I want to know." She chuckled.

"Coward!"

"Yes, you're probably right. I'm also famished and I don't think as well when I'm hungry. I need to be sharp, really sharp, to match wits with you."

"I bet our Willie boy will have some strong computer knowledge. Working in the office of the senator, he could get access to classified information and major resources. The only other question would be—is the senator somehow involved?"

"We might just have to work on that. Where would you like to go for dinner?" She put her car into gear and pulled out of the parking lot.

"Patterson's sounds good to me." He clicked his seatbelt on and adjusted his arm.

"Patterson's it is." She looked at him. "Is your arm bothering you? Your pills are in my purse. I remembered to grab them."

"It's aching a little. I don't want anything now. I need a clear head."

"So you think suffering will keep you more clear-headed?" She grinned.

"If I remember correctly, a certain beautiful young lady wouldn't take pain pills because she didn't like how they made her feel," he teased.

"True, but she did take plenty of over the counter stuff." Her eyes crinkled at the corners, her dimples showing. "I have some of those in my purse, too, and I suggest you take them now. You do want to sleep tonight, don't you?" Her eyes sparkled.

"You are too damn pretty, you know it? You make it hard to say no to you. Do you mind if I look?" He motioned to her purse.

"Be my guest. I brought you a bottle of water, too. You don't have to wait to take them." She pointed to the bottle in the cup holder and laughed at his expression. "My mama taught me to be ready for anything."

"Thank you, Jess." He popped the pills in his mouth and took a swig of water. "We lost another person during the night. Steve was an intended target, I believe. I'm not sure about the senator's wife. Maybe they were aiming for him. I'm pretty sure though Mary Wentworth was just in the wrong place at the wrong time." He raked his hand through his hair.

"You'll get them. I know that for sure. You're good at what you do." She glanced over at him, his head was leaning against the headrest, and his eyes fluttered shut "Are you sure you want to go out? You look tired."

"I'm fine. I can always relax when you're around me."

When she finally parked the car in front of Patterson's, Matt woke up. "Did you have a nice nap?" She grinned at him.

"I wasn't sleeping."

"You could have fooled me. Who was that snoring while I drove for the last twenty minutes?" She laughed.

"You're kidding me!" He took off his seatbelt and turned to look at her.

"Nope…" She placed her hand over her mouth to hide her smile. "I didn't have the heart to wake you. I would have still been driving or have just taken you home, but I got too hungry."

He opened his door, walked around to open hers. "Sorry, I don't usually fall asleep on my dates."

"I must be one of the privileged ones. I make you sleepy. I wonder if that makes me boring." She glanced sideways at him, her eyebrow raised. "Bombs go off, people get shot at, and strange things happen whenever we're together. I think you may need a more docile female companion."

"I like it just the way it is. You shake things up. Contrary to your thinking, that's not boring, sweetheart." He opened the door to Patterson's, holding it open for her.

Joe Patterson rushed forward to greet them with menus in hand. "Where have you been keeping yourself, pretty lady?" He smiled at her. "I'll seat them," he said as he waved off the hostess. "I haven't seen your pretty face in my restaurant for a while."

"Aren't you happy to see me, Joe?" Matt grinned.

"You're always welcome, but you're not as charming or as pretty as your friend here."

"You'll get no argument from me on either count."

Jessie blushed. "To answer your question, I've been a little busy the past few days. You know I love your place, though." She leaned up and whispered something in Joe Patterson's ear making him laugh.

"You always make me happy to see you." Joe smiled at her and patted her cheek. He seated them at a table near the front window. "Here you go. My best table for one of my nicest customers."

"Joe, are you trying to compete with me for the admiration of the lady?" Matt chuckled.

"If I was younger, I might give you a run for your money." His booming laugh drew eyes toward them. "For now, all I give you is my best table. The rest is up to you. Don't ruin it."

Jessie shook her head. "You're both incorrigible!"

Jessie liked this side of Matt. He was relaxed and fun to be around. She would use that to her advantage. It was for his good after all! She wasn't being deceptive. At least, she didn't think she was. She smiled at him and went to work, laughing at something he said. All of this observed by two men sitting in a white car that was parked just out of sight across the street.

Chapter 29

"I hate waiting! Why are we waiting?" Jed shifted on the car's front seat and glowered at the front of the restaurant. "We could take them out when they leave." He flicked the safety off on his .38.

"No, we can't. From now on, we do it my way. We can't have any more slipups." His eyes were cold and steely. "I don't like to kill anyone that I'm not paid to kill. That was a damn messy job last night. You made too many mistakes." He smirked. "My jobs are perfect. They always go off without a hitch. They don't draw any attention until it's too late."

"What are we supposed to do?" Jed wiped his face, sweat soaking his collar. "The place is crawling with feds." His eyes darted back and forth between his partner and the restaurant.

"We sit tight and wait. The feds will get tired, and go home. They've got no leads." He shrugged. "We can get the job done right in a few more days. With no one the wiser." He looked over at Jed. "You'll do nothing, keep your freaking mouth shut, and do what I say."

"Don't tell me what to do! I'm the one who brought you into this." Jed flipped his gun over on his lap.

"Stop messing with that gun before you shoot your damn leg off." He reached over and grabbed it. "If I wanted you dead, you wouldn't stand a chance and you damn well know it." He pointed the gun at Jed's head. "You'll wait and you'll keep your mouth shut. Do I make myself clear?"

Jed gulped and nodded.

He studied the couple sitting near the window. Nice set-up for a shot. The cop wasn't too smart. The woman laughed at something the cop said. It was a damn shame to have to waste her, but it was necessary. She'd been trying to hack around in their system and was getting too darn close. Pretty and smart. Yeah, too bad. He smirked. The cop was a different story—the world could always use one less cop. He'd let the little weasel beside him think things were fine and he would get rid of him, too.

"So what are we supposed to do for the next few days?" Jed fidgeted with the keys.

"We'll lie low. When we see the press and the feds roll out, we'll drive right back in." He looked at Jed with disgust. "You and your friends thought you were so smart. Look who's bailing you out."

"We're all rich." Jed looked down his nose.

"What good is that?" he snorted. "You're a wanted man and the rest of them are in jail or dead. Where can you spend that money, Mr. Rich Guy? Hell, you can't even go home." He chuckled. "Me, I'm a ghost. They know my signature, but I'm always one step ahead of them. You have to plan, man." He grinned as Jed squirmed. "You've got to know your subjects' every move. You wait, you watch, until you know their thoughts before they think them. And then..." He pointed the gun at Jed. "Boom, it's over and you're off to your next hit." He snickered. "I know for a fact, Jed, that you may have money, but you have nowhere near what I have. So tell me, jock, who's so hot now?"

Jed glared at the windshield and shut up. He watched the couple until they stood up to leave. He snapped a couple of pictures of them. *Everyone has a weakness. What is yours, Mr. Cop?* He knew it now, yes indeed. *She* was his weakness! This might be entertaining after all. At least for a little while. He sat there a few more minutes, thinking, and then they drove away from the restaurant.

Chapter 30

Matt stretched out in bed. He was bone weary, his sore arm twitched, and sleep eluded him. He was in her bed again, and she was in the next room on the couch. It was impossible to sleep with her so close by. He smiled slowly. She had outmaneuvered him once again. Those blue eyes of hers pleading as she listed all the reasons why he needed to stay one more night. She'd had Dylan bring his clothes by earlier, his dog was taken care of, and she insisted what he really needed was a good night's sleep. He chuckled silently. Yeah, she could probably get him to do just about anything. If only it would be this easy when his arm healed!

Where was Jed hiding out? How did he convince Travis or was it Willie to work with him? For that matter, who was working for whom? Who had hired the brothers? It just didn't make any sense. Steve was dead. Why was that? Was the senator somehow involved or had he just been at the wrong place at the wrong time? Too many things to think about! He could feel that they were close, but still a ways from solving this deadly little mystery. Something was nagging at him. He rolled over, winced as his arm protested. He was missing something. Willie worked in the senator's office in New York, but he had never been in trouble with the law. Travis was a hit man with a lengthy record who would kill anyone for money. When had they gotten together and where? Then there were the Evansville friends, those from Rocky Pointe. How did all of this go together with human trafficking?

Finally, he drifted off. Through the fog of sleep, he heard her scream. He jumped up. His foot tangled in his blankets and he fell hard against the wall with his sore arm, knocking the lamp off the nightstand. He stubbed his toe trying to find the door, yanked it open finally, and charged into the hallway. By the time he got to her, Jeremy was sitting beside her with his arm around her. Matt frowned. "Is she all right?"

Jessie sniffed and hiccoughed as she looked up at him. "She has had a nightmare!" She emphasized every word.

Jeremy stood up, and Matt grinned as he took his place. "I'm sorry about your lamp."

She looked puzzled. "What about the lamp?"

"I took it out when I jumped out of bed."

Jessie smothered a giggle. "It's okay. I've been meaning to get a new one anyway. I'm sorry I woke you. I really wanted you to rest."

"Let's hear about the dream." He rubbed his hand up and down her back trying not to grimace. His injured arm hurt like hell.

"You and Jeremy were in it. Someone was about to kill you. I tried, but I couldn't stop him. He's watching us, Matt." Her voice rose. "I can feel it. He was watching us tonight, calculating how he's going to do it." She shivered. He held her closer and Jeremy tossed him a throw to wrap around her. "I will never forget the cold dead look of his eyes."

"We'll have to be careful. All of us!" Matt looked at Jeremy. He nodded. He knew better than to discount her dreams and premonitions. They'd been too darned accurate.

"Matt." She pulled away from him. "He was watching us tonight when we were at Patterson's. I didn't feel it then, but I know it now. He's not like Jed. He is scary. It's going to take us being smart to outfox him."

"Then we'll have to be smart. I'm not going to let anything happen to you."

"It's not me I'm worried about." She grabbed his hand. "I'm not going to let anything happen to you or to my friends. I need your help to keep you all safe. You have to tell me what to do just in case." She buried her face in his shoulder, mumbling a few incoherent words.

"Okay, sweetheart, we'll work on it together." He looked at Jeremy and shrugged his shoulders.

"I know how to handle the gun, but I've never had to shoot at a real person before. How do I drop if I have to? What do I do when there is only a moment to figure it all out? I need a plan." Her whole body tensed against him.

"I'll help you. You don't need to worry about it."

"Yes, yes, I do. Your life may well depend on me." She sniffed and grabbed for the tissue Jeremy was handing to her.

"I know just the person to work with you for the next several days. Now, don't worry!" He reached over and turned off the light. "Close your eyes. I'll sit in the chair for a while."

He stood up, and she stretched back out. He heard a sniffle or two and the rustle of sheets, soon followed by the sound of her easy, steady breathing. She was asleep. Sleep wasn't going to happen for him. His arm was throbbing, and the pain made him twitch. Where had he put those blasted pills?

"Is she all right?" The sound of Jeremy's voice startled him.

"Yes, she's sleeping like a baby."

"How about you, is your arm okay?"

"That's another story entirely. It hurts like the devil. I don't think it helped that I hit it dead-on when I fell into the wall."

"Probably not…" Jeremy held up his bottle of pills. "You might want to take one of these."

"Where were they?"

"Jessie told me to hold on to them in case you needed one. She didn't think you would appreciate her telling you to take one." He tossed him the bottle. "She thought you'd be more receptive to it coming from me."

"Does she always worry over all the little details like that?"

"Yep, that's our girl, just a tad on the obsessive side." Jeremy leaned against the wall, silhouetted by the light from the guest room in the background. "She's worried about something. I've never seen her like this before."

"This is crazy; she hasn't been trained for this kind of work." Matt watched her sleeping form. "She almost died last time. Did she tell you? I barely got there in time. I still have nightmares over what Anderson had planned for her."

"You've both told me," he replied, trying not to smile, "but you saved her."

"I almost didn't though. It was way too close, man. If we had gone anywhere else first, it would have been too late."

"Matt, give yourself a break. She's a big girl. She walks into each story knowing the possibilities of what can happen when you stir things up. She's a lot stronger than she looks."

"I know she's strong, but she also has a lot of stuff happening inside her head. She doesn't get it, and it has her worried."

They talked a while longer, and Jeremy let Matt know a few things that didn't add up regarding the two Booker brothers. In spite of the talking and his fatigue, Matt still couldn't fall back to sleep. What Jeremy had told him supported his current theory. Now all he had to do was prove it. He didn't think it would take too long. Blast his arm; it kept twitching from the pain. He tossed and turned. He could not get comfortable. What about Jessie? He would have to think this through. He needed a plan. He smiled into the darkness. How many times had he heard her say that over the past few months? It was getting contagious.

****

The sound of a closing door awakened Jessie. Matt and Jeremy had left for their morning meeting. It was Sunday, and she planned to do nothing. She needed to quit over-thinking everything. If the time came for her as Reba had said to take care of her friends, then she would just have to do it. She jumped up, stripped the sheets off the couch, and headed to the shower. Then it was on to the hospital.

A few hours later, she was still thinking about that visit to see Josh Harris and Lindsey Adelson. Josh had confirmed Eddie was the one who had beat him as pieces of his memory returned. Eddie scared the kids and seemed to take delight in using that fear as his weapon. Josh hadn't been as scared of Jed. He had called him mean several times. The only one that seemed to be decent to the kids at all was Karl. The other two men ridiculed Karl for being weak.

Her research told her that molestation diminished their sale value. She shivered. These guys wanted the money. It was too bad that neither Karl nor Eddie were alive to face the music. She could think of a few choice things that they should experience, especially Jed and Karl, seeing as they were both fathers. How could someone who had kids get involved in such terrible stuff without thinking about their own kids?

Something Sammy had said about Travis made her stop and think. It triggered something else, one thought lead to another. The sites she was finding supported it. She sat back from the computer screen, stunned by what she was finding. She had to make sure, before she told Matt. For all she knew, he might already be thinking along these lines. She smiled. He was a great cop and always at least a step ahead of her in a case. Maybe she should call him. She chewed her lip. Or should she wait until she had solid proof? The phone's ring took the decision out of her hands.

"Hey, Jess, are you busy?"

"Doing the research you asked me to do. What's up?" She jotted down a quick note from the screen in front of her.

"You want to hook up at Mindy's Waterfront Grill with me for dinner? Jeremy and Katie will be there."

"Sure, what time?"

"Just a minute…" She heard him talking to someone in the background. "How about six o'clock?"

"Six it is. How's your day going?"

"It's crazy! Just a minute, Jess." His voice sounded muffled. "I need to go. I'll see you later, Jess."

"Okay." She smiled; she rather liked it when he called her Jess now. No one else had better try it, though!

She turned off the computer and turned on the TV. An action cop show was in order, something she would normally have no interest in at all. She needed an idea how to protect her friends and maybe by watching an actor do it, she could imitate his actions. It wasn't very sound, but it was all she had for now.

Chapter 31

Jessie finished dressing. She took one last glance in the mirror as she put on her lip-gloss. The gun in the holster over her shoulder was the only thing she saw. It was strange seeing it there, but she was determined to wear it until it became second nature. She smiled and wrinkled her nose. On the count of three, she had dropped to the ground and rolled out of the line of fire. At the same time, she had to draw her gun, aim, and fire. Of course, there was no telling whether she would have even come close to hitting a target. She made a face at her reflection. She smiled. She fluffed her hair out over her shoulders and put on her boyfriend jacket. She buttoned the middle button and called it finished. What they didn't know couldn't hurt her. You have to have a plan. She chuckled and walked out the door.

Katie was waiting for her when she got to the Inn. "You're finally here. I thought maybe I would have to call."

"Why? I'm not late." Jessie frowned at her.

"I know. I'm just impatient." Katie lifted her hands. "I'm so jumpy and it's driving everyone nuts, including me."

"Dr. Gilbert, I'm telling you, she can help."

"Yeah, yeah, I know you're right. I just have to make myself. I never thought I would ever need a shrink. I'm so well adjusted."

Jessie rolled her eyes.

"Well, fairly well adjusted."

"She can help! Believe me, I know it's hard to get through it alone." Jessie grabbed Katie's purse as she started out the door without it.

"Oh, thanks." Katie took it from her hand. "I don't seem to be able to remember anything these days."

"She can help."

"All right, already, I've got the message." She let out an exasperated breath. "I'll get her number from you and call her tomorrow."

Jessie smiled at her. "Sounds like a plan to me. You've always got to have a plan."

"No, that's you. I just like to roll with it." They giggled and laughed all the way to the restaurant. Neither one of them noticed the car that followed them at a discreet distance, turning when they did. Katie parked in front of Mindy's Grill, one of the small buildings on the wharf. The other car passed them, unnoticed, and pulled into Anthony's parking lot to wait.

Stepping through the door was like taking a step back in time for Jessie. Mindy's had a seaside cottage feel with warm sun-washed floral fabrics and ginghams in blues and whites. The colors were soothing and easy on the eyes. Flickering candlelight and fresh flowers adorned each table. Spices scented the air. The cozy picture looked somewhat strange with Matt and Jeremy sitting at a table.

"It's not quite their atmosphere, do you think?" Jessie whispered in Katie's ear.

"A lot of guys like this place. The food is great! It's like eating at the Inn." Katie waved at Jeremy and headed toward them.

Jessie followed; she noticed Matt looking at her. A flutter tickled her stomach, and it had nothing to do with hunger. "Hi, how was your day?" She smiled at both of them.

Matt stood to pull out her chair for her. "Hi back at you." He leaned close and whispered in her ear, "You're the best part of it so far."

She was glad that it was dark, her face felt warm. "What did you boys do all day?"

"Are you any closer to finding out who planted the bomb?" Katie interrupted their answer and pointed a finger at Matt. "The sooner you get it solved, the better, as far as I'm concerned. It's hard to function knowing that guy is out there and might do it again."

"We're working on it. It takes time." Matt handed Jessie a menu. "It's all good here."

"Let's talk about something different." Jessie gave Katie a quick look. She could hear frustration in Matt's voice, and Katie would keep pushing it. "There should be a general rule; no talking about cases during dinner."

"That's just plain stupid, Jessie, and you know it." Katie lifted her chin. "It's the only thing people are talking about in town."

"We don't have to." She nudged Katie under the table with her foot. "They've been working on it all day, maybe they need a break."

"Okay, I get the message. You didn't have to kick me."

"Believe me, that wasn't a kick."

Jeremy signaled time out. "You two are really something." He grinned. "You fight just like my kid sisters used to."

"You mean this measly little argument?" Katie tossed her head. "This isn't fighting. I could tell you some stories about fights if you want to know what a real one looks like." After the waitress took their orders, Katie proceeded to do just that. It turned out to be a fun, relaxing evening.

The evening air had a brisk chill to it by the time the four of them stepped outside after dinner. Waves slapped against the shoreline with a hypnotic rhythm. Jessie shivered, but she wasn't cold. Someone was watching them. The sense oppressed her, clogged her mind. Her legs suddenly felt heavy, as if she was rooted to the spot.

"Are you cold?" Matt was watching her closely.

"I'd like to get in the car." Her eyes darted up and down the street as she started toward it. Jessie stepped out into the street to get in the driver's side. The next thing she knew Matt had pushed her to the ground and he was on top of her. "You have to really stop landing on me like this," she gasped as soon as she could get her breath. "Why?"

"A car was headed toward you." He pushed off her with his good arm.

"I think you just like pushing me around," she whispered and he laughed.

Matt threw Jeremy his keys. "Take Katie home and I'll ride with Jessie." Jeremy nodded at him.

"Are you okay, sweetheart? I'm sorry. It seemed the only thing to do to get you out of the line of fire if the driver had a gun."

"Sure, that's what all the guys say before they shove me face down into the asphalt." She glared at him, but his words shook her.

279

He helped her up, opened the car door, and closed it after she got in. "What was going on in your head before that car came at you?"

"Why do you think something was going on?" She inspected a fresh scrape on her elbow.

"Oh, I don't know. Your eyes glazed over, you started shivering, but said you weren't cold. Then you walked out into the street and just stood there almost daring the guy to hit you."

"No, I didn't." She frowned at him.

"Yes, you did! It was out of character, even for you."

She told him about the strange feeling she'd had when she walked out of the restaurant. "I didn't say anything, because I didn't want Katie to worry. She's having a hard time with all of this."

He reached over and lifted her chin so he could look in her eyes. "Any feeling, dream, or ghostly impressions you get, tell me, do you hear me? I want to know so I can anticipate how I'm going to keep you safe. I can't let anything happen to my girl." He started the car.

"Are you okay to drive?"

"Yep, I'm fine." He turned in the seat to look at her. "I mean it, Jess, tell me! It could save someone's life."

"I will." She hunched her shoulders. "It all makes me feel just a little bit out of control. I don't like feeling this way at all."

"I understand that, but you have to admit something happens every time you have them. I don't understand or get it. We do have to be smart about it though. I know that much."

"Whoever this guy is, he tries to get inside your head. He's studying our every motion trying to figure us out. He's smart, methodical, and almost spellbinding in his approach. I...I felt myself captivated by it." Her face really was hot now.

"Geez, Jess, what are you talking about?" He ran his hand through his hair.

"I mean I could sense, I'm not sure that's the word I want, what he was doing. The strange thing, I was too occupied with his thoughts to be aware of anything else. I didn't see the car at all. Which has me wondering...? He wouldn't be that careless or miss for that matter." She grabbed his arm, her face lit up.

"What are you thinking?'

"I'm wondering if Jed jumped the gun. I might be hearing the thoughts of one of them, and Jed is doing his own thing."

"You blow my mind." Matt shook his head. "Enough said. You're right about Booker, whichever brother he is. He is methodical, and he wouldn't jeopardize the job. Jed on the other hand, might try something on his own, in which case he might become the next victim."

"I can't imagine our hit man letting him live when this is over. He wants to be the only one left standing."

"I need to get you home. If I forget to tell you later, thanks for taking care of me the last couple of days. It was nice." He pulled out of the parking space and made a U-turn.

"We may be dealing with two men coming at us with two different approaches."

"As crazy as it seems, Jed may be the hardest to anticipate. He'll just spring it on us anywhere and at any time. Your head just might help us with the other guy." He stopped to make the turn onto Main Street.

"How's your arm doing?" She turned her head to look at him.

"You mean after I pushed you to the ground and landed on you?"

"Yep…" She grinned at him. "You really need to find another way to save my life. Your arm will never heal at this rate, and I already have enough bruises." She smiled at him. "It's not that you're a big man. It's like having a tree land on me." She tried not to laugh.

"Nothing personal, Jess, but I can think of other things I'd rather do than taking a bullet or rescuing you from a speeding car. But I'll take what I can get."

"So what's the plan?" She let her smile fade.

"We keep our eyes and ears open. I don't think we'll have to wait too long before they try something." He looked over at her with a lopsided grin on his face. "Sweetheart, just be prepared for me to do almost anything to keep you safe."

"Why do I detect a hidden meaning in that statement? I think I might have to keep my eyes on you, too." She glanced at him, making eye contact for a moment.

"Time out…unfair tactics…flirting is against the rules unless you want what comes with it." He stopped at the light and looked her over slowly.

"And just what might that be?"

"That's for me to know and you to find out." He gave her a slow grin. "Believe me, I'd be happy to show you."

"I think I'll pass for now." Oh yes, her cheeks were definitely flaming now! Good thing it was dark in the car.

"All kidding aside, Jess, keep your eyes open."

"I will, and you, too. I can't have anything happen to my rescuer." She dug through her purse to find his keys.

"I enjoyed tonight even if it ended with a hard landing." He pulled Jessie's car in next to his. She started to open the door. "Don't go anywhere yet. I'm walking you to the door."

They walked quietly together and at the door, she handed him his keys and thanked him. He lifted her hair gently from her face with his finger. She couldn't take her eyes off him. The look he was giving her caused her insides to flutter. He leaned nearer and brushed his lips seductively back and forth across hers. "Sleep tight, sweetheart, dream about me." Then he turned and walked away.

She watched him get into his car and waved when he drove away. He would probably be in her dreams. He often was.

Chapter 32

By the middle of the week, Matt's concern was growing. The window of opportunity was closing fast for finding the kids. He found himself going through every theory again. He replayed every possible scenario, came up with nothing. Tom had worked tirelessly with him for the past few days, questioning suspects and pouring over transcripts. Even with all of the tips that came in by phone, they had very few solid leads. They followed up on every one, but nothing had turned up. Hell, they were all on a wild goose chase.

Matt closed the file that he was reading and set it off to the side of his desk. He turned his chair to look out the window. What he needed right now was one solid lead that could give him a break in the case. Sammy was cooperating in every way that he could, but he knew very little about what the group was up to. Sammy was exactly what he thought he was—the hired fall guy. He had minimal information only.

Josh had filled in a few missing pieces on Lutz, Hampton, and Johnson. Matt learned more about the places where the kids had stayed and how they were treated. The FBI had questioned each of the suspects a couple times, but no one would give up the name of the head of operations. Either they were afraid or they didn't know. Mike Pearson thought that maybe it was Steve Murphy. He was the only one that Mike ever talked to or saw. Steve had given them their marching orders. Matt felt in his gut that he wasn't the top guy. He had been one of the hits on the night of the ball. Probably he knew too much. The top dogs were in self-preservation mode now. They would let the others take the fall so they could live to play another day. Unless something major changed, they'd get away with it. Matt pounded his fist silently on the desktop. The operation was set up to protect those at the top.

"Matt, can we talk to you?"

Matt turned his chair to see Jeremy and Jessie standing there. "Sure, come in. What's up?"

Jeremy spoke up first. "We've been searching and I think we've found something pretty interesting. We put it together in a timeline to make it easier for you to read." He handed several sheets of paper to Matt.

Matt slipped his glasses on and started reading. "Are you sure about this item right here?" Matt pointed it to out to Jeremy.

Jeremy nodded. "Someone in the senator's office has been passing information along and doing things on the computer. There is no way to know yet how much the senator knows, maybe nothing at all."

Jessie watched him flip to the next page. "This is where it gets interesting. Do you notice the discrepancies surrounding the Booker brothers' early years? It gets more interesting the further you read. There are many inconsistencies in the last few years."

"I can see that. I'm going to have to think about what all this might mean. I've been toying with a similar idea for a while." He frowned.

"I was sure you probably had been." Jessie smiled at him. "I didn't think we would find anything that you hadn't considered in some way. We've only found the tangible evidence to back up your theories."

"I'll take a little time to study this. Is it possible for us to get together later on to discuss your findings?"

"Sure thing!" Jeremy stood up to leave.

"Will six work, at my house? Jess knows the way, don't you, sweetheart?" He smiled at her as a rosy blush tinged her cheeks. "I don't want to be in a public place when we talk. I'll take care of dinner."

Jeremy headed out the door. Jessie stood up to follow him. Matt jumped up, grabbed her hand, and pulled her back in the room. "See you, Jeremy." Matt closed his office door. He leaned against his desk pulling her gently into his arms. "I've missed you. This is the first time I've seen or talked to you since Sunday." He watched the way her face softened when she looked at him and groaned inwardly. Wrong time and wrong place. "I needed to hold you close for a minute. Thank you," he whispered in her ear.

"For what?" She tried to twist out of his arms, but he held her fast.

"Well, for all your hard work, of course. You make my job easier, and besides you're much better to look at than any of the mugs around here." He let her go. He gave her a playful push toward the door. "See you at six."

After Jessie left, Matt sat back down and began reading their research. It was the ace in the hole he was looking for. Now he had enough powder to blow the lid off this case with the potential to take several people down with it. Up to now, he had no proof. None at all. This changed everything. He could interrogate his suspects again, armed with some damning evidence.

****

Jessie walked out of the station, alone; she suddenly had that feeling someone was watching her again. She could feel *him* spinning his web, probing her head, but she wasn't afraid. He was playing games with her. She decided it was time to get in the game and give it back to him. Jessie had no idea what she was doing. Instinct kicked in. She pictured herself dressed as a goalie; she went for the block. She dodged his probes and threw some random thoughts back at him. She could feel his confusion. He was throwing one thing after another at her, none of it making any sense. She refused to let him get inside her head. Finally, he gave up. Feeling suddenly exhausted, she got into her car wondering what had just happened.

She would have to talk to her grandmother about this. It seemed to be a new place for her once again. She could talk to Reba of course, but no one else besides them. She wasn't sure if anyone would understand this. Who would believe her anyway?

She took her sandwich out of her lunch cooler and ate it as she headed back to the church. She felt a near-hysterical urge to giggle. Life had certainly played a few tricks on her lately. She had moved to Blue Cove to have a nice quiet life and what had she gotten—a ghost, a girl in her head, strange dreams, and now some crazy man trying to waltz through her mind. She felt her arm, yep, it was still real. *I'm still me!* she told herself and smiled. Sort of! Why anyone would want to do this for a living was totally beyond her.

She pulled into the church parking lot. She should have known. She smiled again as she turned off the engine. Reba was standing by her car waiting for her.

"Jessie girl, you're just the person I wanted to see." Reba walked toward Jessie as soon as she stepped out of the car.

"Nothing should surprise me anymore." Jessie shook her head and laughed. She met Reba halfway between both cars. "What's up?"

"I could ask you the same thing. You've been on my mind all morning. You have questions, and I have the answers."

"I'm not even going to ask you how you know. I think I can understand just a little."

"You're learning." Reba nodded, her eyes sparkling. "Only those who need your help should be allowed to enter the world of your thoughts. You must find ways to stop those who are there for the wrong reasons. You are the gatekeeper." She grabbed Jessie's hand. "This should only happen when there is great need for it, as in the case of Gina or Abigail. You may or may not hear or see something again in the future. Do you understand what I'm telling you?"

"Yes, I believe I do." Jessie paused to gather her thoughts. "My grandmother told me similar things happened to her at different times as she worked on special projects. Her grandmother before her also had the same experiences."

"Ah, now that makes sense." Reba smiled at her. "I had wondered where you'd come by the ability and why it had so randomly shown up."

"I felt twice lately that someone was trying to probe my thoughts. The first time almost got me killed. Today was the second time, and I managed to keep him out. He didn't belong there."

"Good, good! This is the person who will challenge

you." Reba looked around. "I don't need to tell you to be careful." Reba had a serious look on her face. "Watch over your friends, too."

"I will."

"You should get to work. Be safe." Reba hugged Jessie and they said their goodbyes.

****

A few minutes before six, Jessie pulled her car into Matt's driveway. Jeremy got out and walked around to open her door. Something smelled wonderful. She couldn't wait.

"Wow, this place is amazing." Jeremy looked around the grounds and at the view. "How does he do all this on a cop's salary?"

"This was his parents' home, which they gave to him. They live in the Boston area now." She rang the doorbell. "He did most of the work inside himself. Wait until you see it. It's like a show home."

Matt opened the door. "Come in. Dinner is ready."

Jessie noticed the nicely set table. "Did you make dinner?"

"I did and before you get worried. I'm considered to be a pretty good cook." He grinned at them. "At least no one has left hungry, yet, or complained for that matter." He drizzled the dressing on the salads he had prepared as he talked.

"Tell me who would complain the chief of police was an awful cook. You could be bad, and no one would ever tell you." Jessie took the three green salads he handed her and placed one at each table setting.

"I'm willing to give it a try. I'm starving." Jeremy sat down at the table.

Matt poured a light fruity Chardonnay into the

wine glasses. "Go ahead and eat while I get the rest together."

"This dressing is really good. Did you make it?" Jeremy looked up at Matt when he walked in carrying their plates.

"I did."

"Well now, I am impressed." Jessie grinned. "A chief of police that's a gourmet cook."

"It's called therapy! I work on my house and I cook. It gives me other things to think about besides work all the time."

"I, for one, am glad." Jeremy finished the last of his salad.

Jessie thought the wine was perfect with the herb grilled chicken and grilled veggies. The entire meal was wonderful. "Impressed twice in one evening, that's a record. Can I have a doggie bag for the rest of my dinner? I don't want to waste one bit of it." She sipped her wine.

"You have to save room for the dessert, which is equally good. I always serve it with coffee. And then we'll talk."

He served the light chocolate soufflé with a raspberry sauce. "Please tell me you didn't make this. No woman in her right mind would want to compete with this cooking."

He grinned sheepishly. "Sorry, I can't take credit for this. This wonderful dessert is compliments of Roger Blackman and the Chowder House. I don't bake or do desserts."

"Whew…" She dramatically placed her hand to her forehead. "I thought for a minute we wouldn't be able to date again. I have to have one area in the cooking department where I excel, and you're simply too good. My female pride couldn't take it if you could do it all."

"Well, you can tell that Roger fella for me this was a damn fine soufflé." Jeremy licked his fork.

They spent the next hour going over the papers and putting together a plan. Matt asked the questions he had, and Jessie and Jeremy answered them with clarity. The plan was that Jessie would bait them with an article. They'd see if anyone went for it. Now all they had to do was play the waiting game.

Chapter 33

Jessie's article came out in the following Monday paper. Matt folded it open on the table at Joe's where he'd stopped for a belated breakfast. He hadn't seen Jessie since the dinner at his place last week. Tom was running him ragged. He didn't have his usual time to think through the case the way he liked to. Something didn't feel right to him. They were going in too many directions.

Jessie's article zeroed in on Tot's Togs & Toys and the possible link to a human trafficking ring. It put before the public once again the names of the children and the known kidnappers in hopes that someone would remember one little thing that could help them solve this case. It also focused on the group of eight men who worked for the company in case someone knew something about them, which would lead them to the two unknown people and anyone else known to work there.

So far the snow had held off, and they were a having a typical New England fall. He hadn't had time for football games or anything else fun lately. Hell, he hadn't even claimed his second date with Jessie. He sipped his coffee. They had talked a few times, but he hadn't seen her. Jeremy would be leaving this weekend, so he needed to think of everything he wanted him to do. He tapped his pen on the notepad. He really should bring Frank back one more time before snow covered up any possible tracks. His phone rang.

He looked at the caller's name and smiled. "Hey, stranger." Jessie's voice sounded real and warm in his ear. "I wanted to see how you're doing,"

"I was just thinking about you. I read your article and I was missing you. Another good piece, by the way."

"Thanks!" He heard her take a breath. "I was wondering what happened to you. You usually come by to talk over the case. I was hoping all those extra hands would take some of the pressure off you this time."

"To tell you the truth, it's made it worse. I haven't had a minute to think." He nodded as Molly paused by the table with the coffee pot to see if he wanted a refill. "Are you in the vicinity's of Joe's? I sure would like to see my girl, if only for a minute." He added cream and stirred his coffee.

"Sure, I have a few minutes. I'll drop by."

Matt watched the door every time it opened. Finally, she walked in. Man, she looked good. He smiled and waved her over. "Hey, sweetheart, Molly will bring you a coffee and scone. I've already taken care of it." He liked it when she wore something that showed of her gorgeous long legs. This skirt did it quite nicely and the blue sweater made her eyes look like sapphires, bluer than normal. Was it even possible? "Are you doing all right?"

"I am. I've been spending a lot of time with Jeremy and Katie. Things have been a little quiet as of late. I think Jeremy is closing in on the partners of the store. We should have that information for you soon." She paused as Molly set her coffee in front of her along with the scone.

"I haven't seen either of you in here for a while. It's good to see you both." Molly smiled down at Jessie. "Wasn't the shower fun the other night?"

Jessie poured cream into her coffee. "It was great! I really liked your family. Your sister kept me laughing most of the night."

"We're best friends—even when we were growing up we were. Of course, we got into some major sister wars as well."

"I thought you got some really great gifts. You'll have fun getting your new place decorated."

"I know." Molly tapped Matt on the shoulder. "Don't forget the rehearsal is a month from Friday right over there at her work place." She smiled and pointed across the street at the church. "Kenny really likes Pastor Kevin. He's been doing the premarital counseling with us."

"He's a super great guy. I'm glad you like him." Jessie felt the hair on the back of her neck stand up. She looked around but didn't see anything. He had to be somewhere close by.

"Both of the pastors are going to be a part of the wedding. I guess I'd better get back to work." Molly started to walk away but then turned back to them. "I'm happy we were able to change venues on such short notice since the marina won't be ready in time. The Chowder House offered us the restaurant for the reception for the same price. Cool, don't you think? Enjoy your coffee." Molly waved at someone who had just walked in and went back to the kitchen.

"I've been practicing with the lady from the FBI that you got me hooked up with. I think it has made a difference. I feel a lot more confidence in using the gun, now." Jessie straightened in the chair and crossed her legs.

Matt noticed. "I talked to her the other day, and she said that you were catching on. You're quick on your feet, agile, and smart at picking up things. She told me you had learned to drop and roll as you fired. She said that you hit your target almost every time, too." He gave her an approving smile. She really was something. "I have cops on the force who have to work to pass that part of the recertification every time."

"I'm supposed to take the test tomorrow or the next day. I'll have to hit all the targets in order to pass." She smiled at him. "I'll just visualize you cheering for me, and I'll do fine." Jessie paused, her brows creased.

"What are you thinking?" He reached for her hand.

"I was thinking how things have changed since we first met. I would have visualized you as the target then."

Matt laughed. "Yes, I believe you would have." He had been an idiot, back then. He was darn lucky he hadn't lost her to someone else. He continued to chuckle.

"You can always stop by and talk about the case, even if it's late." She took the last sip of her coffee.

"Let's do dinner and talk tonight. I'll just leave early." He touched her hand lightly. "You want to meet at Patterson's after work or somewhere else?"

"I don't care. Whatever sounds good to you is fine with me."

"How about a good burger or a great salad?"

"Sounds good."

"I know just the place. It's in Seaside Village. I'll

text you all the particulars in a few minutes. Better yet, I'll meet you at the church and you can let me drive your sweet car." He watched her stand. He stood up beside her and without stopping to think he pulled her into his arms and hugged her.

He watched her until she pulled her car out of the parking spot. It was getting harder for him to be patient. Life was too damn short to mess around. He wanted to spend whatever life he had loving her.

****

Jessie smiled the minute she'd walked out the door of Joe's. The smile continued through the morning at work, and through most of the day until the phone rang that afternoon, right before Matt's arrival.

His deep raspy voice came across the line. "Are you Jessie Reynolds, the writer?"

"I am." She felt oddly hesitant.

"You don't know me, and you've no reason to trust me. Hell, I wouldn't. I'm the one who tried to run you down the other night outside of Mindy's Grill. I also was driving the car the day you were shot at."

"Jed Johnson!" Her heart beat rapidly. "Why are you calling me?" She grabbed her pen and notepad.

"It's like this. I'm as good as dead, and I sure as hell am not going out alone. I want to take all the double-crossing bastards with me. I read your article in the paper, and you are getting close. There are still things that will take time to figure out. When it comes to the kids, you don't have much time. You get my drift."

"What do you want?"

"You and I are going to meet. Right there in the church parking lot Friday night at eight. Nobody and I mean *nobody* can be out there with you. You can tell them you're meeting me. Hell, they can plant a wire on you and be in cars nearby. I don't plan to hurt you. I just want to talk to you and tell you everything I can before they kill me. Be there!" He hung up the phone.

Jessie couldn't believe what had just happened. Should she trust him? Matt called to let her know he was waiting in the parking lot. She closed up the office, walked down the hall and out the side door of the church.

He was standing beside his patrol car. She walked toward him and he met her halfway. "Okay, let me have the keys." He opened his hand in front of her. "I like driving this car, anytime you let me."

She dropped the keys into his hand and waited for him to open the passenger door for her. "How was your day?"

"Too busy!" He closed the door once she was inside.

He got in and started the car. "It purrs like a kitten." He grinned at her. "How was your day?"

"On a scale of one to ten, I'd say this was a ten. It was a very interesting day."

He adjusted the mirror and looked over at her. "Why is that?" He put the car in gear and started to drive.

She smiled at him. "Let's just say I had a call from a murderer!" She studied his face for a moment. "Jed. He set up a date with me for Friday night. It looks like you'll have to cancel our reservations again." Jessie's seatbelt held her when he slammed on the brakes.

"What the hell, Jess?" He frowned and she proceeded to tell him what Jed had said. His frown increased with her every word. "You aren't going to do it. You've got that?" His face was stormy. "Not unless I'm sitting in the car beside you with a gun pointed at his head."

"Matt, you're not thinking like a cop. If it was anybody else, you would wire them up and do just what he said."

"Damn, Jess, you know how easily things can go bad. You've experienced it before. What if he walks up and shoots you dead? I can't get to you in time to stop him." He raked his hand through his hair.

"I'll have my gun." She smiled sweetly at him. "Besides you'll keep me safe. I know it." She touched his arm. "How can we possibly pass up the chance to hear him out just in case he's telling the truth? This may be our chance to take down the others and possibly find the kids. He knows you'll be sitting in the dark with guns trained on him. I don't think he's suicidal. We have to try, and you know it." She smiled all the way to the restaurant in spite of his frown. She was right, and he knew it.

Chapter 34

They ended up at Sally's Place. According to Matt, it was the best place in town for shakes, burgers, and fries. She went with a simple cheeseburger. He went all out ordering the blue cheese and bacon number, topped off with a chocolate shake. He wasn't doing a whole lot of talking. Jessie tried hard not to laugh. What he *was* doing was grumbling. Growling might be a better word. She bit her lip and hid a giggle in her water. He wasn't making it easy on her.

"If this is your attempt to charm me, I would just give it up if I were you." She finally gave up and the giggle emerged. "Let's forget about it for now. You can think about it, and we'll talk about it at another time. We have four days to decide."

"I'm not going to change my mind." He scowled.

"I think you will, after you think about it. From the beginning, this hasn't been about *us,* it has been about those kids. We have to do everything we can to get them home safely to their parents."

"I know you're right, but I don't have to like it."

"No, you don't, but you do have to think like a cop. This might be our only and best opportunity. You even said that this guy would kill Jed in the end. And Jed knows that, too. Obviously." She leaned toward him. "I've got a feeling this is the break we've been looking for."

"Aren't you just a little bit afraid, Jess?" He grabbed her hand and held on to it.

"I'm not afraid of Jed, and I can't tell you why exactly." She frowned. "I don't think he will harm me. He's afraid he's going to die. He wants to get it off his chest." She paused as the waitress set their meal in front of them.

"Okay." He picked up his mountainous burger. "We'll talk about something else, and I'll think it over."

"Thanks, Matt, that's all I'm asking."

"What else did you do today besides talk with Jed?"

"Oh, you know, the usual in the exciting world of a church secretary." She dipped a crispy fry into ketchup. "Write the bulletin, exercise my coffee-making skills, and regulate the church calendar." She sipped her chocolate shake. "Mmm, this is really good."

"I told you so."

"So, Mr. Parker, you haven't been doing much impressing lately." She grinned at him. "I mean, it's hard to be impressed when I hardly get to see you."

"Feeling a little neglected lately, are we?" He smiled when she nodded at him. "I'll have to try and remedy that. I'm sorry, Jess. It's just I go a little crazy thinking about you anywhere near a guy like Jed Johnson."

"I know! I appreciate your concern for me. The moment I heard from Abigail I was hooked. The other day when Josh opened his eyes while I was there, I knew I would do *anything* to help those kids. Besides we're a team." She placed her burger back on the plate. "Tom and all the others will be gone when this is over, but you and I will still be watching over our town."

"That's what has been missing. I haven't had the time to bounce things off you. You're right, we're a team." He finally smiled. "I'll be by every night to talk things over with you. We started this case together and we're going to see it through." He took a big bite of his burger.

"I have to admit you were right about this place. I can't tell you when the last time was that I had a shake this good. I mean it! It's worth every mile I'm going to have to run tomorrow to burn off the calories." She smiled, wiping up the mustard that had plopped onto the table from his burger.

After dinner, they strolled through the village to the water's edge. They sat together on the beach, watching the waves lap the shoreline and shimmering moonlight dance across the water. It was a moment of contentment for her. There wasn't much conversation; there didn't need to be. She looked out of the corner of her eye at him. He was handsome, and he might just be easy to love. She shivered. He wrapped his arm around her.

"You're cold. I guess we should get you home." He stood and pulled her up. They walked hand in hand back to her car.

****

If it were anyone else, he wouldn't be struggling with this so much. Matt stared at the bedroom ceiling. Not true! He was always serious when anyone's life was on the line. Man, he couldn't believe he was even considering letting Jessie do this. He didn't know if he could keep her safe. Maybe Jed *was* suicidal. His stomach churned at the thought. He rolled onto his back. Jessie had said from the beginning it was all about the kids. She knew the risk and was still willing to meet Johnson. Frustrated, he sat up. His first priority was to keep her safe and to bring the kids home to their families. No small task. He exhaled. What he needed was a great plan. She was rubbing off on him and truth be told, he liked it.

Matt rubbed a hand across his face. He couldn't lose her now. Couldn't! He would plan. He lay back down on the bed and tried to get into the mind of Johnson. Jed was cornered, afraid, and therefore hard to gauge. He said he didn't want to hurt her. Maybe that was true, maybe not. Things could always go bad and you had to have back-up options just in case. A sharp shooter hidden at the scene was one part of the plan. Jessie would wear a listening device, with Gary and Jeremy monitoring. He would keep several guys close to move in at a moment's notice. He would work her tail off with gun training every night until Friday.

The only thing he couldn't account for was the outside factors. The unknowns, like someone moving when they shouldn't, an itchy trigger finger, who knew what? Anything could go wrong. Finally, his mind quieted down and he dozed off.

****

Just as Jessie was walking out the door, her phone rang. "Hey, this is Jessie."

"No kidding." She heard Matt chuckle. "Pick me up after work before you go for your training class. I want to go along and see how you're doing. I might allow you to do this if I think you're ready."

"Allow me? I don't like the sound of that. If I want to do it, I will do it and that's all there is to it, mister." She barely stopped herself from hanging up.

"Excuse me, Jess, but I'm in charge of the case, I

have the ultimate say." His tone was surprisingly gentle. "This isn't personal. I have to know you're ready for any eventuality. I would do the same with anybody. I'm going to go over some important instructions repeatedly. You'll get sick of hearing me, but I'm hopeful it'll stick in your head if you need it."

"I know." She let her breath out in a rush. They were both under pressure here. "I just don't like you telling me what I can or cannot do. You're right, of course, this case is yours, and I'm lucky to be a part of it."

"No, Jess, your skills earned you the *right* to be part of it. All I want to do is sharpen them so you are absolutely on your game. Are we okay?"

"Yes. I'll see you after work." She smiled as she hung up, then locked, and closed the door behind her.

Chapter 35

Matt had pushed her hard the three remaining days. He smiled thinking about it. She had impressed the hell out of him. She was also good and angry with him. Tomorrow night would be the true test. He hoped it would all go down smoothly.

He rode back with her to the station. She didn't talk much. That was his first clue not all was well. He leaned in her open window. "Jess, come here tomorrow after work. We'll get you wired and turn it on when you're in the parking lot of the church. Then we'll all go to dinner. I want you as relaxed as possible."

"Sure, whatever…" She scowled at him.

"I know I've been hard on you. I wanted to make sure you're ready. Damn, Jess, you've done everything I asked of you and more. I'm impressed. You're good." He ruffled her hair and grinned when she slapped at his hand.

"Does this mean you'll stop growling?" She peered up at him. "I surrender." She raised her hands.

He nodded. "Go home and take it easy."

"I wasn't this tired when I ran my first marathon. I hope I can stay awake tomorrow for the interview with him." She waved and drove away.

On his way back into the station to get his case files, Tom stopped him. "Is she ready?"

"She's not bad, I mean good, but that's without the

stress of a fluid situation. You can only hope training kicks in and takes over." Matt leaned against the wall. "I rode her pretty hard and she didn't blink, although she did snarl a few times." He laughed.

"What's so funny?"

"At one point, if memory serves me right, she told me if I didn't knock it off, her next target would look a lot like me. She would explain to the police it was accident and that I had gotten in the way."

Tom laughed. "She's game, I'll give her that. I don't know too many women who'd be willing to do it."

"She's got spirit, intelligence, and the skill worthy of some my best officers on the force." Matt grinned and leaned against the wall.

"Maybe I should see if she wants to work for the Bureau." Tom turned his head and smiled.

"If I were you, I wouldn't go there. She belongs here." He pushed away from the wall and stood, feet apart.

"Shouldn't she make that decision?"

"I know her, and she's here to stay." Matt frowned at him.

"You've got it bad, man!" Tom laughed and slapped Matt on the back.

"You've got that right, but I'm happy." He grinned. "I don't share well."

"With her looks, you're going have to put a paper bag over her head or fight jealousy all the time." Tom paused and grinned back at him. "You're not half as pretty as she is."

"That's for damn sure." Matt laughed and walked back into his office to close up.

****

By the time Jessie got home, her legs felt like rubber. It took everything she had to walk up to the door. Her first destination was to the tub, kicking off her shoes as she went. She filled the tub and eased her weary body into the hot water. It went to work like magic fingers soothing her tired muscles. Even her hair felt sore as she worked the shampoo through it. She nearly fell asleep before she could rinse it.

When the water got too cool, she grabbed for the towel and stood up to dry. She put on her robe and made it as far as the bed where she promptly fell on it and went sound asleep.

****

She was hearing something. Light tapping became knocking. Through the sleep fog, she heard the loud banging. She tried willing it to stop, but it was persistent. Jessie sat up, rubbing her eyes. Matt. He was calling her name, banging on the door. She pushed her hair out of her face, wiped the drool off her cheek. Stumbling toward the door, she pulled her robe tightly around her.

"Why didn't you answer any of my calls? Are you all right?" He stared at her, his jaw clenched.

"I was fine until you woke me. But now that you have, you may as well come in." She walked toward the bedroom. "Make yourself at home, I'll be right back." She quickly put on some clothes.

"Did you eat anything?" He looked up as she walked back into the room.

"No, I barely made it out of the tub to the bed before I fell asleep."

"I'm sorry, sweetheart. I didn't mean to run you

into the ground."

"I know." She didn't try to stifle a yawn. "Is there a reason why you're here? I mean you did wake me from a very sound sleep."

"Sorry again, I wanted to make sure you're okay." He looked her over. "Even a mess, you're pretty."

"So you came to insult me too." She frowned at him.

He shook his head no. "Believe me that wasn't an insult. I don't know how you do it."

"Do what?" She shrugged her shoulders at him.

"Look like a million bucks no matter what."

"Now you're just being a suck up after you insulted me." She stuck her tongue out at him.

He grinned and opened the refrigerator, sticking his head in for a look. "Let's see what's in here. I'm going to make you something to eat. It's the least I can do."

"I'm not hungry."

"Sure you are, and you're going to eat." He took out a couple of eggs and some veggies.

"So you're here to boss me around some more." She propped her head up with her bent arm.

"Sweetheart, I'm only here to take care of you. That, and to satisfy this need I have to see you." He made an omelet while she stood and watched. "Sit!" He smiled at her as he fixed her toast and tea to go with it. "I'll let you sleep when you're finished, but I'm going to hang around just in case you need something."

She stared at him, her mouth falling open. "Why?"

"Okay, I admit it I'm feeling a little guilty for working you so hard." He gave her a lopsided grin.

"You should!"

Chapter 36

Jessie looked at the clock for the umpteenth time. She would be meeting Matt in fifteen minutes. There were butterflies in her stomach, but she wasn't afraid. Her jacket covered her gun, her badge was in her slacks pocket, and she had a small tape recorder in her handbag. She was excited. Smiling, she got up from her desk and went to shut off the coffee. "I've come a long way since our case together, eh, Gina!" she whispered.

She cleared off her desk and took the bulletin to the lobby for Sunday. She stood at the Sanctuary door remembering the first time she had heard Gina singing. Since Gina's murderer was dead, her ghost was gone. She shook herself. That was then, and this was now. The children were waiting for them to find them. This was almost the end for those who were responsible for all of the kidnappings and murders. She could feel it.

She ran a brush through hair and put on some lip-gloss. Locking the church door, she stepped outside and strolled to her car. Was she being a little too cavalier? No way! You can't hurt children and win! This was the bad guys' time to lose.

Jessie arrived at the police station ten minutes later. Jeremy held the door open for her.

"Are you nervous?"

"Not yet. I might be later." She smiled at him. "Is Matt in his office?'

"I'm not sure where he is." He frowned, running his hand through his hair. "To tell you the truth I've been trying to stay out of his way." He added under his breath, "So is everyone else. He's been doing a lot of growling today."

"I'll go find him." She brushed past him.

"I think you're the reason he's like this." Jeremy tapped her on the shoulder.

"Why? I didn't do anything." She turned around to look at him. "Don't worry. He always gets super serious in the midst of a case."

"This isn't his game face; he's nervous. He doesn't like sending you to meet with Johnson, and the closer it gets to game time, the more he's grumbling. Once he gets a look at you, it'll get worse."

"What's wrong with the way I look?"

"Not a blasted thing. You look as if you're ready to teach a freaking Sunday school class. Looking the way you do won't make it any easier on him. I have to say I'm with him on this."

"You're both going to have to get over it, because I'm doing it." She put her hand on her hips. "I'll just have to reassure him, won't I? And, you'll have to keep your opinion to yourself. You, of all people, know that I interviewed some pretty notorious people in New York for my job."

"Yeah, but none of them had tried to kill you twice."

"It's going to be okay. But if not, I'm going in with my eyes open, and I'm doing this to bring the kids home. I won't let them down." She turned to walk away. "I'll just have to reassure Matt, won't I?"

"How do you plan to go about that?" He followed

her down the hall.

"I don't know. I'll think of something." She got to Matt's empty office, went in, and sat down. She could hear him coming up the hall, and yep, he was growling.

"Has anybody seen Jessie? She was supposed to be here at least ten minutes ago. Nothing good is going to come out of all this." He mumbled something else. She couldn't hear it.

"Yes, I've seen her!" She spoke up just as he reached the doorway. "She's been patiently waiting for you for about ten minutes." She watched for his reaction.

"Jess, you're not going to some church picnic. Couldn't you have worn something else?" He leaned his hip against the desk.

"I have on what I wore to work, and you can live with it. That's what Jed is going to expect me to wear." She scowled at him. "What did you want? Camo fatigues?"

Jeremy coughed. "I think he would like it better if you wore a paper bag over your head." He laughed and started to walk away when Matt frowned at him.

"Matt, it's going to be okay. I know it. So give it a rest." She smiled up at him.

He tapped his fingers on the desk. "I guess I've been behaving badly. Let's get Jeremy to get you wired. I want to go over a few things with you and the group, and then we'll eat."

She stood and put her hand on his arm. "I'm sure it will be fine. I won't do anything crazy."

"Let's hope Jed doesn't either." He studied her face. "Okay then, let's roll."

****

Matt made sure everyone knew what his or her job was. He felt calmer now. He knew everyone wondered what had happened to him. It was seeing her that did it! Hell, he couldn't explain if he tried. Her face showed no sign of concern. And, if she was confident, she could do it. That was good enough for him. At least it had to be. End of story!

Matt had Jeremy run a check on the sound levels. Everything was set, including men who were already in position along the church perimeter. He had covered all his bases and now he had to hope nothing went bad.

"Are we done here?" He looked at Jeremy.

"We're ready." Jeremy gave Jessie a playful push. "Be careful, sweetheart, don't play heroine. I don't want anything to happen to my best girl."

Matt's hand fisted and cheek flexed. "We have to eat at Angelo's or Patterson's so we can be parked with the equipment in place. Jed gets to the church at eight. Jeremy, you can drive the van. I've already talked to the pizza place. They reserved the first space in the parking lot for you." Matt handed him the keys.

"Patterson's is fine with me." Jessie grabbed her bag off the table. "I have to drive, too. Do you want to ride with me?" She looked at Matt.

They walked out to her car together. He opened his hand, and she handed him the keys.

"You wouldn't want to sell me this baby, would you?" He opened the door for her.

"It's possible." She smiled at him. "Anything is possible. It's not very good in the snow, you know. When I lived in New York, it wasn't a problem because I never drove it in the city. I used taxis most of the time. It's a little different here."

"You could always get some little car for the snow, and this could be for the summer. I sure love driving it. If you really want to sell it, I want it." He adjusted the mirror. "Are you buckled up?" He looked at her and she nodded.

At seven thirty, after dinner, Matt and Jeremy got in the van. He had her turn on her equipment. They talked to her as she drove around Blue Cove.

"Jess, it's time to make your way to the church. We have your back, sweetheart, just be careful. Everyone is in place and waiting. It's your case now. Go get him, let's see if we can't find out where the kids are."

Chapter 37

Jessie pulled into a space in the church parking lot. She had been there about ten minutes when a white car pulled in beside her. She turned her small recorder on. He got out and jumped in the passenger's side of her car.

"I guess you know who I am." He stared at her. "I'm sorry I tried to kill you, but I was told to. I'm glad I missed both times."

"I'm kind of glad you missed, too!" She watched his lips curve into a slight smile.

"Here's the thing, I'm not sure how much time I have." He handed her a sealed envelope and put a finger to her lips. "Do you already know about the group of us from Evansville?"

"Yes." She glanced over at him. What a waste! She was sorry for his wife and kids.

"What you don't know is about the three others. There was Steve Murphy who hired us for what we thought was a legitimate business until we were in too deep. The owners of the store were Willie Booker and our illustrious Senator Douglas Brinkman. No one knew that, of course."

"Why was that?" She watched him closely.

"Steve was the fall guy for the organization. He was meaner than blazes. He had a two-bit criminal working for him, T.R. Booker. Willie and Travis were twins separated at birth. They found each other a few years ago or so everyone thought. But they were together in high school. Willie often posed as his brother when he committed a crime. Willie looked like the good guy and Travis took the fall and even did time for it. It was hard for me to believe that Travis could be a hit man. He didn't have the smarts upstairs." Jed pointed at his head. "I think I might have figured it out. Willie was the real hit man and posed as T.R. Booker."

"Do you know that for sure?" She watched Jed shake his head no.

"It's just a theory of mine."

"What's Willie like?" Her brows arched up.

"He's real smart and a Harvard graduate. He got a job as a staffer in Senator Brinkman's office. He inherited a lot of money when his adopted father died a few years back. That's when he became a partner at the store." Jed wiped the sweat off his brow. "But, he's mental, with a screw loose, if you know what I mean." His leg twitched. "Willie was the one who shot up the Marina. I was the one who placed his bomb too close to the window. I'll pay for that. I probably won't live to do any time." He looked around the parking lot.

"Is everything okay?"

"I've got to hurry. Do you have a pen?" He grabbed it out of her hand and wrote something on the envelope. "I didn't know when I first got involved that we would be stealing kids. Only after a few months did I learn the truth about what they were doing with the kids. There's a lot of money in this, lady, and we're only one small cog in the wheel."

She read the words on the envelope, "Here are your answers." She nodded at him. "Was it you signaling from the dock that night at the Marina?"

"Yes." Jed's eyes darted around the parking lot. "You must have seen me signaling Willie, when he was bringing in his boat." He looked at her. "It was ingenious to do everything from the water so we could make our getaway by sea in the confusion, don't you think?"

She frowned at him. "I'm hardly impressed with the whole plan! You killed and wounded innocent people."

He frowned and looked away. "The kids are still in the area. If you get the dog back, I bet you'll find them. But they won't be here much longer."

"Do you know their exact location?"

He shook his head. "There's a dirty cop in Maxwell's team." He talked faster, looking around nervously. "Brinkman hired the hit on his wife and—"

The window shattered, spraying Jessie with glass. Mouth open, Jed slumped toward her, his eyes wide open and empty.

Jessie ducked and screamed as she shoved the door open and slid out onto the ground. She heard the shots now, and bullets were hitting her car.

"Jessie, can you hear me?" She heard Jeremy speaking through the earpiece.

"Yes. I'm okay, but I think Jed is dead. I didn't wait to find out."

"Matt's coming, don't move, Jessie! Did you hear me? Don't move!"

"Like I could if I wanted to!" she yelled. "I'm not going anywhere. I'm glued to the spot." She watched as Matt scurried around the white car and fell to the ground. He crawled toward her, swearing as he came and she reached her hand toward him.

"How can I help?" Blood was soaking through his pant leg and already pooling on the blacktop. Too much blood. Way too much blood.

He pulled off his belt. "Here tighten this around here." He pointed to the spot.

She followed his directions. "Jeremy, can you hear me? Matt's been hit. We'll need an ambulance." She talked into the piece. "Kip, are you there? Can you see the general area where he's firing from?"

"Yes! It's up behind the church."

"Cover me."

"Jess, don't you even think about it." Matt grabbed at her arm.

She crawled closer to him. "You need a doctor and I'll be right back. I know where he is. It's not Willie. I would know! It's someone else out there."

She kissed his cheek and smiled at him. He looked gray. Better hurry. She waited until Kip started to fire and drew the gunman's attention, and then she crouched low, crawling along the ground until she was out of the line of fire. He probably figured she was too scared to move, wasn't even looking her way. Good. Out of his line of sight, she stood up and started running.

She cut through the cemetery. It was dark. She could hear someone following close behind her as she wove through the headstones. "Wait up, Jessie." Dylan's voice startled her. "I'll take it from here."

"You can come if you want. Hurry, I know where he is." She picked up her pace. "If you're coming, you'd better keep up." She ran along the trees at the back of the church, remembering that night where she had run not so long ago. Slowing down, she tried to feel her way. That darn tree root was somewhere around there. Closing in on where she thought the gunman was, she got down on the ground and crawled quietly toward the ledge. Matted wet leaves, soggy grass, and mud muffled the sound of her progress. When she came to the ledge, she carefully peeked over the edge. There he was, the snake, stretched out on the ground ready to strike. A dark figure clothed in black, just sliding another magazine into his semi-automatic. She could barely make him out. He had shot out the light in the church parking lot. She slipped her gun out of her holster and took aim, and felt Dylan grab her foot to let her know he was there. Good she had back up.

"If you pull that trigger one more time, mister, it'll be the last thing you ever do." She kept the gun sighted between his shoulder blades. Startled, he yanked his head around toward her voice, his night goggles making him look like a sci-fi character in the shadows. He started to reach for his gun, and she aimed a hair to the right. The warning shot scuffed the leaves six inches from his arm. "I won't miss the next time. So anything you do from this point needs to be slow and easy." She watched until he put his hands up. "Lay face down and spread your legs. Away from the rifle."

Dylan started down the slope to the ledge. He gave the agent his rights as he cuffed him. Jessie held the gun trained on his torso as Dylan collected a rifle, a handgun, and several magazines. "The suspect is apprehended." He spoke into the radio.

"Good job, Dylan. Is Jessie okay?" Jessie heard Matt's voice over the radio and relief flooded through her. He was still alive!

"She's fine! Jessie apprehended him." Dylan smiled at Matt's choice of words and then grinned at Jessie. "Between you and me, girl…" He paused. "You did a damn fine job." Dylan stood the agent to his feet. He pushed him up the small hill walking behind him. At the top, he shoved him to a sit. "There's nothing I hate more than a dirty cop." He stared down at him, looking as if he wanted to spit. "You guys give us all a bad name."

Tom and one of his team came up behind them. "I believe he's one of yours." Jessie pointed to where he sat.

"Mabry, what the hell?" Tom clenched his fists.

"We'll take him in." Dylan nodded. "You can collect the guns and equipment. I know what you're feeling, Tom. I won't beat the crap out of him, even though I would love to. Jessie will keep it all legit. It'll give you a little space before you have to deal with this scum." Dylan yanked Mabry to his feet and gave him a shove.

By the time they all got back to the parking lot, Mabry was in a cruiser on his way to the jail. Jessie made her way toward the ambulance. She hung back a little, her heartbeat unsteady. Matt was lying flat on a gurney in the back of the ambulance. She heard Dylan telling him she did the force proud, which made her smile.

"Jess, are you going to come in here, or do I have to get up and come out there." He craned his neck to peer in her direction.

She popped her head in the door. "Is he restrained?" She looked at the paramedic. He laughed and shook his head no at her. "How are you feeling?"

She studied his pale face.

"Like hell. And you didn't help me much either."
He frowned.

She cut him off. "Is the police department going to
pay to fix my car? I know I said I might sell it to you
but I won't be able to get near as much for it now. Did
you have this planned so you could get it for a cheaper
price?" She glared at him with her hands on her hips.
She could use a diversion too!

He grinned. "I'll see that it's as good as new."

"You do that." She patted his hand.

"We need to get him to the hospital." The
ambulance driver came up beside her.

"I'll be there in a little bit." She smiled at him.

"Jess, you took a few years off my life tonight, but
I'm real proud of the way you handled yourself out
there."

"Why, thank you, Mr. Parker." She stepped away
from the door. "I was trained by one of the best." The
driver closed the door, got back in and drove off.

She watched it until she couldn't see it anymore.

"I'll take you to the hospital once we get back to
the station and get my car." Jeremy gave her a hug.
"He'll be okay."

She shivered, and it was hard to stop. "I can't
believe I did that." She looked at him. "And the guy we
need to worry about most is still out there. Who knows
which Booker brother he is."

Chapter 38

By the time Jessie, Dylan, and Jeremy filed their paperwork and got to the hospital, Matt was out of surgery and in recovery. Kip walked over to them. "The surgeon was here a while ago. He said that the bullet entered from the side, spinning, and narrowly missed the big artery. There was some subsequent tissue damage and repair work necessary. He should be as good as new in time for Molly's wedding and the holidays. So you can smile." Kip tapped her chin. "You can breathe now."

"I never saw so much blood in my life." She took a deep breath and settled into the chair next to him. "I can't believe it was one of Tom's team who shot Matt. Mabry was on the team to protect the kids, and he was one of the ones hurting them."

"'I'll never understand what makes a guy turn like that." Jeremy stopped pacing and took the seat beside her.

"Money!" Kip and Jessie said at the same time.

"I suppose you're right, but it all seems pointless. He won't be able to spend it now." Jeremy jumped up and answered the ringing phone in the waiting room. "Okay, thanks. Matt is in his room. It's room 255. You go on up. I'll be up in a minute." He squeezed her arm. "I could use some coffee."

"Wait up!" Kip jumped to his feet. "I'll go with

you. Do you want something?" He looked at Jessie.

"A bottle of water would be nice."

Jessie went up to Matt's room. The nurse was fluffing the pillows behind his head. He still looked pale, but conscious.

The nurse smiled at her. "Come on in, honey, he's groggy, but awake. I don't know for how long, though." She turned to look at him. "If you need anything, ring for it. Don't be hero when it comes to pain. And don't try to get up on your own." She gave him a stern look. "You hear me?" She smiled and left the room when he nodded.

He squirmed and then winced. "I hate being laid up here like this when so much is going on."

"I know. They have Mabry in custody. He's the one who shot you." She pulled a chair over to sit beside his bed.

"I wonder how many times he tipped those guys off." He closed his eyes for a minute. "How many kids did we lose because of that piece of scum?"

She pulled the envelope that Jed had given her out of her purse and handed it to him. "I haven't had a chance to read it. I thought you should have it first."

He set it down. "Do you suppose you could come close enough for me to give you a kiss before this room fills up with people? You can't imagine what I was thinking when you went after that guy."

"I bet I can. You didn't know whether to wring my neck before or after you shot me." She grinned at him.

"That pretty much covers it." He chuckled. "Come here, be kind to me, sweetheart, I'm in pain."

"On one condition…" She frowned at him.

He raised his eyebrows. "What might that be?"

"That you post a police officer outside your door."

"You can't be serious, whatever for?"

"Willie Booker. He's still out there. There's enough evidence to arrest Brinkman, Mabry, and whoever has the kids but Willie—he's trouble."

"He may just go underground and live to play another day."

"I'd like to believe that, but mean boys get crazy when you take their toys." She bent down and kissed him. Thoroughly. And smiled as she felt his surprise.

"Now that's what I'm talking about." He grinned up at her and then kissed her back. Leaning back against the pillow, he closed his eyes, taking her hand in his. She wiped her eyes and sat back down, content to let him hold it.

Those were the last few quiet minutes that they had together. Dylan showed up, followed by Tom, Kip, and Jeremy. They talked about the case. She went to sit in a chair away from the guys. She needed time to think.

When all the others left, she decided to stay. The senator's arrest was already on CNN but not Mabry's. She wondered about that. Jessie was restless and didn't want Matt to be alone. She couldn't convince him, or Dylan for that matter, that he needed police protection.

He did. She knew it.

Booker was angry. She could feel it. The life he had created so carefully was all coming down around him. He blamed Matt and would try to kill him.

She didn't know when, but she knew it was only a matter of time.

****

He saw her when he first awakened. Curled up in the chair with a pillow and blanket, she looked uncomfortable, but beautiful with the morning sunlight shining in on her through the big window. He was going to see her every morning when he woke up. At least that was his plan. He stretched his leg and winced, then glanced at the door. Maybe he should take her warnings seriously. She didn't throw them around lightly.

"I see your guardian angel is still asleep. She was here all night and awake for most of it." Dr. Brown looked at Jessie as he walked into the room. "How are you feeling this morning?"

"Morning, Doc." Matt managed a thin smile. "Outside of the nagging pain in my leg, I'd say happy to be alive."

"That's how most shooting victims feel about it." He chuckled. "I think your leg will heal nicely. It will hurt and that's what those pills are for. The stitches will dissolve on their own. I had to do some repairs to the surrounding tissue torn by the bullet's entry. It barely missed a big artery. You could have bled out. You're lucky." He frowned, looking over his glasses at Matt. He checked Matt's pulse. "Pain and tenderness are to be expected. I know we like to avoid pain when possible, but it's what happens when people and bullets collide." He listened to Matt's heart. "You will need to be on antibiotics for a while. The biggest threat from an invasive wound like this is infection. You get past that, and you're home free." He sat on the edge of the bed. "You're young, you should heal quickly. The nurses will get you up today to walk with crutches. You'll hate working with the nurses, but they're used to it. And believe me, they won't let you bully them." His eyebrows rose. "You'll need to walk with a cane until your leg feels strong again. Any questions?"

"Only one…when can I get out of here?"

"I'd say tomorrow afternoon if you do everything the nurses tell you to." He turned to Jessie as she stirred. "Good morning, little lady. Can I trust you to keep this guy in line? I don't want to see him with any more bullet wounds."

"I'll do my best." She smiled at him. "Since he's in capable hands now, I'm going home to freshen up." She walked out of the room.

"Matt, I've known you since you were a little boy." Dr. Brown peered at him over the rim of his glasses. "Enough with the bullets! What's happening to this town anyway?"

"Crime has a way of moving beyond the cities. I guess it finally caught up to us, or maybe it was here all along and we just woke up to it."

When his doctor left, Matt picked up the envelope Jessie had given him. Most of it was just what he had heard Jed tell her but in a little more detail. With a sigh of relief, he found what he was looking for, the place where they could start looking for the kids. He would call Frank.

After a walk up and down the hall with the drill sergeants dressed as nurses, Matt could hardly keep his eyes open.

Dylan kept him up to speed on the fast breaking case. Mabry's arrest was kept quiet and away from the press. They needed him. He was singing like crazy. He was the one who had worked with Willie to fix the police records. Mabry told them that four men they had hired after the arrests of Pearson and the others were watching the kids now. They were waiting for the all-clear from him.

Tom had Mabry arrange to meet them at their usual place so he could give them the money for relocating the kids. It was to take place today at four o'clock.

"You have to let Jessie go with you," Matt told him. "She has to be there to see the kids rescued."

"I knew you'd see it that way so I already arranged it." Dylan shook his head. "Matt, try to take it easy. You've run a tight ship, and we're ready to do our jobs. Two bullets in a couple weeks could set anyone back. So give yourself time to heal. We'll let you know as it's going down."

"Thanks, Dylan." Matt's tone became serious. "Keep her safe."

"Hell, she'll probably save me. I wish you could have seen her last night, all bold and sassy, telling Mabry that if he pulled the trigger again it would be the last thing he ever did." Dylan chuckled. "I'll call you, as soon as the operation concludes."

Four was still a few hours away. He would just take a little nap. Weary, he laid his head back, closed his eyes, and was sound asleep within minutes.

****

Jessie was waiting. She kept popping up and down to look out the back door. She saw Dylan the minute he pulled into the place where her car usually was. It was a shot up mess. It made her cry to think about it. She grabbed her jacket, putting it on as she walked out the door.

"You ready?" Dylan asked as she opened the door to get in.

"Of course." She closed the door and put on her seatbelt. "Have you notified the parents?"

"They're all on their way to the hospital now. Let's hope everything goes well, so we can bring every one of them home alive." He backed up and started driving. "It's not too far from here, but we have to find a place to stash the cars and hide."

"I'm excited to be a part of it." She looked over at his grin. "Are you sure Matt told you to take me?"

"His exact words were 'You have to let Jessie go with you. She has to be there to see the kids rescued.' " He peeked over to see her smile. "Then he told me to keep you safe." He grinned when she frowned.

"I know he's just looking out for me, but..." She sounded disappointed.

"I told him you'd probably save me." Dylan laughed outright.

"I know I could if I needed to." She sat up a little straighter in the passenger's seat.

"I believe you could, too." Dylan glanced over at her. "Jessie, you need to keep your eyes open. Mabry told us there might be a woman with them. She's a sister of one of the suspects. He wasn't sure if she'd be a part of it this time. Her name is Selena, and he said she was a mean one."

She was quiet for a few minutes. "I will." She frowned. "I'm concerned that Willie is going to go after Matt. I can feel his thoughts. Don't look at me like that. You know I'm an oddity by now." She stared through the windshield, not really seeing the light traffic. "He's blaming Matt for everything." She twirled a strand of hair between her fingers. "Jed said he was mental, which to me means he's unpredictable. He might feel he can just walk into the hospital, take him out, and slip away never to be caught. The truth is I don't know if

Willie is the one who is alive and he posed as Travis or if Travis is alive and Willie is dead. Either way, the brother who is living is the real hit man."

"All right, you've convinced me. Let's see what we can do."

They arrived at the site in plenty of time to stash the cars and hide. Jessie hid in a thick group of bushes on the other side of a grove of trees. She was to remain there through the operation. That was the condition. She waited and she remembered! It had all started with Abigail. Now, here she was. She wanted to see some of the faces she had seen in her dreams. She sucked in her breath and her body tensed when the vans pulled off the road. Boy, she would love to do some damage to a couple of these guys. Mabry was sitting in his car. She watched him open the door when he saw the vans. Several guns with sights locked in on him. With his briefcase in hand, Jessie watched Mabry head toward the three men who had gotten out of the vans. "Where's your brother?" Mabry looked around.

"He's in the van with the kids." The man looked around him.

"Go get him. I need to talk to all of you. Is there anyone else?"

"No, only him and he's keeping an eye on the kids."

"Dammit, get him out here!" Mabry yelled. "Threaten the little brats and they'll stay put."

He went and got his brother, waving his gun and yelling at the kids. Jessie could hear their whimpers. She knew exactly what she would like to do to him. To all of them! Mabry handed the tallest man the briefcase with the money. That was Tom's cue. He leaped out of his hiding place followed by the others. "FBI, you are under arrest." The FBI surrounded them.

Jessie saw Selena when the others couldn't. She had slipped out of the van and made her way toward the back of the vehicle. Jessie didn't stop to think about it. She moved from her hiding spot, following the same path the woman had taken. She took her gun out, aimed. "If you fire that you might hit someone, but I guarantee you'll be dead." The woman spun around and for an instant, their eyes met. Jessie stopped breathing, time slowed, and her finger tightened on the trigger as the woman's eyes narrowed.

"Damn!" She dropped the gun, lips pulling back from her teeth. "You bitch!"

"Jessie, I'm glad you saw her. No one could see her from our position." Dylan trotted around the van.

"Thanks for the warning earlier." She held the gun steady on the woman as Dylan cuffed her.

"Nice job!" Dylan escorted the woman to a waiting cruiser. She cursed him all the way.

The kids were dirty and scared, but alive. Tom popped his head in and showed the kids his badge. We're here to take you home. You don't have to be afraid anymore."

"He's a cop," the tall boy told them. "He's going help us get home." They all began to chatter at once.

Jessie remembered his face and several others. So many emotions! Tears, drat these blasted tears. She swiped at them. She walked around to the other side of the van to get control before she really cried. A few minutes later, she got into one of the vans with Kip. She wanted to be near the kids she had seen in her dreams. They drove the kids to the hospital for evaluation, and then to be reunited with their parents.

It took a while to get them back to Blue Cove and to the hospital. She waited. She walked over to Tom who was standing against the wall. "Thanks for all your hard work. This is a good day."

"If I remember, you were the one who started all this." Tom smiled down at her. "It's a very good day."

She looked around the room as the parents filed in. One by one, she watched as the freshly scrubbed children began to trickle in and went right into the arms of their waiting parents.

Soon, everybody was crying.

Someone had heard that today was Lily's birthday and a couple of nurse's aides rolled in a cart with cake and punch. A nurse opened the door. "Before you cut the cake, I brought a few more guests for the party." She wheeled in Josh followed by Abigail and Frank with Radar.

Jessie watched the children's faces light up as they gathered around Josh and Abigail, excited and giggling. Full of questions, each one approached the two, and they repeated their stories several times.

"How'd you know to come?" Jessie stood beside Frank who watched some of the kids pet his dog.

"Matt called me this morning and told me what was going down. I didn't want to miss this for nothing." Frank grinned. "He also has something he wanted me to do at the morgue so they can release Booker's body.

"Doesn't Josh look good?" She pointed him out.

"He sure does. I didn't think he'd make it. And look at Abigail with Radar." He listened to Abigail tell the others how Radar had found her. "You did it, Jessie. Thank God, you heard Abigail's call. Take it all in and enjoy! Now you can take it easy."

"Not just yet." Jessie watched the happy reunion scene. "There's still someone out there. I feel he's coming after Matt." Her eyes filled with moisture.

"Hey, doll…" Gary walked up and handed her a set of keys. "Matt's car is in the parking lot. He wanted you to have it to use until yours gets fixed." He noticed the tears.

"That was nice of him to remember."

The room became crowded and stifling as more family members arrived. "Jessie, we're headed up to Matt's room. Do you want to come along?" Tom passed her on his way to the door.

She shook her head. "I'm going home to freshen up. But let Matt know I'll be up right after dinner."

Chapter 39

Jessie finished dinner, ran the brush through her hair one last time, and put on her lip-gloss. As she looked in the mirror, she suddenly felt a sense of urgency. She needed to get to the hospital. She put her gun in the holster, grabbed her jacket, and got into Matt's car. She called Dylan as she drove past the Inn toward the highway.

"Where are you?" she yelled into the phone.

"Home...What is it, Jessie? What's wrong?"

"We need to get to the hospital. Something is wrong."

"I'll meet you there."

Jessie drove as fast as she could. She pulled into the hospital parking lot just as people were running out.

"What's going on?" she called out as she ran by a man and his daughter.

"An explosion rattled the hospital. We didn't stick around to see what it was."

He was here. His MO. It was his diversion tactic. She took the stairs two at a time. She had to get to Matt's room before he did. She pushed the door open to the second floor, looking cautiously around. The hair on the back of her neck stood up. He was close, she could feel him. She crossed the hallway to the corridor where Matt's room was. He was just getting off the elevator wearing surgical scrubs. He spoke to one of the nurses briefly. Jessie heard her tell him room 255.

She picked up her pace, but he was closer to Matt's room than she was. She pulled the gun from her holster and saw Dylan coming from the other direction.

"Travis, you can stop right there." She watched as he turned toward her, a gun coming up in his hand. Aiming at her.

She dropped to the ground and rolled behind a cart in the hallway, firing a shot. Time seemed to stand still. He cursed her. She heard a shot and something struck the wall slightly above her head. Her finger was still on the trigger, but her hand wouldn't quit shaking. She couldn't fire! She heard another shot and rolled over against the wall. Trapped!

Silence.

A woman screamed. She peeked around the edge of the cart just as he folded forward, to land face down on the floor with a sickening thud. Dylan ran up from behind him and kicked his gun out of reach.

"Jessie, are you okay?"

She sat up, too shaken to answer and waved at Dylan. When she finally stood up, she saw a doctor bending over Travis giving orders, and hospital personnel scurrying to get what he requested. She also saw Matt in the doorway of his room with a gun in his hand, leaning on a walker.

****

Matt watched her walk toward him. His heart was just beginning to beat normally. He had never seen a more beautiful sight in his life. She walked around those working on the suspect and straight into his arms.

"I didn't know if I could get here in time." She started to shake.

"But you did." He rubbed his hand up and down her back.

"Did you shoot him?" She looked into his eyes.

"No, baby, you did, and then Dylan finished it." He pushed her hair off her face.

"I don't remember doing it." She shivered again.

"When you dropped to the ground, you fired and hit him. That slowed him down, and Dylan had time to get him." He held her close. "How'd you know?"

"I felt I needed to get here and I called Dylan..." She stared out the door at the white-coated figures working on Travis.

"Come in, I need to get off my leg." He pulled her into the room and shut the door.

"You saved my life." He looked at her, not letting her go. "I knew something was up, but I couldn't have moved fast enough to save myself. If I hadn't heard you call his name, I wouldn't have even known he was here." Matt made it to the bed and sat down, pulling her down beside him. "Thank you, sweetheart." He held her while she cried.

She helped him get his leg back up on the bed. Dylan came in to check on them.

"Did you see her? She was great!" Dylan smiled at her. "It looks like our hit man, whichever brother he is, will live to stand trial."

"It's Travis, we know that for sure now. Willie wanted to be the hit man but Travis was our real guy. Frank's dog confirmed it before the DNA results came in. Willie died that day out on Old Homestead Road. Willie had an identifying scar and Radar hit on his scent. Travis was also there that day. He hid in the bushes across the street. He had been hired to kill

Willie, his own brother. Travis' bullet is the one that took Willie out…Jed thought he had done it and that Willie had joined forces with him. Ballistics told us a different story, and the facts now back it up. It wasn't Jed's gun that killed Willie, it was Travis' gun. Jed would never have willingly joined forces with Travis, there was bad blood between them. If Mabry hadn't killed Jed first, Travis would have killed Jed when he was done using him." They talked for a little while more, and Jessie fell asleep in the chair. Matt had a nurse bring in a blanket and pillow. He let her sleep and watched her most of the night.

****

Tomorrow, he was going home. Matt's youngest brother, Jason, was coming to help him out for a few weeks. He wasn't going to let him within ten feet of her. Jason was in that stage where every girl was a challenge, another notch in his belt. Matt frowned when Jason walked in early in the morning, with Jessie still sleeping in the chair.

"Who's that?" He eyed her.

"That, brother, is my girl, which means hands off." Matt grinned at him. "She saved my life last night, and I'm letting her sleep so keep your voice down."

"Too late." Jason walked toward Jessie as she sat up and stretched her cramped muscles. "I'm Matt's brother Jason." He grinned at her. "Why settle for the old man when you can have a younger version?"

"As tempting as that sounds, I think I'll let you two settle this in your own way. Keep in touch, Matt." She walked over to the bed, gave Matt a kiss, and walked out.

Matt looked at his brother. "See? I told you, she's

my girl."

"She's too fine for the likes of you." He chuckled.

"You aren't telling me anything I don't know already."

"How do we break you out of here, old man?"

"He'll leave when I sign his discharge papers and not a minute sooner. Why don't you go get some coffee, pup?" Dr. Brown walked in the room in his surgical scrubs. "I'll give your brother his check-up! Then we'll talk about his release." He smiled at Jason.

By the time Jason got back to the room, the doctor had discharged Matt. He was dressed and had his doctor's final instructions and paperwork. He wanted to get back to work as soon as possible and follow this case through to the end. He had no clue when Jessie left that morning he wouldn't see her for several weeks.

He was so busy, with work and rehab on his leg that all he could do was talk on the phone with her and fall exhausted into bed each night. He had a friend and his brother working on a surprise for her while he supervised them. She had stopped by a couple of times, once with flowers, once with homemade chocolate chip cookies—his favorite—and a few kisses.

Chapter 40

Jessie looked at her reflection in the mirror one last time. She was finally going to see Matt tonight. Either he had been busy with the reports, court appearances, or she had been busy with showers and story deadlines. At least he would be at Molly's rehearsal and dinner. Maybe she had taken too long to come around, and he had grown tired of waiting. She scrunched her face.

She walked over to the Inn, buttoning her coat. It definitely felt like snow wasn't too far off. Katie had insisted that they drive together, and she was somewhat glad. If Matt was upset or something, she could always have Katie bring her home. She went in the kitchen door and saw Katie sitting at the small desk. "Are you ready?"

"I am. Did I tell you that Jeremy will be coming for the wedding tomorrow? I'll have a date tomorrow. Can you believe it? I hate to go to weddings like a pathetic dateless bridesmaid." Katie smiled. "Besides you know what I think about Jeremy." She fluttered her eyelashes. "I'm pretty gone on him. I've almost convinced him to come and live here."

"I know." She smiled. "He talks about it a lot when he calls."

"I'm glad he's talking about it with you, too. That means he's serious and not just being nice to me." Katie opened the door, and Jessie followed her.

By the time they got to the church, Jessie had worked herself into a state. She didn't know what to expect until she walked through the door and saw the way Matt was looking at her.

"It's been way too long since I've seen you." He met her halfway, walking with a slight limp and took her hand. "I finally got rid of Jason and finished all the paperwork from the case. You can't imagine how much I've missed seeing you." He flung his arm around her shoulder and drew her into his side.

"What?" She looked at him, moisture filling her eyes.

"It killed me to stay away so long, but every spare moment I had was taken up with court appearances and paperwork." He paused. His thumb stroked her hand. "I have a surprise for you." He turned as the Pastor called for the groomsmen to take their places. "We'll talk at dinner. You're with me." He walked to the front of the church.

When the rehearsal was over, he grabbed her hand and walked with her out to the parking lot. He had parked her car under the lights so she could see it. "What do you think? Looks great doesn't it?" He gave her a lopsided grin. "Jason, my friend Chris who does body work, and I spent all our spare time restoring it. Actually, I supervised, but I was there. I wanted to surprise you tonight."

She started to cry as she looked at her car. "It looks great." She never took her eyes off him as he took her around the car telling her everything they had done.

He opened the door for her and closed it after she got in. "One last drive and the keys are back in your safe little hands."

"Thanks, you had to have really worked around the clock to get it finished so fast."

"You know me, I cracked the whip, and they did most of the work. It was therapy. There were so many times that I wanted to punch those guys in the face for what they did to those kids. This is how I punched them. It will take those kids a while to be normal again and to live without fear—if ever."

"So what has happened the past few days since we last talked?" She watched his handsome profile.

"Before we talk about that, I'm going to collect something you owe me."

"Oh, yeah, what's that?"

"Our second date. Tomorrow night it's you, a wedding, and me. How's that sound?" He smiled at her. "You've got to do it, you owe me."

"I don't know about that." She smiled at him. "After all, I did save your life."

"I figured you might say that so that's why I had your car fixed. So you still owe me."

"I guess since you put it that way, sure, we're on." She glanced flirtatiously over her shoulder at him. "You might have to work to get a third, though."

"No way. You'll be begging me to take you out." He laughed at her expression. They didn't have much time to talk at dinner, so he drove her home. He parked her car and turned to look at her as he handed her the keys.

"I went to see the Adelsons the other day, but Sammy had been discharged. What happened with them? I had just missed seeing them," Jessie asked.

"Sammy was given probation because he took a plea deal. He'll testify for the state. Steve Murphy hired him to take the fall. He knew very little about the operations over all."

"I'm happy to hear he won't be going to prison."

"He won't if he keeps his nose clean and stays out of trouble. Lindsey will be good for him there." Matt took off his seatbelt.

"Did Lindsey have her baby yet?"

"Sammy was with Lindsey when she gave birth to their daughter." He opened the door and walked around to open hers. "She looks a lot like her mother. They named her Jessica Lynn."

"That's so nice," she sniffed. "I'm glad they'll be a family." Tears rolled down her cheeks, he handed her a tissue.

He walked with her to the door, his limp a little more noticeable, and unlocked it. He helped her remove her coat and walked over to the sofa, holding her hand. He sat down and pulled her into his lap. "Now I'm going to tell you everything, and then I'm going to kiss you breathless and be back here tomorrow promptly at two to pick you up." He looked at her. "I would start with the kiss which is what I'd prefer, but I'd never get around to telling you anything. And tomorrow we aren't going to talk shop at all."

"Anything you say." Her eyes softened as she held his gaze.

He cleared his throat. "Okay, this is the short version. You know about our six high school friends. Add to them Steve Murphy, Travis, and now we know Willie, too. Brinkman and Steve met up with Willie at a dinner party and offered him a staff position in Brinkman's New York office. He was smart and great with a computer. Willie blackmailed his way into a partnership at the store, holding his knowledge over their head. Brinkman was one of the top guys and already into trafficking, along with Steve and the others. They knew Travis and Willie were brothers. And though Brinkman was afraid of the Bookers, he needed someone to control Steve who was out of control with his anger." He felt her shiver and held her tighter.

"How did Mabry get involved?"

"He was one of the nameless guys from Evansville. He was friends with Jed and went to college with Willie. They all had some connection through high school or college. Even Brinkman did. He was a senior at Rocky Pointe High when the others were freshmen. The strangest thing of all is the one guy who we thought might talk, Mike Pearson. He got them all into it. As sick as this is, he preferred children. I know you understand. He went on a several trips to South America, across country, and overseas. A connection informed him about the demand for American children emerging in several markets and the money that was easy to make. He lay low because of all his travels, but he was the richest of them all. He found the markets. Brinkman and Murphy already owned the store, which became a perfect front and a place to collect addresses for families with children. Pearson convinced them about the ease with which they could all be rich. Mabry and Willie covered the tracks with the computer, and Travis took out anyone they needed to eliminate. It was an entirely smooth operation until recently, when Lutz messed up. Their computer gave us lots of valuable information, the names of children, locations of porn-rings and people waiting to buy children. The FBI has several sting operations ongoing." He smiled at her, pulling her closer. "Now, sweetheart, I'm going to make good on my promise." He bent his head to kiss her. She turned her head and he got a mouth full of hair.

"Not so fast. I have a couple of questions. Why did they use that bomb?"

"Johnson messed up. He placed it in the wrong place. His improvisation cost lives. Travis was only there to take out Brinkman's wife and Steve. Brinkman's wife was asking too many questions from what I understand. Booker always uses a diversion, but he never killed anyone unless the money was in his hands for a hit. Booker was angry, and Jed would have been killed eventually."

"Why? How could they do it? I don't get it. Unlike with the Harvest Club who thought they were doing it for good, there was nothing good about taking kids from their families." Her brow creased as she crinkled her nose.

"We may never know all the whys, but money, and the power of being in a group of friends doing the same thing is a strong pull."

"What a waste." She tilted her head up and gazed into his eyes.

He didn't need any other invitation. He kissed her. This was home to him.

****

He was there promptly at two, looking handsome in his wedding tuxedo. Her dress was red, and the other girls each had on different color of a New England fall. The wedding was beautiful. Molly was a glowing bride. The day flew by. The dinner was eaten, the toasts given, the first dances danced and the cake cut. She felt there was something different about him today. Her breath caught when he looked at her. The air crackled with excitement around him. The music started to play, the dance floor was open to everyone, and he stood, holding out his hand.

"Are you sure your leg can handle it?"

He nodded and grinned. "I worked hard for the past three weeks in rehab to have this one dance with you." He walked with her to the dance floor, and he pulled her in close. "It has to be a slow one I'm afraid, with not much movement, but I like them best."

She gazed into his eyes. "Me, too."

"I asked them to play this song. They agreed because Kenny requested it too. The last time we danced to this song, gunfire interrupted the moment. Let's finish our dance, sweetheart, they're playing our song. It says it all for me, Jess." Etta Jones' voice came through the system. *At last my true love has come along. My lonely days are gone and life is like a song.* The lyrics were weaving their magic. He turned her and brought her close once again.

"It was like that for me, Jess, the first night I looked at you, I knew I was home. You smiled and you cast a spell over me. I was lost to the magic of your smile." They danced close, her head resting on his shoulder, lost in the moment. He whispered the last words of the song in her ear. *"For you are mine at last."*

She pulled his head down and brushed her lips across his. "Casting a spell indeed..." She smiled, the music had ended, but she didn't move.

He grinned. His smile faded, replaced by a look she had never seen before. He gently lifted her chin and gazed into her eyes. "Jessica Lynn Reynolds, I love you." His body tensed. They stood motionless.

She smiled, tracing his lips with her finger. "That's Jess to you." She leaned closer to him and whispered, "I love you, too." He shuddered and his body relaxed.

A word about the author...

Iona Morrison is the author of *The Harvest Club*, the first book in A Blue Cove Mystery series.

For the research on *Not for Sale* (the second book in the series), she got to watch a team of bloodhounds working a track. The dogs did an amazing job and so did their handlers.

http://www.ionamorrison.com